DOVE
KEEPER

This is a work of fiction. Names, characters, businesses, places, events, locales, and incidents are either the products of the author's imagination or used in a fictitious manner. Any resemblance to actual persons, living or dead, or actual events is purely coincidental. Except when it's not, but again, these people are used in a fictitious manner and emerged only slightly scarred from the experience.

This is for the victims.

Prologue

The Boy

The boy swallowed a scream when he stepped on a nail. The pain couldn't matter. He had to keep running. His throat was raw, and the thunder of steps behind him faded. He only recognized his feet slapping against stone. All he tasted was copper and smoke.

Only what was before him mattered. With his remaining strength, he pushed himself over a short wall of crumbling bricks, remnants of a house abandoned before its foundation was complete. He stumbled down a slight incline and fled into the forest. The leering canopies cut up the horned moon, and the boy staggered as far as he could without tripping over exposed roots.

The veil of night shadows, the sweat, and the tears obscured the branched labyrinth. Even if the boy found himself lost forever in the woods, it'd be better than where he'd been an hour before. As his limp worsened, the forest's thorns and low oak claws clamped around him like a wolf on a girl's shawl. Briars snatched off the fabric of his coat sleeve. His blood fell on the leaves, the forest sticking to his skin.

The boy hobbled to a tree with bulbous joints and a dark split up its skirt. When he touched the rough, unyielding bark, all he could see were the half-rings on his wrist where teeth had cut his skin, the black crust under what fingernails he had left, and the bruising blue-yellow of cold moonlight.

Falling to his knees, the boy crawled as far into the hollow as he could. The bark scraped his exposed elbow. He made himself small like he did when he and Papa played hide-and-seek before the war. He did his best with his broken body. It had been such a long run out of the pit, out of Hell. Without help, he couldn't have made the steep climb out of the place, with its howling and decay and lanterns. With its stench of sulfur and something worse than burning trash, worse than a slab of forgotten lamb meat. It hurt leaving the others who'd been dragged and flung into the pit.

The boy's mind was clear, if only for a small shard of time. The pounding in his ears faded. If he could, he would sleep, stay lost forever, but a realization soured in him. No, he couldn't, not when he survived an ordeal others could die from. He had a duty graced by God to save those who helped him escape.

Not only that. Maman was preparing for his birthday before the monsters took him. Maybe she still had the cake and its eleven candles ready. She would've spoken to the police by now, the boy knew it, and Papa would be pacing and worrying his hands, crumpling his hat between his fingers like he always did.

The boy could only pray he would find help before anyone else died. But that meant moving after his prayers.

God help me, God help me. Mother Mary, please. He needed to get the Lord's prayer out quick like Maman. *Father in Heaven, hollowed be Thy name.* What was it, again? *Give us our day bread. Your king dumb comes. Your wheel be spun.* He clutched the silver crucifix at his neck. *Forgive us our deaths, as we've forgiven our deaders.* His thoughts fractured into webs of half-forgotten Latin litanies Maman had taught him, and they went on until he couldn't tell if he was praying or cursing.

He needed to move, but he didn't.

Something growled. God, his stomach hurt. The woods had the stink of rain settling on dirt. When he was in the pit, he heaved, but nothing came out after a few days. The filth had wrung him clean. He'd heave and cough and sob now, but he couldn't.

The devils had been stupid to keep his hands free. After one had found him alone at the edge of town, they liked chasing him in the dark tunnels with the marks from their hard fists staining him like wet ash. Their hands. Reaching, tearing, groping. No, it did no good to dwell. He had lives to save, a birthday to prepare for.

When the boy exhaled, it came out as a snort. He froze, and his world was the forest rustlings and the violent *throom doom throom doom* against his ribs. He was both present and away, as if his soul scrabbled up the tree trunk and peered above him like a yellow-eyed owl.

Something crunched like bone to the left of him. The boy couldn't tremble. Sensation drained from him, and he'd never been closer to God before his eyes snapped up.

Only then did he find his screams when he stared at two fanged slants of light, a pair of grinning eyes.

1

Rosalie

When her husband returned home from work, Rosalie asked who he killed. They had agreed before they married on the acceptable amount of details, and Anatole allowed her to read his little black diary chronicling every execution. His lists were absent of pomp, and, like most else, they shared those notes, those names and dates and prayers and final glasses of rum. Anatole scraped the pages, burdened them with whatever stains he carried in from work, and left those black feathers on the desk.

Before he left for his work, Rosalie kissed his carnation and placed it in his breast pocket. Beyond that, she could do little but send her husband off and hope he returned home unscathed. At five in the morning, before he slipped away to fetch the guillotine parts from the barn, he'd lean down and kiss Rosalie, and she'd tell him she loved him if she wasn't too sleep-heavy to move her lips.

This wasn't one of those mornings, but the morning after. She shook her head and straightened the fabric pooling in her lap. The living room smelled of citrus and pine potpourri, a strange combination for the first of October. The hearth warmed the room, though Rosalie couldn't suppress a chill. The light from the fire did little to brighten the burgundy walls and mahogany bookcases of the study. She folded the newspaper and laid it on the cushion beside her. It sickened her, the story of the butcher's boy who disappeared. Rennes, never much for news, buzzed with fear for numerous missing children. With the war, split families were nothing fresh, but not this. Rosalie hated reading the news, but she did it anyway with daggered curiosity. She loathed the pictures the most, the new, hulking monstrosities, the tanks and the improved Gatling guns. The sickly men in gray uniforms and rounded beetle hats studded with hobnails, the earth clawed open, oozing clay and blood.

The past few months, she checked the windows and doorknobs often. She was Bartleby in the dead letter office, and to survive, she made herself focus on smaller fragments of life that seemed trivial in the vastness of God's creation. A moment ago, while peering outside the study, she had seen Anatole and their daughter Marcy in the rose garden, and the tightness in her heart lessened only a fraction. Rosalie cast a baleful eye on the pitiful molting birch by the fence. Marcy leaned against her papa's arm, and they both patted Jolie, the graying cocker spaniel with coils as black as Rosalie's.

Rosalie didn't mind mornings, mostly. She couldn't help but admire how, whether the day was bright or gray, the songbirds sang with full-throated ease as daylight drifted between the curtains. That was why she left the study, to listen to the chirping. The birds were one of few consolations when the dead swelled the banks of the Somme and children went missing. Throughout the day, the trains' cries and the church knells mourned the war's fallen, and Rosalie discreetly grieved with them. It was the morning tree chorus that kept her by the window, and it was only when Rosalie set the paper down and lifted her head that the birdsong faded. Outside, she saw a man she first took for Anatole because of his dark clothes.

It wasn't Anatole standing out on the front path with a resting frown. Leaner, no beard, no gray beyond his ruffled waistcoat. It was their nephew, André, with hair as dark as his mother's, her sister's, that same shade of magpie. Just as well, Rosalie needed to speak with him, but before that, his hair caught her attention again. There was something in the way it was parted.

Juliette. Rosalie inhaled and kept the breath until she felt warm again. *Sister.* The space behind her eyes tightened when a shadow met André on the path. Marcy. *Daughter.* The girl's dress scuffed the dirt, her face and bright, blue eyes as round as Anatole's, her hair the same red as his before his hair lost its vibrancy.

Rosalie leaned closer to the window, keeping half her face obscured by the curtain she clutched with an ache.

Their mouths moved, and though Rosalie could read the I's and me's, the conversation wasn't clear. Marcy bent forward and clasped her hands together as if praying to Mary. André shook his head, brow low as Marcy brushed his sleeve and stood on her toes.

He cast his gaze to the side, and Marcy shot up, her lips meeting his. Shock iced Rosalie's veins, and while she watched, André pulled away, setting his hands briefly on Marcy's shoulders. Marcy bowed her head, shoulders heaving once and eyes shrinking. Then, as quickly as she had cast her gaze down, Marcy straightened and broke into an uneasy smile. She said three words.

Sorry about that. Her face was as red as one of Anatole's roses, and when she darted to the front door, André followed at a slower pace.

Rosalie quickly adjusted herself so she looked as if she was simply pondering, not spying.

When the front door opened, Marcy whispered something like an apology and averted her gaze after flashing Rosalie a forced grin, and Rosalie's brow furrowed in pity, but it was gone before Marcy could turn around.

André came in and gave a start when he saw Rosalie on the couch. "I didn't see you. How are you doing?"

She struck him with a cold stare. "Please come with me." When Marcy took a step, Rosalie raised a hand to halt her. "No, poupée, just him. Go back to your papa."

Rosalie led André to the study, which smelled of Anatole's roses and the yellowed pages of decades-old books.

She closed the door. "Sit."

André was a man, a man who wandered and went to war, both with mixed results, but he knew better than to disobey. He settled in the oak chair with its sharp edges and wicked gleam in the yellow lamplight.

Rosalie crossed her arms. "Where were you last night?" She knew André's habits by the strange, cloying perfume the nights gave him.

"What does it matter? I haven't killed anyone, so it's of no concern."

"So you say."

He gave her a white smile. "I was just going about the town."

Rosalie sniffed. "All right, then explain to me what I saw out there."

Her nephew took a new interest in the shine of the study desk. "What do you mean?"

"Don't pretend."

He raised his hands, as if offering a sacrifice. "Am I on trial?"

"You aren't so fortunate." André's jaw twitched, and he stared at his aunt with shadowed eyes. "Marcy proposed to me and gave me a kiss."

"Why?"

"How should I know?"

Rosalie kneaded her knuckles. "Are you two . . ."

"No!" André paused. "She's too young for that."

He was right. Rosalie didn't care if Marcy's age, thirteen, meant she could marry. Most women waited until late adolescence to start a family, at the very least, if they married at all. Damn the law in this instance. If Marcy were to fall pregnant now, she and the baby might not survive.

"Is that the only reason?"

"No, no, of course not! I would never! She's practically a sister to me."

Rosalie's fingers lingered on her neck. "You weren't going to tell me about Marcy."

"I was in shock." André stood and paced. "It's not every day you learn your cousin wants to marry you."

Rosalie checked the window. Anatole was still out there, checking the roses as Jolie wagged her tail and nudged his palm.

She muttered, "I don't know if I can believe you, you and your secrets."

André stopped, and his ice equaled her own. "You're the least open of us."

"I have decorum."

André tilted his head and cocked a brow. "You have your reasons, I know, and I have mine. I don't see what makes any secrets I have different than anyone else's."

"Oh, really?" Rosalie narrowed her eyes. "You never explained to us why you were discharged from service in Strasbourg, what you did, what you went through."

"I didn't perform well because I was distracted. I don't know what else to say. It's really nothing, and it's in the past."

"By what? Women? How can that be? You can't be the only soldier who spends your time in such a way."

"I can't tell you."

"Why?"

Rosalie opened the desk drawer and pulled out an opened envelope. She postured it like Judas before flinging his bag of silver. "André, what is this?"

Dryly, André said, "It seems to be an envelope." However, he lost his humor when he judged her expression. When provoked, Rosalie excelled at not blinking until her nephew and daughter acquiesced.

She offered the envelope, and André snatched it and examined it like a curious trinket.

"You never go to the mailbox," he said, unfolding the letter from the open envelope and looking down.

"I'm adapting."

As he read on, André flushed. He looked so fully like the boy he was not that long ago.

"Explain this to me. Tell me this is somehow wrong. Tell me you didn't make a woman pregnant. Tell me she's lying or mistaken. Tell me she and her parents aren't caring for your bast—your child and that you didn't keep this from us."

"You read a letter addressed to me. Wonderful, at least we trust one another." As if affronted, André added, "My daughter's name is Guylaine."

You fool. "We cannot afford this. Have you told your uncle?"

"Yes, earlier. I'm sure you'll have words on it. I didn't intend for it to happen. It's not as if I calculate how to inconvenience you."

Rosalie flicked a finger on the letter. "She's asking you for help."

"Yes, so I read." She grit her teeth. That mouth of his. "But I'm working on a solution so I can help you, Oncle, and them." André motioned to the letter in his hand. "It was a mistake, I know, but—Tante, I'd never marry Marcy, but if I did, I'd do my best to care for her. I'll prove to you I can help."

Thorns stung Rosalie's throat like she was a nightingale. "I'd rather see her dead than with you." *Than with a future executioner.*

Rosalie swore footsteps padded close to them. She looked out the window for Marcy, but it was only Anatole again, alone except for the dog. A twinge of dread skittered across her heart like spider legs.

André scowled, but his eyes were off somewhere far behind Rosalie. The letter was balled in his whitening hands. "I see."

"I only want what's best for you and Marcy."

"Of course you do."

Rosalie clenched her jaw. "I do."

"What is it about me that perturbs you? What would make you say such a thing, that you'd rather Marcy die than marry me? I'd never hurt her."

"I thought you said you don't plan to be with her, so this shouldn't be an issue." She arched a brow. "Should it?"

André smoothed out the letter, but it was permanently wrinkled. "There's something, something about me."

Rosalie replied, "You're reckless."

"What else? I'm doing all I know to do to prepare myself to help you and Oncle with money." André slapped his knuckles on the letter, which still hadn't recovered from its crumpling. "Oncle teaches me as best he can. He's good, and I'll be the best."

"Ending a life isn't like slicing through a bale of hay." With or without Anatole's company, practicing with the Widow's blade in the barn wasn't the same as suffocating under a circle of crows' eyes, multiplying like coupling spiders. One day he'd learn.

"You don't think I know that? I'm fast, fast and efficient. Oncle said so himself."

"And there's nothing else you could do? Your mother wouldn't want this for you."

"It's a shame she has no say."

"How could you say something like that?"

"What else is there? What would make you happy? What would make my mother happy when her father was an executioner, and his father before him?"

"Would your uncle's job make you happy? Would you enjoy it?" Voice soft, Rosalie said, "You'll kill men. Husbands, fathers, sons. People will hate you, people you've never met. You'll come home with specks of blood on your boots." Blood in the house, blood in the bed, blood on the sheets. "Blood will spray your coat, stain your hands, and you'll try to scrub it off, even when it's not there. You, your wife, you'll both try to scrub it away."

André's face grew soft. "I feel like this is a conversation you should have with Oncle." André looked away and added, "It wouldn't make me happy, I don't think, but it'd make the world better, and only those who haven't lost someone violently and unfairly would oppose it."

"You know I'm not one of those people." Rosalie only cared about her family's safety; the morality was indisputable.

The shallow lines of André's mouth and forehead dimpled in something like pity. The lift in his brow and the color of his hair, that hair that never quite remained in place, it reminded Rosalie too much of—she needed to breathe—

Her sister, her little sister with blood welting her sheets, the pillow, drying on her mouth the morning she died, and Anatole holding André away as he, not even half a year old, cried for food. Even now, Rosalie sometimes woke up with a chill stiffening her body and Juliette's name on her lips.

She stumbled, and André started, but she raised her hand for him to stop and steadied herself with a bent arm on the desk, the burnished knob of a side drawer imprinting like fire on her hip. Rosalie chewed the inside of her cheek and bit back the scream squirming in her lungs, begging for release.

Don't bend. Don't bow. Don't break.

Gesturing with his empty hands, André asked, "What can I do?" He'd dropped the letter, from surprise or disgust, Rosalie didn't know because she only saw the aftermath, not the letter's pitiful descent.

"You should've never found those postcards."

She and Anatole never would have had to reveal to André and Marcy what Anatole did, and André, eager to follow Anatole's steps since he could manage an unsteady waddle, wouldn't have wanted to be an executioner.

André showed her his profile, his shoulders hunched from the lead weight of their conversation.

"André, I—" He swiveled to leave, and Rosalie rushed to meet him. "Please don't—"

But he did, leaving in such a flurry of movement Rosalie stood stunned until she heard a door close with more force than usual in their quiet home. The only sign André was there rested at Rosalie's feet.

When all she had left was the clock clicking its tongue, Rosalie sat where André had been, the cushion warm.

If André kept assisting Anatole, and if Anatole wished, one day André would eagerly settle his uncle's mantle on his own shoulders, and Marcy would be Rosalie, the executioner's daughter made another executioner's wife. Rosalie's heart ached with its incessant murmurs. It said what she couldn't.

Oh, my love. If you want to live, don't marry an executioner.

Rosalie tapped her nails on the study desk. Doom clouded Rosalie's relationship with her nephew as it was, this note of finality hanging, visible but never playing. When André was much younger, he displayed more fondness toward Rosalie. On an acute summer morning, when he was eight and she was bedridden with a fever, he offered her a strawberry muffin. That made her heart swell with love for him, though they drifted away from one another as he grew taller. It was always Anatole who was better with André, Anatole who accepted André as a son and his protégé. If Anatole died before his retirement, God forbid, Rosalie would choose his successor, and she'd pick anyone else, and André would despise her for taking what was his.

What else was there?

Rosalie drifted into a memory after André had found the guillotine postcards, the images of Anatole at an execution, even when such images were prohibited. Her husband sat in the study, on the very chair she sat in now, with his head cupped in one palm. She stood by his side, and though she hated to do it when Anatole was in distress, she said, "I don't think he should have that life. God, it isn't me, you know that. Juliette wouldn't want this for André."

Anatole slouched, his fingers in his thinning hair, his countenance doused in orange light. Outside, the austere day waned as clouds hid half the sun and darkened spots of uncapped grass. "But what else can I give him? No one will hire an executioner's nephew."

Rosalie had lied. Even though she didn't mind if the men who killed an old woman for fifty francs or raped children died a too-merciful death from the Widow's blade (because, after all, their odds of repeating those actions lowered significantly with death), there were those who did. And those who claimed to care for life might not be so lenient toward the man who pulled the rope and killed their father or son. After Anatole's family had migrated from Augsburg generations ago, committing the Frenchmen's bloody work for centuries did little to endear them to the townspeople, nor did their Jewish heritage. Pieces of themselves were stolen over time, if those pieces ever belonged to the family to start with. Rosalie and Anatole chose to live on the relative outskirts of town because of that, far from the flocking jackdaws. The sneers. The cameras.

Rosalie and Anatole kept Marcy safe from those teeth, and Rosalie told herself for two decades that their home's blessings outweighed the costs, the seclusion. Despite executions not straining much from the government's fickle pockets, she and Anatole were not poorly off, and therefore Marcy and André could thrive for the time being. Their family owned an auto before any of the surrounding (but reasonably distanced) families, and Anatole was one of the first Frenchmen to obtain a license. It seemed exciting, owning a rare technology, and it made his trip to the prison or the town square less strenuous, though he admitted to missing train rides. The rickety vehicle made Rosalie's stomach lurch. *You can barely feel the air,* she had complained. Why would anyone want to be trapped inside a moving mechanical nightmare? It was a metal wagon only good for transporting the Widow.

Nothing was wrong with a good cycle ride, watching the wind shiver through oaks and red maples as one's heartbeat thundered in their ears. Rosalie missed the crisp mornings where she took a cycle and rode along the hills. In many official races, Rosalie beat most men when it came to speed. If it weren't for her love of racing, she never would've met Anatole.

That time was gone, though. Now, as the study gathered dust and age, Rosalie rewound her words with André until fiction sank in, and she worried her sentences like teeth on tobacco.

And then there was Marcy.

Marcy was still an adolescent girl, while André was grown. Rosalie was in the right; she meant to protect her daughter from the war, from the world. Marcy had years left before she needed to navigate what remained of her life, as it should've been. She was a gem, bright and confident. All the possible wrong paths for her daughter leered before Rosalie, the needles and pins. She didn't want to hinder Marcy, but she didn't want the world to smother her daughter either, didn't want her daughter to fall where Rosalie couldn't reach her. It was like Talia from the old Italian tale: the cursed, sleeping beauty had been peaceful in the woods before a king crept upon her helpless body. No briars kept Talia safe, and no matter the lengths Rosalie and Anatole taken to fortify their home, Rosalie dreamed of those kings, dreamed of their bruising hands and the thundering hooves of their dead-eyed horses.

2

Jehanne

When Jehanne opened her eyes, the light burned, and she screamed.

A child's cry echoed in her mind till it became laughter. Thrashing, Jehanne snapped her head to the side, her cheek wet with tears and black soil. The sun blazed into her, dribbled down her ears like candle wax, and the river by her fingers was as silver as mercury. Her skin itched. A suit. Wrong suit, wrong skin.

Warmth embraced her, and she was lifted closer to Heaven, and there was blue, soft blue against her cheek, and a man's aching voice pierced her. Before she could speak, her world darkened. A wolf stalked her dreams, its claws clicking against the inky black of her brain.

Jehanne's sickness lasted for days, and she couldn't tell wakefulness from dreams.

She rested in a bed, and her mind was fog. A man knelt by her side. He prayed, wept, cried out, but when she called to him, he melted into the shadows. Feathers scattered like snow on the ruddy sheets. Was the red her blood, her heart?

Sweat dripped down Jehanne's forehead, her nose, and cold wetness made her jump. She blinked, and an unsmiling woman leaned over her. She had thin lips and thick, black hair like pinned wires. The shadows under her eyes were purple and stern. The man was behind the woman, but no, his face was unlined and wrong, not sad enough to be the same man. Soon, he melted into a gray wash and vanished.

Jehanne asked without hearing her own words, "Where did he go?" The woman rippled away like a pebble drifting to the bottom of a pond, and Jehanne smelled smoke.

The next morning, she sat up and rubbed her eyelids till dark lashes fell on her knuckles like mice hairs. A tightness bothered her neck, and when she lifted a hand there, there was only the cotton nightgown with its collar snug against her neck. When she pushed it down, her fingers raked across a long, narrow scar horizontally lining the side of her neck.

"Drink this," a woman's voice said, and a cup was thrust into Jehanne's hand. Her vision adjusted, and there stood the wire-haired woman with a simple black dress and white apron.

Jehanne's focus drifted to the woman, to the cup of what looked like tea, and then to the woman again. "Who are you?"

"I am Mademoiselle Clair, a humble servant of this estate, and your father sent me to attend to you." No *How are you feeling?* or well wishes. No smile. Besides the faint frown lines around her mouth, Clair had smooth and pale skin.

Jehanne's room, even with the red and gold wallpaper and ornate canopy, was a bit dreary. She asked about her father, "Where is he?"

"He fears his presence would excite you, and your fever broke last night, so he doesn't want you to see him until you're better."

"Which will be when?"

"Soon, hopefully."

"His hair was gold, I remember that." Jehanne's attention drifted to the cup of liquid in her hands. "What's this for?"

Clair stared at the spot beside Jehanne's elbow. "The tea'll help you regain your mind. Drink it."

"If you're a servant, you shouldn't order me around."

Clair's frown deepened for an instant before returning to its normal severity. Brow rising, she said blankly, "I'm sorry, you're correct. Drink it, please."

That wasn't much of an improvement. "If it'll help." She had won, and she didn't want to concede, but she also wanted to stop the aches that weighed her to the mattress. Jehanne lifted the cup, sniffed, and wrinkled her nose. "It smells funny." But she drank anyway, and alongside the strange odor and dark color, the tea had a bitter taste. "Who . . . ?" No, the woman had already said her name. Clair, right. And Jehanne—yes, her name was Jehanne. How did she know?

She was nineteen, she knew that somehow, maybe from a dream, and she supposed this was her bedroom. To the servant, she said, "Why don't I remember you? And when I saw my father, I didn't know he was my father. That was my father crying here, right? Him and another man who looked like him."

"Your sickness almost killed you, and my mas—your father warned me that your mind might not be in the same place it was before you were ill."

"What was I sick with? How did he know?"

"I can't say the exact name, only that you'd been complaining of headaches and like your mind had caught on fire. Some sort of swelling, I presume."

Jehanne rubbed her temple. "I was in dirt, and water, I reached for water." She dragged her fingers down her cheeks. "Someone carried me here." Home, carried her home, carried her here with the golds, browns, and reds, the deep burgundy of her sheets. When she looked at her pillow, it was clean except for strands of hair.

"Yes, you were gone one morning, and your father and Monsieur Moreau, one of the other servants, went to find you. You were on the Vilaine's bank. You were covered in dirt and grass and scratches; it was difficult to keep the bed clean."

"How long have you been here?"

"As long as your father commands."

Jehanne rubbed her thumbs together. "How long is that?"

"Seven days."

"Really?" Jehanne's forehead crinkled. "Where do you sleep?"

"At the end of the bed."

Jehanne motioned to the sheets by the dimly shining footboard. "There?"

Clair pointed to the floor, expression unchanging.

Jehanne winced. She felt fleshy and tender, especially behind her eyes. She rubbed the line on the side of her neck. "I—do you know where I got this scar?"

"No."

"Do you know when Father will come see me?"

"I do not."

Jehanne huffed. "Helpful. Can you find out? What time is it?"

Clair tilted her head, her eyelids heavy, as if smacked blank by the sheer number of questions. "Do you mean the time of day or the time of year?"

"All of it, I guess."

"It's the morning, and we're a bit into October. Are you hungry?"

Jehanne frowned. She probably should be, but she was a little queasy, if anything. "Not really."

"Do you wish to take a bath?"

22

Jehanne's scalp crawled. She had the distinct feeling of not belonging in her own body. She must've looked like death. "Yes, I think so."

Clair nodded, her back so stiff Jehanne didn't know if anyone else could ever be so perfect a line. "We'll do that then, at your request. Before that, I'll tell your father how you're faring."

Before Clair could escape, Jehanne's hands rose. "Wait! Are you sure Father can't see me today?"

"I'll ask him."

"And my mother? What about my mother?"

Clair's eyes darted from Jehanne to the door, then to the carpet. Jehanne's heart sank, and she licked her cracked lips.

"I'm sorry," Clair said, her hands seeking direction.

"She's dead, isn't she?" The silence was answer enough. "How did she die?"

"I don't know." Clair looked to the carpet again.

Jehanne launched herself up and wrapped her fingers around the bedpost. Somehow, she knew her mother was dead, but she wanted to at least know why, to materialize a stark image in the mist. "Tell me! How can you not know? What do you know? What was it? Illness? Bitten by a bug? Cracked her head on the stairs? Kicked a sleeping wolf? Ate bad cheese?"

The servant faltered, her trembling left hand tightening on her collar. "I wish I could say. When I—I started working for your father, he was alone." Clair cleared her throat. "Besides your presence, of course."

"Would Father tell me what happened to her?"

"I suppose he could, once you're well enough."

Jehanne's limbs hurt from inactivity. To her left, by a curved wardrobe, was a curtained window, the drapes stippled with fleurs-de-lis. She uncovered herself so she could cross the room.

"What are you doing?" Clair said before Jehanne's bare feet hit the carpet. The servant followed her gaze and went to open the curtains herself.

"I know how to open curtains," Jehanne muttered, poorly hiding her pout.

"You mustn't exert yourself."

Had she always been this meek? "What was I like before my sickness?"

Clair blinked. "Just as you are now, I suppose."

Jehanne tasted those words, and they rubbed her gums wrong like cotton. She didn't feel like her whole self, whoever that whole self was. "Confused?"

"Stubborn."

"Oh, quite—"

"A fighter," Clair finished. She went to leave the room again.

Jehanne said to the servant's back, "Can I go with you?"

"Your father insisted that you stay in your room now." Clair didn't bother to pivot around. "The manor's too large. You might get lost or hurt yourself."

Jehanne's teeth ground together, and she tasted blood from her cheek. "I know how to walk. I remember that much."

"I'll tell your father you want to see him."

"Could I go outside one day?"

"I'll tell him you want to do that as well." Nothing in the servant's voice changed. What a strange woman.

Jehanne opened her mouth to thank her, but Clair left too soon.

Jehanne's mind still scattered and flounced about, an impasto of gold walls and ghost hands. Eyes where there should be hands and hands where there should be heads. And teeth for fingernails. The only person who drew her away from these images was Clair, who would attend to her, bathe her, dress her, feed her, fold her clothes in silence unless Jehanne spoke. Tonight, the chore was mending clothes at the end of the bed, and all Jehanne could do was watch and try not to sigh and shuffle her feet.

While working on the shoulder of a gown, Clair's brow was knitted in frustration, and her work was slow. As Clair struggled with the needle, Jehanne scratched her neck, which twinged slightly, as if she carried stories beneath the skin.

"You don't know how to sew," Jehanne said, just as an observation. "You're awful at it."

The servant paused. "It's been years."

"How did you learn?" An itch crawled from Jehanne's neck to the crown of her head.

The shadows under Clair's eyes darkened. "Father would make me mend his clothes before . . ." She swallowed, not looking up. "The way to move my hands, the patterns, it should come back to me if I think hard enough."

The movement, the patterns, yes, and a fire sparked in Jehanne, so she flapped her hands in an odd fashion.

Jehanne crawled forward and tapped the servant's shoulder. "Give me that."

"Why?"

"I can do it, I think. Just give it here."

Though Clair was hesitant, she complied, and Jehanne pinched the warm thinness of the needle for a moment, and though she only remembered movements and not a full memory, mending the gown came easily to her.

Clair warily eyed Jehanne's handiwork. "Your father would kill me if he knew I let you do this." Jehanne stared at her, startled, so the servant elaborated with what seemed to be a laugh under her breath. "I mean that it is my place to mend clothes, not yours. It wouldn't take so long if the master invested in a sewing machine, but I am, of course, glad to do honest work."

Jehanne didn't want to give up the gown, but she supposed she didn't need it now. "Here you go then." With a grunt, she returned the gown, the needle, and the thread. Clair cast it all aside and stood. She crossed the room, and after Clair pulled books off the shelf to the bed's left, Jehanne asked, "What are you doing?"

Clair sat on the edge of the mattress, which released a soft groan, and gestured curtly to Jehanne. A book was open in the servant's lap. "I've been instructed to help you read."

Jehanne sat beside her and looked at the pages, and it burned because none of the lines made any sense. She clapped a hand over her mouth. "Oh, dear Lord." Symbols, letters, words, yes. What they needed to be was obvious, yet she couldn't understand them.

Clair searched her face and the page. "What is it?"

Words, tiny little black worms crushed together, squirming and slipping away until they gave Jehanne a dull headache. "I don't understand." She clutched her hair and tugged on it, hoping an errant piece of mind would fall into place. "How gone am I that I can't remember how to read? What happened to me?" As her voice rose, Clair maintained her calm, expression straight and unyielding.

"All will be well, you'll see, but first we must start. You've made it this far. Best not to linger on the past, only recovery."

"I haven't done much at all. It's all too much."

"Let's take it step by step. I'm sure you'll learn again in little time." The encouragement was rigid. Dejected, Jehanne pressed and balled her hands together, and she flushed with heat at the persistence of Clair's stare.

"Please stop looking at me," Jehanne said, and the servant shifted and lowered her eyes.

Before Jehanne could dismiss her servant, Clair opened her mouth. "Your father told me to take you to him tomorrow."

Jehanne flooded with light, her melancholy forgotten. "Really?"

Clair beamed, or rather it was her version of a smile where the corners of her lips dimpled for a second before smoothing. "He's what a father should be. You're blessed to have him." Her pseudo-smile faded. "Some fathers sell their daughters, you know."

Jehanne wrinkled her nose. She couldn't let this matter rest, especially when she'd never seen this sort of wistful sentimentality from her servant. "What do you mean?"

The chill slinked back into the servant's voice. "It was just a meandering thought, nothing of import."

"Oh? And what's my father like? I hope he won't sell me if I'm too mouthy."

"If he ever did, I suspect the buyer would return you shortly."

Moving to the head of the bed, Jehanne threw a tasseled pillow, and it landed far to the left of Clair. "You are the worst servant in the world. In history, even."

"I'm certain I am, as certain as I am of your historical expertise." Jehanne ruffled. "Anyhow, to answer your question, your father's kind." Clair paused, and her mouth twitched like she wasn't sure what to say next. "He—he's a bit scrambled from the war."

That tickled Jehanne's head. "What war?"

Clair pursed her lips, she did that a lot, and gripped a book page so hard it tore a little at the top. "The Great War against the Germans and their friends. Your father served for a time."

"Is the war still happening?"

"Yes."

"Then why did he leave?"

"He had a nervous breakdown, so you should be gentle with him."

"But he'll be okay, won't he?"

Clair narrowed her eyes, maybe noting the strangeness of someone recovering from an illness being more concerned for another's health. "I'm sure he'll be fine."

Jehanne resolved to focus on her lesson.

When Clair finished, she let Jehanne keep the book and left for her own quarters, which she had mentioned were in the attic when she didn't need to watch an unconscious Jehanne. That stirred Jehanne's pity, but for now, her eyes stayed on the pages and pictures before her. The book was heavy on her cramping leg, and when she went to rest, she couldn't help but have it beside her and mouth what words she did know.

Though her eyelids drooped, she leafed through the hefty book and stared at the blurring words, those black, thorny little secrets on the yellowing white. On one page, there was a single vibrant picture: a red-haired woman leaned on a tree with a solemn frown. Sobbing women circled a dead crowned man covered in furs. One of the women with a gold cloak and gold crown cradled his head in her lap, and another in black cradled a tome next to him. The king wore a white tabard with a black dragon sigil.

As Jehanne closed her eyes, the dead king and the mourning women imprinted the black with red and purple. She drifted into a half-dream with a sword and fire and men singing, and she was sitting cross-legged on the dirt.

A howl broke over the hills, and Jehanne snapped awake. Clair's name rose to her lips, but the sound didn't repeat itself, so she settled her head down again. Though the room was quiet, she couldn't bring herself to turn the bedside lamp off, and she stared at the door, at the knob's bronze, churlish gleam. A sound echoed in the back of her mind, a boy's scream.

3

Marcy

I'd rather see her dead than with you.

Marcy stood in the kitchen and choked back the pressure bubbling up her throat. She was thirteen, old enough to marry and have children. In the eyes of the laws that made her father execute men, she could consent to be with André like any other woman. Really, marrying young would be considerably less bloody than other family habits.

The day had been going splendidly too before she made her mistake. Before she kissed André and saw Maman in the living room with her hard stare and frosty blue dress. Marcy had only her back to defend herself from the chill, then.

But before that, she joked with Papa as they always joked, as he never acted with anyone else, except maybe Maman when she was more relaxed. They played with Jolie and brushed her coat. Papa referred to Marcy as an old woman, since she found herself to be more mature than she'd ever been, which was not *in*correct. She had replied, "Your birthday's closer than mine. How old will you be?"

"I'm hurt you don't know."

"I can't think that far back," Marcy had said.

Papa mussed up her hair, not that she kept it spectacularly well-kempt at home. She saw no need to keep it pinned up and perfect all the time.

Marcy's mind wandered as she leaned her cheek on Papa's arm. "Can I learn to drive?"

"Why would you want to do that?"

"I don't know."

"You should ask your mother."

Marcy sighed against his warm sleeve. "Why?"

"Poupée." Papa shifted and cupped her chin in his gentle hand. "She loves you."

"I know, but you know she'd never let me do it." The dog nudged her hand. "She'll look at me like I kicked Jolie."

Marcy faded back to the kitchen, feeling like a shade. The soft morning made the room pink, which was Marcy's favorite color. That was good. She could do this; she could ask Maman to go to the park. With a war and old anxieties coming true, Marcy's acute pangs weren't the world's end, but they hurt like the pinch of moving a hand stuck with a splinter. War, death, sadness, and still, Marcy couldn't tell if her feelings for André were true or a need for something different, something exciting that'd touch her core. She couldn't discern when jokes became possibilities.

All she wanted to do was kiss him because he looked like sea salt, but he tasted like old coffee.

One foot after another, avoiding where the kitchen tiles were the creakiest, Marcy edged herself to the kitchen's threshold, where it met the living room entrance. Maman was on the couch reading. Since Marcy had stood in the kitchen hiding, the pink had gone silver, which made Maman look unreal in her blue dress. Maman looked pretty this way, Marcy thought. Her mother was beautiful, no doubt.

When Marcy checked the bedroom earlier, Papa was gone, maybe for groceries, maybe for a job, which was a shame, because he gave her yeses easier.

"Maman."

"Good morning, poupée." Maman gave her a tired smile, though that was normal; her mother never looked fully rested.

"I had—I have a question."

"I would presume I have an answer."

Marcy looked down at her shoes. "I want to go to the park. On my own. To, you know, walk around."

Maman frowned. "You can't walk around here?"

So it began. "I just want to go somewhere different."

"Poupée, there are children going missing. Did you read the paper, the story about the butcher's boy?"

"I'll be careful."

"And he wasn't?"

"The butcher's boy disappeared at night, didn't he? I won't be out when it's dark, I swear." Marcy swallowed. "Maman, please, trust me. I wouldn't make you and Papa worry." She should've touched Maman's shoulder, or maybe Maman should've come over and touched hers.

"I'm not so certain you should leave unsupervised. It's improper for a young woman to be out alone."

"You would do it, wouldn't you?"

Maman stared at the space behind Marcy's head. "Years ago. Everything was different then."

Marcy persisted. "Then it's fine now. It's not that far, and Papa's been letting me do it for a year. I've been doing it for a year, and nothing's happened, has it?"

"No, but—"

"Maman, I know how to be careful. I'm not stupid."

With a sharp breath, Maman raked one hand through her hair and furled the other in her lap. "Have you ever thought it's not *your* actions I worry about, but everyone else's?" That was a possibility, yes, but it seemed like a lie. When Marcy was little, Maman would keep her distance, flinch away, and wear gloves when holding her. It was as if Marcy was diseased and Maman tried to keep herself clean.

Deep down, if Maman hated her and wanted her gone, she wouldn't care if Marcy disappeared, and she wouldn't worry at all. Yet, something was broken, something Marcy couldn't fix on her own.

"André can come with me."

"No, he cannot."

"Why? He's grown. He can probably fight." He probably couldn't, but Marcy could run quicker than him if someone assaulted them, so Maman really couldn't argue with her there. André had never caught her when they played as children.

Shaking her head, Maman curled a hand on the couch arm. "I don't trust him with you."

"Why?"

"I don't see why I should explain myself."

Marcy muttered, half-intended for only herself, "Papa'd let me." She wanted to run to him now, to smell the tobacco she hated and the wool coat and cologne she loved, the

34

cologne Papa made himself. She wanted to continue to goad him to stop smoking because of his doctor's orders and lean against him in the garden. He understood her.

By the look in her eyes, Maman had caught what Marcy said under her breath. "I'm not your papa."

"I can take care of myself. If I'm ever in trouble, I know how to find help. You know that, don't you?"

In less than a minute, Maman had gone from stiff and impassive to slouched and fraught. Her face was an arrangement of knots and dark shadows, and she was no less distant, no less lost within herself. Maman could have this faint, ethereal charm, but her head was stamped with last century's ghosts. Marcy wanted to understand. She knew what Maman had gone though, but that knowledge wasn't enough. It was like lightning had split Babel open when Marcy was little, and their one shared language had been lost.

Marcy stepped forward until she was by the couch, and her mother looked wary. This could or couldn't work. Marcy put a hand on her mother's knee.

"Maman, please."

Please, so I can be away from you.

Maman faltered. "I don't want anything to happen to you."

"I promise nothing bad'll happen to me. You taught me too well."

Maman looked helpless and small when she averted her eyes and pinched the bridge of her nose. "But that isn't enough, and you know it." Marcy could only watch as Maman rubbed her eyes with her fingers and released a heavy sigh. "If you must, just please go soon, while it's brighter."

"Thank you!" Marcy embraced Maman, pressing her cheek against her mother's. Maman stiffened, before raising her arms to return the gesture. "You have no idea what this means to me."

"Yes, well, you must promise me you'll take your coat so you don't become sick."

They separated. "I will, Maman."

"And your hat—"

"I will."

"And in case it rains, you'll need your boots so your feet won't . . ."

Weary, Marcy nodded. "I know, Maman."

Maman bowed her head, looking to the side at something Marcy couldn't see.

Marcy's victory was a little sour. With the unspoken walls between her and Maman, she suspected, even if this ended well, this wouldn't be their last quarrel. The next, she suspected, would not go as well as this one.

4

Jehanne

The second Clair entered the room, Jehanne pushed herself off the pillow and said, "Did you hear something last night, something like a scream?"

"Let's prepare you for the day," Clair replied, retrieving the hairbrush on the vanity.

"And now, back to my question. The one you just glossed over." Jehanne may've been bedridden for days with little recollection of past events, but she surmised someone hearing about screaming would express concern. Intrigue, at least.

Clair's brow furrowed as she strode to the side of the bed. "Please." It shocked Jehanne how soft her voice was, a different kind of quiet. "Let's get ready for the day."

"You know, I don't need a maid."

"You wouldn't have said that if you saw yourself covered in sweat and excrement."

Jehanne's face flooded with heat. Her illness, her near-death, her loss of memories.

"You're the servant, and you think it's proper to talk to me like this? I could tell Father."

Clair shrank as if preparing herself for a blow.

"I didn't mean disrespect."

"Oh? You used my sickness to avoid a basic question. I take that as an insult."

"I don't know. Is that what you want to hear? I don't know if I heard anything."

Jehanne grabbed her sleeve. "You know it isn't. Why would I want to hear that of all things? Who would be satisfied with that?"

"Besides the typical creaking of the manor—no, I heard nothing. Are you sure you weren't dreaming?"

Jehanne pulled away. She wasn't sure. "I don't know. I don't know anything when I'm disallowed my own memories, my family. What about when I thought I saw Father? He cried by my bedside, didn't he?"

Clair sniffed and put down the brush so she could straighten her sleeve. "You'll see him soon, so no use pondering on it."

"Soon? You said today."

"I know, and it'll be today, but there needs to be prep—"

"Right now. I'm going. Goodbye." Jehanne tossed off her covers and, after momentary dizziness, stormed away from the servant.

Clair followed. "Your hair—you aren't even dressed— your father'll be furious with me if I let you leave now." When Jehanne reached the bedroom door, her servant showed remarkable new speed and stood between her and freedom. "Please, you must be patient. He's worried. He hasn't come because he was afraid he might provoke your senses too much, and you'd have a fit and end up right where you were."

Jehanne squinted. "Why? I'm not having a fit right now, and aren't I upset enough?"

"It's stupid to overwork yourself when you shouldn't."

"I'm not stupid!" Jehanne shouted, raising both hands. Clair flinched and jerked up one hand, as if defending herself from a blow. Jehanne paused. "What's wrong?"

The servant lowered her hand. "Calm down. You'll give yourself a fit. I'm here to fulfill your father's wishes. To protect you, to keep you safe and happy. You'll have shelter, food, and comfort. That's more than most can ask for in an hour, much less a lifetime."

"I don't need you to tell me what I have to appreciate, and I most certainly don't have to listen to you, especially when you called me stupid."

Clair's throat moved as she swallowed, and her temple had a cold sheen to it. "Very well, my apologies."

Jehanne stiffened and dropped her hands from her hip. "As you should be."

"Could you find it in yourself to forgive me?"

"I'll have to think about it. It's a terrible thing to say."

"I didn't mean—"

"Don't try to take it back. You should at least claim it."

Clair rubbed her forehead. "You mustn't exert yourself, but, if you wish, I'll ready you to see your father." Jehanne's eyes widened, and Clair met her gaze warily. "Isn't that what you want?"

It was, and though Jehanne didn't want to let the energy building in her dissolve, she returned to the bed and let the servant brush her hair.

Jehanne realized her right hand was clenched shut, and when she opened it, there were red moon marks. "You said Father's nice, right?"

Clair made a noncommittal noise, but didn't stop her duty. "He is."

Jehanne's hand was slick when Clair guided her down the hall, but if the servant was disgusted by the wet nervousness beneath her grip, she gave no sign. Lions, wolves, flowers, and crosses marked the oil paintings lining the walls. Beasts obscured in dense brush beside flourishing carnations and sad, pale women mourning Christ. Then another with a mud-brown acrylic bowl where grapes draped down like fat, green rosaries.

Jehanne's attention wandered to her servant, to a silver glint in Clair's apron pocket, the fabric too weighed down for the object to be a sewing needle.

"What is that?"

Clair followed her gaze. "A knife."

Jehanne frowned. "What is it for?"

"Protection."

"From what?"

"Anyone who intrudes."

"Does that happen a lot? Intruders?" Jehanne adjusted her fingers in Clair's hawkish clutch.

"Preparations don't hurt."

"Do you expect—" They halted to a stop outside an open door.

"This is your father's study. When he's not in his room, he spends time here."

They entered the study. The room was lit by a roaring hearth and smelled of book must. There were many armchairs, with two in the center by a polished table that had a half-empty glass of wine.

Both chairs were occupied. A man—Father, yes, the one who had cried by her—held another's hand. At least, that was how it appeared at first, two men reaching across the distance, but on a second glance their hands weren't touching, only moving as hands did in conversation. The other man looked so much like Father, with the same golden shine to his hair in the firelight, the similar pleasant, lupine features. Father's hair and skin were so fair she didn't see his beard at first. His tunic was Heaven-blue.

The two men looked to Jehanne, her heart stopped, and they whispered, so even when Jehanne strained she couldn't hear. But it was when their lips stopped that Father shone in the firelight as she met his eyes. He graced

41

her with something close to awe and disbelief, and all she craved was to close the distance between them.

The younger man, she guessed, was the servant Clair mentioned before. Moreau. He wasn't dressed as plainly as Clair. His scarlet tunic alone was much different than a simple apron and dress.

Standing, Father said to Moreau, "Will you go feed the doves for me?" His voice was honey, and Jehanne felt complete for the first time since she had awoken after her sickness. Moreau bowed and obeyed, not looking at Jehanne, but passing a glance at Clair as he brushed past them. Clair's hold tightened before she let go of Jehanne.

Overwhelmed, Jehanne did what came to her first, and she rushed forward and swept her arms around Father's shoulders. Though he was taller than her, he'd bent a little like he anticipated her action, like the shore molded by sea waves. With his nose buried in her shoulder, he inhaled as though suppressing a sob, and he embraced Jehanne like she'd turn to salt the moment he released her.

As an afterthought, Father said to Clair, who had taken an interest in the floor, "You may go." The servant bowed, as much as one could when her head was already inclined, and left.

"How are you feeling, pup?"

Jehanne pulled away begrudgingly. "I'm all right."

"Good, good." His breath smelled of wine, but his lingering hand was soft on her cheek. "You gave me quite a scare. I imagine you have questions. Come, let's sit."

When Jehanne settled down, she asked, "Why isn't Mother here?"

Oddly enough, despite his previous suggestion for them to sit, Father stood close to her.

Just a day ago, Jehanne had felt a warmth she connected to her dead mother, warmth as honest as Heaven's fires. The warmth of being a tiny child and resting against Mother, yes, and a scent, a taste settled in the back of her throat. Hay? She had attempted to weave her senses into coherence, yet the memory was cramped, scratchy, and gone before Clair gave Jehanne her special tea. The warmth she felt now was similar, but stronger.

Father scrutinized her like she was a porcelain doll he didn't want to break. "Ah, straight to the point. You must be my daughter." His smile was sad, and Jehanne thought he wouldn't answer, but he did. "She passed." Clair had told her that, though maybe she wasn't supposed to.

"What happened?"

"She was sick."

"Was it the same illness I had?"

The lines around Father's eyes became more pronounced. He hadn't looked terribly old until now. "I'm not sure. I'm not a doctor."

That led to another inquiry. "Why don't I see a doctor, or why doesn't one come here?"

"You can never trust them. Charlatans, the entire lot. Most of them don't even believe in God, you know."

"No, I didn't know, but a doctor heals the body. I don't expect a sermon." She didn't think a doctor needed to believe, unless the illness came from something wrong with her soul too.

Father settled his large hand on the crown of her head; he seemed unable to keep his hands off her. "There's not a disconnect between the body and soul, I don't think."

"Another question." Jehanne pointed to the side of her neck. "How did I get this scar?"

Father followed her gaze and wet his lips. It took him a moment to answer, and only the crackling fire filled their silence. "You tried to chase a feral cat in the garden when you were a child, and I'm afraid the cat won." That was probably before Clair worked here, since the servant hadn't the slightest clue about Jehanne's scar.

"What other rooms are there I can explore?"

"Hmm, come with me. I have something that might interest you."

He took her hand, a touch Jehanne welcomed, and led her to a smaller, emptier room just across the hall. The room had dusty bookshelves, but in the center lounged a strange device beside a green armchair with clawed feet.

She asked, "What's this room for?"

"It's a bit of a neglected second study."

"What's this?" Jehanne lifted the strange device, or part of it, which was connected to what looked like a long pig's tail.

Father seemed to hide a chuckle, but not an unkind one. "A telephone."

Jehanne fit her chin between it. "What does it do?"

Father took the telephone from her and put it against her ear. The cold shocked her. "You can speak to another person by moving the rotary dial over the numbers." He pointed to the wheel with holes.

"Really?" Jehanne couldn't hide her awe. This couldn't be real. "What's our number?"

Father's face broke into a fond smile, likely from her enthusiasm. He told her the four-digit number and their address, but when she tried to enter the first one in with her tenuous remembrance of numbers, Father tenderly took her free hand in his. "No, pup, it'll do no good to call ourselves."

"Who could I call?"

"No one, as of yet."

"Do you call anyone? Can I go outside and meet people?"

Father's brow furrowed. "So soon after you've gotten out of bed?"

"I would've left sooner if it weren't for the servant keeping me there." Jehanne couldn't help her pout. Clair could be tiresome with all her rules and demands.

His words were good-humored rather than admonishing. "Now, pup, she only does as I ask, and I pay her exceedingly well to do just that."

"It makes me feel bad that she does so much." To be honest, it didn't really. She enjoyed having someone do things for her, but it felt gracious to say that. Her father would be impressed with her.

Father's smile didn't waver. "Nonsense. You are within your rights to ask the servants to do anything. If you want to leave, there's a park nearby, just across the road, but I wouldn't want you to go so soon and without supervision. And I wouldn't want you to exhaust yourself staying out too long."

"Well, when could I go?"

His knuckles brushed her temple, and he leaned down to kiss her there. "Let me think on it."

"Father, please?"

"I won't leave you pining, pup, I swear. Now, would you like breakfast?"

Jehanne eased her breathing once she closed the manor's white-stained front door. She really shouldn't. It was a bad, no, terrible idea. To betray Father's trust while he read in his study, to go out into the unknown. Even the front yard was strange with its globes of violet weeds and yellow wildflowers. Just off the segmented path, parked to the side of it, was this odd mechanical thing with cataracts in its eyes, a hood covering the interior, tentacled grooves running along its side, and wheels for feet. When Jehanne squeezed her way past the front gate's needle teeth, she swore the bushes along the dirt road stared back and that the red dots she saw weren't unpicked berries, but a bushel of alien eyes.

The road was hard and gray, a flattened snake. An old couple smiled at her beneath the crescent-shaped French pussy willows draping their fuzzy, pink hair on the road. Jehanne smiled back, life brimming deep in her, yet she couldn't suppress the shiver that rattled her shoulders. With their matching black garbs, the couple would have looked like two elderly, oversized crows if it weren't for their ghost-white faces, like they'd burrowed their noses in flour. The whiteness crinkling around their eyes and mouths reminded Jehanne of a dream where flames engulfed her.

In that dream, she cried out. Little blackbirds sifted around the burning, bone-white earth, and she screamed for them to fly away, to keep away from the fire. She prayed to the Virgin for their protection and her release. An angel hung above her like a weeping portrait.

Jehanne begged for help. *Jesus, Jesus, Jesus.* The angel had five pairs of eyes, at least on its face alone, and stars dripping down its sable mantle. When she touched its iron skin, the coldness became wet sand, squelched and funneled between her fingers. What she thought were wings were wisps of sky, a white, spired horizon, and she was falling below herself, sinking into water as black as pitch.

As Jehanne reached the silty bottom, she met another creature, a hunched, emaciated giant with skin white as the clouds and teeth like a jackal's. A long tongue and a vulture's half-clipped wings. Its eyeless face was like a skull without flesh, and its long, pale body was a cross between a human, a horse, and a dog; spindles poked out of its arms and spine like it was part-fish. Thick, black worms shivered on its back and side.

Instead of moving to attack, the giant waited on its haunches, and Jehanne had the inkling that she was witnessing something both profane and godly, though she could only guess what. Jehanne woke before dawn with a little blood cresting her pillow, which she had tossed under the bed because she had ten more. With a ringing in her ears, she had suffered a thundering headache and wiped off blood where she'd bitten her lip.

After her recollection, Jehanne realized the old couple was gone, and she was alone with her thoughts and the brisk, howling wind. She walked, and besides the wind, she heard only the sound of her shoes slapping the hard road.

It was okay. So long as she knew her way back, nothing terrible could happen. As she continued, she met an expanse of muted, proud birches and oaks; there were also winding dirt paths with benches.

But the most striking image was a girl with red hair trying to climb one of the trees.

5

Marcy

André **was a father, and** she'd do anything to forget that. Even climb this stupid tree. For at least a week, which was a substantial chunk of time, she wanted to at least kiss him, that was all, and she had, yet it'd been empty, not enough.

So, she tried to climb, but the tree was smooth like a scaleless lizard, so gaining traction was hard. Marcy grunted and landed on her rear. Maman would have words if she saw this; her mother often didn't have words for her unless it was a correction of something such as this.

Well, I have the boots, coat, and hat she asked for, don't I? Defeated on the ground, the hat was by her elbow and wings-up like a headsail.

From behind, a voice said, "Hello?"

Marcy hurried to her feet, forgetting all about the hat. When she swiveled about, there was a girl staring at her, and this stranger's face and arms were long like a wolf's. Marcy admired the girl's body, especially the shape of her legs, at least what could be discerned beneath the pants. She wondered how soft the skin there felt. It also felt good when those brown eyes looked at her in curiosity, and like Marcy, the girl's hair was a mess, wind-flustered, but a darker blonde where Marcy's hair was red.

But the girl's clothes were odd. A simple tunic and pants, how strange, especially in public, despite Marcy's limited knowledge of such. That sort of attire on a woman was probably not unheard of, but it was still boyish, though not unflattering.

The girl looked at Marcy like she had sneaked behind *her.*

Nevertheless, the stranger said, "Sorry."

Marcy tried to save face by grinning and brushing herself off. This was the first girl close to her age she had encountered in years, and she wouldn't squander that. "Hi. What's your name?"

Without hesitation, which struck Marcy as odd, the girl answered, "Jehanne." She looked closer to André's age; there was something about her that seemed experienced yet untouched all at once.

Marcy extended a hand and grinned. "I'm Marcy, Marcy Deibler."

Jehanne stared in confusion for a moment before her eyes brightened and she shook Marcy's hand. The air between them grew solemn. Jehanne said, "I'm really not allowed to be out long."

"Oh, me neither."

"I should go soon. I don't want my father to worry."

Marcy persisted, "How often do you come out here? I don't go out much. I mostly look at newspapers to see what's happening outside. Do you read them?"

Jehanne's lips tightened in thought. "I didn't see any on the front steps. I think—maybe the servants throw them out." Servants? Like in those pulp Gothic stories? "And I can't read much."

Now *that* was curious, Jehanne not being able to read much, especially if she could afford servants, but the servants thing came to the forefront of Marcy's mind. "Wait, where do you live?"

Jehanne pointed. "Just down the road, where there are a little more trees."

Marcy frowned. That was where the creepy manors were. Some were even a few centuries old, Papa had told her. Mostly old people stayed in them. "How big is your house?"

"It's pretty big."

"Do you live with your parents?" Her father, at least, based on what she'd said. Marcy was letting her mouth go so she could keep this interesting new girl here.

"My father." Jehanne paused, gazing down at her clasped hands. "My mother is dead."

"Oh, ah, I'm sorry." Even with their troubles, Marcy couldn't cope if Maman died because that'd ruin any chances of them learning to speak the same language. "I could come visit you sometime, if you need someone to talk to." Marcy hoped the bold desperation didn't burden her voice.

"I could ask Father. Maybe. I'd like it. Home could use more noise in the day. But I should go before—"

"Let's climb a tree."

Jehanne's forehead darkened with lines. "Father will . . ."

Panic beat against Marcy's ribs like wings. If she didn't get this girl to stay, she'd lose the one fresh connection she had made in the past several years. She was always kept home and tutored by her parents. She needed Jehanne to stay even if it killed Marcy to make it happen. She sifted through possible ways to keep Jehanne there, the stories she'd read about the ghost barber or the death-bride—no, telling those stories would be a bit gruesome, though it was a guilty pleasure for Marcy to read those kinds of tales this time of year, the time Papa made his toffees and a special orange, caramelized cake with apples, hazelnuts, and raisins.

There was the book she'd read, *Là-Bas*, but it was grotesque too, and Jehanne might not be interested in that. The story had been about a man of Brittany, who was hanged in Nantes because he had sold his soul to the Devil. He had done so with the help of an alchemist and, after, murdered hundreds of innocents, so the demon he conjured up would give him silver to save him from becoming destitute; there were rumors today the man became a demon himself after the Church burned his body.

No, that wouldn't do.

"Please?" Marcy ran and tilted her thumb toward a gnarled branch that was tinged with gold. Best of all, it didn't molt like the birches. "Look! This looks like a good one, lots of places to put your feet." Jehanne walked over and inspected the tree. "It won't take that long, and then you can leave."

Marcy's excitement caught on, apparently, because Jehanne seemed reluctant to crush her hopes. "Okay."

Marcy took note of how Jehanne didn't shake in the cold. "Aren't you freezing?"

"Should I be?"

Marcy lifted a corner of her mouth. "I suppose you don't have to." She tilted her chin up. "Are you afraid you'll fall?"

Jehanne flashed her a grin. "No, I have better faith than anyone."

They climbed until they were both sitting on rough bark, and Marcy laughed once she caught her breath. Both girls stayed like that for a good minute before Jehanne, hands shaking, broke the silence.

"I was sick recently, and I almost died."

Marcy's heart hurt. "If you don't want to talk about it, that's okay."

Jehanne tilted her head. "I have amnesia; I can remember almost nothing about the past."

"I don't really know what amnesia means, except for the memory loss. I've read about it in stories, where people lose their memories and get them back when they need to, those odd little vampire and ghost stories, but I don't think I can be much help."

"Talking helps, I think. I just don't have that many people to talk to." God, Marcy understood that well.

"Is it okay if I ask you questions? Can you just not remember the moments before you were sick?"

"I remember the smell of hay and hearing songs. And smoke. I have dreams of—I don't know how to explain them, but they're connected somehow. I feel it. I don't remember anything else, not clear pictures, and it's not normal, I don't think. I can't place where or when. Or who I was with. I don't remember my mother or anyone. I think I sometimes remember Father, but I can't tell if I'm just recalling dreams."

"That must be frustrating, sorry." Quite odd, especially the hay thing. Father had hay for André to practice with the Widow, the guillotine, but she couldn't imagine someone who lived in a fancy manor needing hay. "Do you have any horses you feed hay?"

Jehanne's knuckles whitened. "Not that I know of, but you're right, it is strange. My mind'll fix itself, won't it? I wish I could know, but I can't crack open my own skull to see."

"That'd do no good for your head."

Jehanne laughed, and Marcy liked the sound of it. Jehanne looked wild and pretty when she smiled, and Marcy found her worries over André dampening. For a breezy point in time, Marcy was not only content, but she had forgotten about the war and the missing children.

Marcy asked, "Do you have a doctor to do tests?"

"Father doesn't trust doctors."

Empathy swelled in Marcy. "I know what that's like. Maman's peculiar about medicine." Maman would administer half, always half, of the instructed dosage. Marcy remembered the pharmacy when she was younger, the way Maman kept her close. The man with the ashen face at the drugstore counter was nice and made Maman pay less, but Maman wouldn't look him in the eye.

("Ten drops, Maman. The man at the counter said ten, not five."

"Pardon my language, but I don't care what the damn fool at the counter said." Marcy remained silent as Maman handed her the dose.)

In earnest, Marcy said, "I'm glad you didn't die though. It's so strange, but wonderful to meet a girl close to my age. If there's anything I can do to help you—"

Jehanne asked abruptly, "Do you want to hear about the strange dreams? They're in my head now."

"Sure." Marcy knew that, at least for her, it was easier to talk to someone she hardly knew, to spill out what she couldn't tell those at home. Maman carried her for nine months, and yet Marcy felt like they were two separate species. Papa would rub Marcy's back, but she almost felt like revealing anything bad, putting words to it, would somehow disappoint him because they took joy from each other's happiness. She couldn't ruin that. But even though she didn't know Jehanne that well, it was like they were connected by the spine.

"Angels, there are angels with eyes, so many eyes and wings and teeth and fire."

Eyes and wings? Seemed normal, not that Marcy was an angel expert. Teeth and fire? That sounded more hellish than any engravings of angels with their flowing curls and long, white robes. But it interested Marcy more than it frightened her. New stories were the best sorts of stories. "How do you know they're angels? The wings?"

Jehanne sucked in her bottom lip. "That's a good question. I just know."

Marcy didn't know what else to say about angels. She'd never met one, personally. "I'm sorry to change the subject—"

"No, go ahead."

"My maman always keeps me in the house, and it's making me balmy." Marcy didn't like bad-mouthing Maman because Maman, like everyone, had her reasons for being strange.

"I know how that is." The wind made the trees breathe.

"Do you have any brothers or sisters to keep you company?"

"I . . . not that I recall." Jehanne knitted her brow, as if confused. "Not that I know of."

Marcy's face scrunched in concern. "What is it?"

"I just had one of these half-thoughts like I remembered something, but I can't tell if it happened or if it was a dream."

"What do you mean?"

"You know the story about the sheep in the Book of Luke? Or the story about the lost son?"

"Yes." It'd been years since Marcy touched the Bible. She was only Catholic because she didn't really know what else to be. She was baptized, and she had gone to church three times in the last decade. That was as good a confirmation as any.

"If a man has one hundred sheep and one strays, he looks for that lost one instead of tending to the others who don't wander. If a man has a son who leaves and sins and a son who always stays, the father gives the errant one more attention than the one who obeys and never leaves."

Maybe Marcy would've understood if she were a better Catholic. "I don't follow."

"I feel like I'm that lost sheep or that lost son, lost and found, but I can't remember anything after returning home."

"If you have faith, then it should all make sense in time, right?" To Marcy, faith was like a cluster of fireflies, like the sparrows that'd perch by her window but fly off if she dared reach for them.

Jehanne opened her mouth—

"Jehanne!"

Startled, Marcy scrambled to keep from falling out of the tree, and it took her time before she looked down. Below them was a woman with pinned-up hair so like Maman's with its curls and dark color. It'd be easy from a distance to mistake this woman for Maman, except she looked young, even with the sad bruises under her eyes and the scowl set on her mouth.

The woman said, "Get down here."

Marcy gave a start and looked helplessly at Jehanne, whose expression was one of annoyance. "I thought your maman was . . ."

Jehanne sighed. "Servant, a bossy one." Conspiratorially, she leaned close. "Should be careful. If I fall on her, I don't think she'd forgive me." She had an odd look.

"What is it?" Marcy asked.

The other girl's nose twitched. "She's never said my name before."

Marcy hurried out her response. "We can see each other again, right?" From below, the woman's eyes burned into her.

What sort of world is this girl from?

Despite the question, Marcy wanted to see it. She had visited the ocean with her family when she was a child, and Jehanne was her new ocean.

With a cheeky smile, Jehanne told Marcy the four digits of her telephone number, and the second her feet hit the ground, the hawkish servant latched on to her wrist. As the two grew smaller with distance, pity and residual guilt welled up; Marcy had let her loneliness convince her it was better for Jehanne to stay with her instead of hurrying home.

But she had made a friend, and surely that'd lead to great things, so she allowed herself to relish that like one of Papa's raspberry tarts, even as the day grew shadowed and a blackbird shuffled on the ground, croaking with unease.

6

Jehanne

Clair was stronger than she had any right to be.

"What were you thinking?" The servant all but barked out as she dragged Jehanne past the front gate. "Do you know what your father would've done if you were hurt? What he would've done to himself? To us?"

Jehanne's teeth clacked together. "You can't talk to me like this."

"You could've died. Do you understand that much?"

"I'm not stupid. I just went to the park. It isn't as if I tried to go to the front lines—"

"That's not funny." Clair opened the front door and propped it open with one hand. "Your father was hysterical, and he would've—"

"But I'm all right, aren't I?" Jehanne yanked away as the door thudded shut behind them. "If you please, I'd like to keep my shoulder in place." Hysterical. Yes, Father, from what Jehanne had seen of him, was frail, like the slightest wind would make him go from brittle to broken. Her servant hadn't been jesting—well, she never jested—when she said the war terrorized him.

Clair raked her hands through her hair, which stuck out in odd places and came loose from her pins. Her eyes were as wide as an owl's and as frantic as a starving fox's.

Jehanne's heart thudded so hard it hurt as she followed her servant to the study. It looked the same as it had early that morning, even down to Father and Moreau whispering together, except, this time, they were on their feet.

As the two men stood beside one another, Jehanne noticed Moreau was taller than Father, by at least a nose, and leaner. He was clean and neat, except for four red lines on his wrist. When Moreau caught Jehanne staring at the scratches, he pulled his cuff down.

Father went over to Jehanne, and his touch on her arms was gentle. "Are you hurt?"

"No."

He looked behind Jehanne. "What was she doing?"

Clair replied, "She was at the park with another girl."

Jehanne added, "She was harmless."

Father snapped his fingers. "Leave, both of you."

The servants departed; once their footsteps faded and Father was satisfied with their distance, his eyes met Jehanne's. Her throat felt as if God had stuffed it with lead.

60

"Why did you leave without telling me?" Father's voice was deep, insistent. He hadn't released her.

"I just needed the air."

"And you had to go that far?"

"It wasn't that far, not really."

"You are my world—"

"And you're mine."

"And to lose you again—"

"I'm not lost."

"Let me finish. If I lost you again, I wouldn't survive." He let her go and paced. "You mustn't leave without telling me again."

"All right, I won't." For his sake. Something burdened him, something that lent a quickness to his movements. "Father?"

He snapped his head up. "Yes?" Even though his voice was rougher than usual, it calmed her, as if Father possessed some sort of mystical charm, some power to sway others to his side. Jehanne wanted to curl up beside him and sleep by the hearth under his steady hand.

Jehanne swallowed, her back losing its weight. "Is there something else wrong? Is there anything I can do to help?"

Father graced her with a morose half-smile. "Only your presence is needed." With caustic humor, he added, "And your consideration."

"I'm sorry."

"Pup, you're flushed. You should go rest, and Clair will bring you food when it's time for supper."

"I don't need to rest."

"Yes, well, I do."

Jehanne couldn't let the matter rest there, so it was late at night, when Clair retired to the attic, that she slipped through the hallways and tried to find Father's room.

She didn't know where to go till she heard deep sobbing.

She encountered Moreau, who wasn't the one crying. He was in a robe, and in the shadows, she couldn't tell if his legs were clad. What an odd thing that he was already undressed. Father must've called for his assistance while Moreau was in bed.

Father, it was Father crying. She heard his voice in the sobs.

She thought she'd be in trouble, but Moreau only looked at her with a sharp curiosity. Jehanne asked, "Does he do this often?"

Moreau rolled a shoulder. "Yes." He said it like she'd asked him whether it'd rain.

"What should I do?"

The line of his mouth was black. "Your guess is as good as mine." Before Jehanne could ask anything else, he tore away.

What a strange man.

Swallowing, Jehanne rested her hand on the cool, dark wood of the bedroom door. It was just Father. Hesitance and fear were nonsensical because Father had shown only love in the little time she knew him in this strange second life of hers. That completeness in her blood when he embraced her hadn't dwindled. Even his frustration after her disobedience sprung from his devotion toward her.

She inched open the door and stepped in Father's bedroom. The room looked like Jehanne's, only bluer, which calmed her. Same wardrobe, bookshelves, bed, and vanity. He knelt not by his bed, but on the floor in front of his wardrobe. On the left door hung an imperious gold crucifix Father kept a fair distance from.

Father balled his hands to his slick forehead. "Forgive us our dead—our debts, as we also have forgiven our debtors. And lead us not—"

"Father?"

His head snapped to Jehanne, and his voice was a timid croak. He was a striking image, like the Virgin Mary, eyes brighter and more piercing from his unshed tears. "You shouldn't be here, pup. I don't want you to see me like this."

Jehanne lowered herself beside him. "Why are you crying?" Even though she wasn't touching him, his warmth settled on her. "Is it because I went too far without supervision? I'm sorry."

"No, it isn't that, pup."

"Can't you go see your doves, the ones you talked to Moreau about? They're still there, aren't they? Will they calm you?"

"Some of them are there, yes, in the dove room, kept locked up and safe. They're sensitive birds." Father worried the hands he'd clasped in prayer. Jehanne took them both in her own.

"I can take you to them, if that'd calm you, give you peace."

"You don't know where their room is."

"I don't know where most of the rooms are, or what they are. But I found you, didn't I?"

His eyes bore a hole in the floor close to her. "That you did."

"Have you eaten today?" He hadn't eaten breakfast with her, and when she inquired, he shrugged it off and said he had no appetite.

He froze at her question, eyes wide and bright.

"Oh, Father, you can't stop eating. What happened? I want to help. Please, let me make you feel better."

"How? What makes you think anything but your presence is needed?"

"I still see tears, so that's not working."

He chuckled, even as the tears still ran. "What do you propose?"

"Something, I don't know. I can't do anything if I don't know what's troubling you."

"I don't mean to worry you." Jehanne's attention strayed to the open, half-gone bottle of wine on his nightstand. "I just doubt you'd believe me."

"Father, I've heard and seen things you wouldn't believe."

"And what would that be?"

"I heard a noise like a howl one night. Or a scream, I can't recall." Maybe she had been dreaming.

"Did you?" Father only seemed curious, not worried.

64

"Yes, and I couldn't tell if I dreamed it."

Father kept quiet for a long thread of time. "You might've been remembering."

"Remembering what?"

Father cast his eyes to the floor. "Do you promise not to be alarmed?"

"I'll try."

He inhaled. "I'm not sure that's enough."

Jehanne wouldn't accept that. If he needed another to shoulder half of his burdens, his memories of the war, those secrets he sweetened or numbed with wine, she'd be that person. "I don't want you to have this burden alone, whatever it is. Being quiet will only hurt."

Father's attention rose to the crucifix and its soft glare. His breathing steadied, and Jehanne's matched it. A pinching in her head insisted she force the issue, but before she could decide, Father spoke.

"There were demons under the house. Moreau and I fought against them and won."

Not finding words, Jehanne went empty. Demons. She might've heard wrong. It could be a euphemism, though what could be terrible enough for "demon" to be the softened word?

After considerable silence, she replied, "Wha—what? I don't—that's—"

"Unbelievable? You believe in God and angels, but not demons?"

He meant actual demons. "Of course I do—I think you're telling the truth." Did she? "But here? Right now?"

"No, not anymore, I don't think."

"Are you feeling all right?"

"I'm many things, but I'm not mad."

"I've heard things about ghosts or vampires haunting places, but not demons."

Father broke his gaze away from Christ. "Vampires are a pagan superstition, pup. Surely you know better than that. Where did you hear about such a thing?"

Jehanne swallowed and fidgeted with her nightgown skirt. If he disapproved strongly of that kind of talk, he might not allow Marcy to visit. At least, she didn't want to risk it. Father's skepticism seemed arbitrary, considering the crux of the discussion, but that wasn't the issue. "Did you actually see these demons?"

"Pup, I fought them."

"What did they look like?"

Father sought comfort from the crucifix again. "I wish I could explain. Maybe one day, but it's too painful now."

Despite Jehanne's frustration, she didn't want to provoke more terrible memories than had already been dredged up. "Is there any way the demons would come back?" She decided to go with it, Father's truth. He wouldn't lead her astray.

"I believe we're safe, so long as we stay faithful and unquestioning. I'm still haunted by them, however. It may never stop."

"Are you sure—about them being gone, I mean?"

Father's tone was amused as he patted her cheek. "And now we've broken one of those rules, haven't we?"

Be unquestioning.

She burned from that and couldn't hide her petulance. "I'm trying to help. I can't help if I don't know as much as I can."

Father's tone was like honey. "Of course, I know you mean well, and I wouldn't have you any other way."

If he had truly fought off demons, Father was more of a hero than she thought when it came to fighting wars, and Jehanne loved him more for it, but she wouldn't stop asking questions until she was dead.

"What is it, pup?"

"I don't remember when I was a baby."

"Most don't."

"Don't be smart with me!" When he leaned back, as if she'd struck him, she relented. If she were too indelicate, the shell shock might crawl back. Hell, she could *give* him shell shock if she acted like more of a pistol. "But after? Surely, I'd remember more. Childhood, adolescence. What happened to make me so sick? Was I attacked by a demon? Is it inside me?"

"I'm sorry this is difficult for you."

Despite herself, Jehanne curled her hands into fists. "Did something—did I—"

Father was only gentle with her, making her regret her outburst. "No, you weren't attacked, and aren't possessed."

"Then how did I get sick?"

His gaze went to the carpet. "I don't have an answer, though I wish I did."

"Not even if it'd help me?"

"If only I knew." He shook his head. "I never thought you'd ask so many questions. I should've known better. There are things I'd rather you not worry about. I have trouble sleeping from what I've seen, and I don't want you to suffer like I have."

"I could stay here with you if it'll help you sleep." Jehanne might need the comfort in the night too.

"I need to leave the room sometimes during the night, and I wouldn't want to wake you."

"But—"

He tapped her chin with his forefinger. "I also have Moreau come here at night, should I need assistance."

"So he'll come back?"

Father frowned, and disapproval crept into his words. "You saw him leave?"

"Yes."

As quickly as Father's demeanor had changed, he calmed. "Well, yes, pup, he'll return to help me."

Still, Father hadn't heard the last of this.

Jehanne said, "I heard a scream once, and I wasn't sure if I was mad. But now, I see we need to keep each other safe." If she told him that when she was out, she had seen things, he wouldn't let her leave in the future, even if it was safer than being in here.

"Nothing will hurt you if you keep yourself quiet and kind."

Then she was already doomed. "How do you know?"

"Even demons are God's servants and know when to keep away from His sheep. They only come when we let them in."

What a strange thing, to blame himself for the infestation.

"Don't you care about me?"

"Yes, never doubt it." His voice carried a new roughness.

"Then why won't you let me stay with you?" She wanted freedom, yet she also wanted Father by her side if it meant safety.

"Sleep is hard for me when—walls have a certain voice to them. I'd be afraid to wake you with my own sleep habits."

"What do you mean?"

"What more do you want me to say?"

"I want you to be more honest."

"I am, I'm trying. Do you know how hard it was to tell you that, of all things, we have demons under our floors? Can't you be patient with me? I saw you almost *die*."

"I, I . . ." She wanted to be freer but closer to Father all at once now.

Father touched his chest. "I'm sorry. I don't mean to be coarse. I'm trying, pup. I'm trying to keep you happy. Can't you see how much this hurts me? I've told you as much as I can, so we can be content."

"But I'm not."

"It'll be better, I swear. Nothing will separate us again." Father took her hand into both his own, then pulled away and ruffled her hair, though his movements were stiff. "Think of something calming. Clair can rest with you."

I don't want him to crack again. If I push too much, he may be the one lost forever. He needed the patience she afforded no one else.

Jehanne met her lips to his knuckles and murmured, "I'll pray for you."

Father's jaw quivered, and Jehanne opened her mouth to say anything to keep him from weeping again, but before she could, Father engulfed her in a crushing embrace.

"I've missed you," he whispered, his cheek damp on hers.

"I've been here."

"I thought I lost you. I swear I won't lose you again, my sweet girl."

"I've just been sick, that's all. My memory should come back, and you'll help me, won't you?"

"I don't know if I can. I was supposed to protect you."

"You can't protect me against a sickness." Afraid more arguing might make Father cry again, Jehanne bit her lip, dissatisfaction gnawing at her.

As night sank into the room, Clair slept beside Jehanne, her light snores drifting through the air.

Worrying her lip, Jehanne admitted to herself that her maid's presence brought solace, though she envied how swiftly Clair fell asleep. Water dripped, a wolf bayed somewhere in the hills. Breathing through her nose, Jehanne traced her hand along the sheet pattern. Wherever sweat pooled, the nightgown stuck to her. She swore a shadow moved in the space between the corner and the vanity. Clair mumbled in her sleep, and Jehanne rubbed her back in case she was having a troubled dream. The back-rubbing was an act Jehanne could do only as Clair slept, or else her servant might think her mistress liked her a little more than she let on with the daily barbs.

Jehanne looked at the vanity mirror, and noticing nothing somehow worsened the insomnia. Closing her eyes only made her dread opening them, so she kept them fixed on the canopy. Her mind was nothing but a wasteland latticed with stars, stars that promised oblivion. Jehanne's tremoring hands didn't ease.

Something pattered. Might've been rain. A groan. Might've been the manor's chilled bones settling. Tapping in the hallway. A shadow grinning over the mirror.

It's not a demon. Father has protected me. But Father wasn't here. *Father wouldn't lie to me because he needs me.*

Why wasn't he here?

Why doesn't he trust me? Why won't he tell me about my mother?

She clenched her fists and worked to control her breathing.

He knows what's best for me. He's suffered a good deal for me. Clutching the sheets until her hands hurt, Jehanne's long exhale was too loud, came deep within her lungs. She cut it off with a squeak. *He knows what's best for me. He's doing his best. Don't think on it. Don't worry over it.* Clair's snores were suddenly everywhere, like an air raid siren, too loud to make note of anything else. Hair clung to Jehanne's forehead like seaweed, and a bitter stickiness coated her tongue. She wondered if Clair had locked the door. She wondered how well Clair could fight.

She wondered if Clair normally spent the night with Father like Moreau did.

Jehanne did not fall asleep until dawn.

7

Rosalie

The moment Rosalie saw André lounging on the hooved, mahogany couch, his polished shoes on the armrest, she said, "I've a matter to speak with you about."

"Indeed," he said, not looking at her. She ruffled. "Go on." The sunlight made him appear boyish.

"When Marcy is near, never mention your . . ."

By the tautness in André's shoulders, Rosalie suspected he'd erupt, and she tensed.

He stood up and spat, "My bastard?"

She sniffed, fidgeting with her cuff. This escalated too soon for her taste. "Your child. Don't mention her in front of Marcy. It'd upset her. And lower your voice."

"Of course. I'd never want to be indiscreet. I'm sure Marcy would crumble."

Rosalie's eyes hardened. "You've never cared to be discreet in the past when you were with women, so I doubt it'd come as any surprise. Nevertheless—"

"Don't talk around this. Tell me, what are you accusing me of?"

She thought it was fairly obvious. In fact, it wasn't a claim if it was true. "It's as I said. You seem content with warming women's beds. You leave and come back smelling of wine and perfume, and it's—it's a sin, and I can't understand it." A twinge stirred in her ribs. Anatole had loved another woman before Rosalie, and she hadn't judged him, but she tried to cast it in the river of her mind, too deep for a net to catch. "But you could at least be subtler."

André pressed his lips together. "I made a terrible mistake, and I wasn't subtle at all about it. I admit it. Does that make you happy?"

"No." Rosalie's frown deepened.

"Of course it doesn't." His eyes narrowed to slits. "It's my mistake. I do try my best to find warmth where I can."

She stepped forward. "What does that mean?"

"I'm not asking you to let go of the past, of those you loved, but you'd think you'd show more warmth toward your sister's only child." She couldn't stand this, couldn't stand the sudden softness in his voice. The pity made it more difficult to keep her fury stoked.

Yet, Rosalie did find enough coal anyhow. "Don't bring Juliette into this."

"Why? Wasn't she my mother?"

"You didn't grow up with her. You didn't know her."

André averted his eyes, his jaw twitching. "You're right. I didn't, and I can't."

Rosalie's heart clenched. "I didn't mean—"

"No, you did, let's be clear. You're not wrong." His eyes, his Juliette eyes, buried themselves in her. "It's difficult to miss a person you can't remember. I miss what she could've done, what we could've had."

I miss it too. I miss that and more. I miss it so much it aches. No, too much. Rosalie straightened.

André continued, "Tante, I know I haven't been the best nephew, but I still have trouble wrapping my head around the fact you think I'd pursue Marcy when she's just a child. She's not as fragile as you think, but, as I said, she's like a little sister to me."

"I wish I knew what to say. You've put us in a difficult position. We'll support you and your child, of course, but it'll hurt us—"

"I'm not asking you to pay for anything. The woman has a home, and Guylaine is safe. I can find a job, a factory—"

"Like your uncle found a job?"

"Is there anything I could do to satisfy you?" Before Rosalie could answer, André's voice broke, not in only sorrow or anger, but both. "I could leave if I'm such a burden. I'm sorry my mother had the audacity to die and leave you with me."

"How dare you! I've never called you a burden. You're assuming, like you have before."

"Oh, have I? And if I walked out now, would it matter to you?"

Rosalie bit her cheek. "If that's what you think will cool that temper of yours, then perhaps time away will do you good."

"You mean it'll do you and Oncle well."

"That's not what I said. Should I be happy with your recklessness?"

"How could I be of more use to you both?"

When André was a boy, he was considerate and always needed a kiss or a kind word. Often, he captured her in an embrace, or a hug, as the Americans would call it (since her people never found a word for this oppressive gesture). It was discomforting, when she considered it long enough, to allow another person so close. Quite frankly, it should be banned.

Yet, in the past, as her arms rested confused by her sides, she couldn't find it in herself to demur. At the start, at least. André couldn't be satisfied until someone made him content. When Marcy arrived, he pouted whenever anyone cooed over her. Rosalie never stopped loving him no matter how he pushed, so she didn't understand why he now thought so little of her and his uncle to think they only cared about his usefulness.

Rosalie remembered the four-year-old André, that excitable boy with his carnation-pink complexion, who held her hand down the stairs and had said with startling clarity, "You look tired, Tante." His head had been tilted, his voice too somber for his age, the front of his hair cowlicked. In response, her eyes stung because, yes, she'd been sore from leaving the bed. Even when she didn't want to be confined, her body punished her.

No, no, that was the past, and Rosalie needed to focus on her new self, on the new André.

She repeated, "I've never called you a burden."

André tilted his head. "It's true. You don't speak much at all."

"I—"

"Do you wish I had died instead of Maman?"

Rosalie leaned back. "What sort of question is that? I'd never wish losing a child on my sister."

"And would you've grieved for me?"

"Of course I would've. Why would you ask me this?" It wasn't fair of him to assume she wouldn't grieve for him if he had died, and she teetered between sympathy and anger. His hypotheticals confused her.

"Would you only mourn me for your sister's sake?"

"I wouldn't know you like I do now."

"I think you know better than me that you don't need to know someone long to mourn them."

No blood in the bed, no blood in the bed, no death in the bed.

"You're right. I do. Why would you bring the past up, especially that past? How could you? Are you trying to make me say I love the dead more than I love you? After I raised you and fed you? How could you do this?"

"If I left this instant, would you leave this house and come after me?"

"You're a grown man. If you need to leave, you should."

"Forever?"

"I won't make your choices for you." Rosalie wouldn't want to make the decision anyway. "You seem to be content to do whatever you want, regardless of what it does to others, regardless of how it makes Anatole or I feel."

She shouldn't have said that, but it was too late to suck the words back into her lungs.

André huffed and raked his fingers through his hair. "That's not fair. Why would I try to learn Oncle's profession if I didn't care how either of you felt? But that's not enough for you, is it? You don't want me to do that. So what should I do, be like Oncle and knock on all the doors in France and have every single person slam a door in my face? Why would I ask you these questions if I didn't care?"

"I don't really know. Why would you make a stupid choice and make a woman pregnant when you were supposed to fight for our country? Why would you act like less than a whore, when at least a whore is working for her own survival?"

Stupid, that was the word Marcy had used.

André tilted his head back a fraction and stared at her with wide, unblinking eyes. For the first time since Rosalie could remember, André was the silent one of the pair of them. Again, her words spilled and stained the carpet, André, herself.

He, God, he was crying. Because of her. "I—I was afraid to tell you because you'd react this way."

"André, I—I didn't. I didn't mean it—"

"What can I do to make you happy? What can I do to make myself worthy? What did I do to make you despise me?"

André fled out the front door before Rosalie could say, "I don't hate you." He was just a boy, and she had hurt him.

Rosalie tried to follow, but once her feet landed on the cool porch, the daylight burned and its weight collided against her all at once. She could go to the mailbox, but no farther, so she retreated, and when she closed the front door, it rattled her soul.

André hadn't even taken his hat. Tension in her chest, squeezing, squeezing, she thought she'd snap in two.

She was poison; if she gave too much of herself to anyone, she'd kill them. Even in all her attempts to keep away, she still managed to cause pain. Imagine how severe the consequences would be if she were more engaged. Hands, hands were the gateway to sickness. Anatole wasn't harmed because he was already sick; they both carried that headsman blood in their families, and so did Marcy and André, but their daughter and nephew were younger, stronger. Rosalie couldn't interfere, couldn't make their lives worse.

Yet she had, despite her best efforts.

And she had no one she could confide in, no one who would listen.

Trembling, Rosalie lifted her knuckles to her mouth so she could keep down her sick. The back door closed, and it could only be Anatole coming away from the garden. He'd wash his hands, pass André's bedroom, and see that their nephew was gone. Marcy was in her room, maybe reading a book, maybe sleeping off her dinner.

Rosalie smoothed her fingers under her eyes and straightened her sleeves. When her husband entered the room, she lifted the corners of her mouth as much as she could manage.

Anatole's forehead crinkled. "What happened? Where did André go?"

She didn't answer, only turned her back to her husband and pretended to dust the end table with a handkerchief she kept folded there. The dust moved a bit, but stayed on the surface.

"Rosalie." Anatole took her hand, curling his fingers around hers gently. "Rosie."

"He left. He couldn't stand to be here any longer." It was a miracle she didn't stutter.

"Did he say something cruel to you?" Oh, poor Anatole, sweet Anatole, diverting the blame from Rosalie when she could only loathe herself. "Please tell me."

"He didn't say anything." Her spine shivered as she lied. "I could just tell that he was in a mood. He'll likely find a woman to stay with. It's what he does, isn't it?"

"I suppose. I've tried to tell him he needs to be more discreet."

Then there's André's child, the one you know about,
yet you don't trust me enough to let me know.

Rosalie didn't need to hear anymore, and she couldn't burden Anatole. She could distract him with love. Yes, that was for the best. Most of all, it was what they both deserved, even with the lingering mist of betrayal coating the chairs and the floor and the curtains.

Anatole pressed, "What did he say, mon cœur?"

Rosalie ran her hand down his arms and brushed his fingers. "I'd like to go to bed now, the two of us. I need to rest my head." He looked reluctant to drop the subject, so she added, "Please, my love?"

Anatole held her to him so her nose rested below his chin, and his coarse beard tickled her skin. She closed her eyes and let breath pool in her chest, and when she shifted, they kissed. Her heart's thorns relented, and he followed her up the stairs when their lips unjoined.

Rosalie's mind wandered to their first married night together. Strangely, while her stomach fluttered, she hadn't been as nervous as she expected; by dusk, in the ruddy pink glow of their bedroom, her cheeks hurt from smiling.

She asked her husband, "Why do they treat us so, when you're performing a service to the country? You don't commit the crimes, nor do you make the sentences. You only carry them out. None of the judges come before the public and watch those horrid men die." Men would dine with judges and lawmen and consider it an honor, but none of them would ever share a meal with her husband.

Anatole rose a brow as he undid his tie. "Funny that killing for your country is admirable until a headsman does so for the law." He preserved an ever-dutiful reputation exceedingly well, kept his work neutral. Death didn't judge. It treated all its subjects the same.

"Yes, funny."

That moment proved to be rare, when he allowed his frustration and scorn toward the public to show. They acutely picked apart the absurdities of social reactions, and Rosalie decided the masses wouldn't take Anatole from her. After all, Rosalie and Anatole first bonded not over death, but over cycling. She was the only woman who participated in races, and they would speak afterward.

Accordingly, theirs would be a quiet, simple home with no blood and strife. Desperately normal, terribly normal. That was their life. In the bedroom, the most feared man in France was Rosalie's. She massaged his arms, laid him on the bed. They spoke about nonsense before Anatole pleased her with his mouth and tongue, and she settled atop him. They made love with her controlling the rhythm. At that time, both sleeping and waking up were easier. She'd seat him deep in her and wake up rejuvenated. Rosalie would grip his wrists and kiss his knuckles. She'd been so vibrant then, the bright-eyed, avid cyclist. The adventurer, the romantic, adamant that if Anatole was her land, her domain, she would be his water. They took the time to explore each other on their wedding night, rather than suffer through a rushed ordeal and call the consummation finished.

This was before she was pregnant. When they joked more.

Now, Anatole rubbed his thumb into her shoulder, which brought Rosalie back to where they rested in bed on their sides.

Ghosting her fingers over his beard, Rosalie said, voice thick with sadness, "What did I do to deserve you?" It troubled her, keeping contact with his steady blue eyes after those words needled her throat.

Anatole caressed her cheek. "I often ask myself that about you."

She beamed, his fingers warming where the skin dimpled. "You charmed me with your cooking." His gardening, his newspaper comics, his laugh. He accrued many talents and virtues. Even in his failed efforts to avoid his father Louis' bloody work, Rosalie had admired him from afar with the perfumes he created and his dashing military uniform. When Anatole courted her, as bashful as he was, she had asked him if he'd ever made love to anybody before, and she couldn't recall all the words. He had spoken about the former love of his life leaving him while he assisted his father. Because of the blood on his hands. Rosalie didn't want to be second, the second love, the consolation, but if she had to be, she'd be the best love he had.

Anatole said to her, "Your brilliance, your resilience, why wouldn't I love you?" It made Rosalie want to cry because, if that wasn't rhetorical, she could easily give him a hundred reasons, but she wouldn't burden him.

After unpinning her hair, Rosalie kissed him and removed his coat. His lips worshipped her cheeks, her neck, her collarbone. This time, when she settled on him and they joined, it was several desperate minutes before they let go of one another.

The slick scents of sweat and rose potpourri wafted through the bedroom. When Rosalie awoke, Anatole slept beside her, and the twilight's blue wash dwindled to complete darkness. She simply stayed in bed. One of her legs was crooked over him, and the side of her face touched his warm cheek. Idly, she stroked the soft hair on his chest.

"Are you sleeping, Brother Jacques?" she whispered. Anatole answered with gentle, slow breaths. Rosalie smiled with a sore tenderness, brushed his cheek with the back of her hand, and kissed the prickly skin there. Normally, she stroked Anatole's hair when nightmares lingered above him, and she would mutter whatever diaphanous prayers crossed her mind.

Rosalie shut her eyes and warded off those pinches of memory falling like petals, brittle and as faded and red as Anatole's hair had been before it silvered. As the petals paled to snow, to white ash, a keen whine sounded off in the distance like a train whistle. The ashes became pillars of smoke, and she drifted away.

Another high noise. Indecipherable, curious. Didn't matter. A wild dog, maybe. André and Marcy were inside, so they were safe.

Weren't they? Had André returned?

The shrill sound sent a chill down to the bottom of Rosalie's spine, and as she turned it into pulp in her awakening mind, what was insignificant, a lash under her eyelid, sharpened like a dagger in her side.

Moving out of bed, she slipped on her taffeta robe and tied the sash.

She couldn't tell if Anatole's eyes were open as she stood motionless. A caterwaul, closer, she squeezed her hands, nails biting into her palm.

"Rosie," Anatole called, his voice gruff with sleep.

She adjusted her robe sash. "I heard something, and I'm not sure what it was."

Anatole mumbled, "I'll come with you."

She allowed herself a grateful smile, even when she supposed he wouldn't see. "Thank you."

Anatole shuffled out of bed. It wasn't that she couldn't go alone, but she found it unwise to investigate a noise by herself at night. Anatole rustled as he fetched his own robe, their soft breaths clouding the air.

Before she descended the stairs, she went to the oak chest at the end of the bed. As she leaned down and opened it, hair fell in her eyes. She produced a handgun and shotgun from the chest, setting them at the foot of the bed. The long snout of the latter weapon knocked against the footboard.

"Which do you think is prudent?" she asked.

He scratched his head, but otherwise showed no surprise. "Are you certain it will come to that?"

"No, but if it should, best to have protection near." Rosalie settled on the shotgun, which was easier to aim.

"Should we turn on the lights?"

"If someone is here, or if they try to come in, perhaps they will be dissuaded to come if they know somebody is home, but the auto's in front of the house, so anyone should know."

Anatole replied, "Not if they're here to harass. It doesn't—it doesn't sound human. It may be only an animal."

Marcy was here, maybe André, and therefore it was Rosalie's responsibility to protect them at any cost.

They turned on every light so they could see their surroundings. They checked the kitchen, the living area, the study, André's room, Marcy's room. Marcy was asleep. Nothing was out of place, but the living room still shifted somehow. The stairs creaked, like a body settling into a molding rocking chair.

"André still isn't here," Rosalie said. "He must've walked to town. Or—is he—"

"He could be visiting a friend for the night," Anatole said, gripping her free hand. Rosalie let him assure her, or it could've been to assure himself.

A knock on the window, another. Rosalie stood still as a winter elm, the shotgun she held weighing her hands down. She'd never shot anyone before. "Call the police," she told Anatole, and he moved to the telephone.

The walls surrounding them gave some semblance of protection from all but dreams. Just the other night, Rosalie dreamed of ambling through the woods, a membrane covering her vision. A chase, many chases, even though no one chased her, she dreamed of it and awoke in a panting, sweating tangle. A destination, she ran to something, but the dream ended before she found whatever it could be.

She shook her head. Of all times, she couldn't lose herself now.

Anatole spoke on the telephone in an unwavering voice, exchanged his words slowly. He looked to her. "The officer has asked for me to look outside."

Moving to the curtain, the telephone cord growing taut and stretching like a pulled sow's tail, Anatole parted the curtain's edge with two fingers, leaned in, and squinted outside. He said, "No, there's nothing."

A shriek splintered the air and weighed her to the spot, her blood chilling like an Irish swamp.

"Yes," Anatole whispered.

Marcy said from behind her bedroom door, "Papa, what was that?"

"I don't know," Rosalie answered.

A pause. Marcy replied, "If somebody comes in, what will we do?" Her daughter's brow furrowed. Not every day she witnessed her mother holding a large gun.

"You'll hide," Rosalie said.

Incessant slamming of a frantic hand on the door, each thud came rapid and hard, and it startled the breath out of her—somehow worsened by not seeing the threat. Jolie yapped until Rosalie told her to hush, the dog's barks turning to low growls. Even in normal circumstances, Rosalie hated when there was a knock at the door, especially when the sun started to descend.

A gunshot resounded as sure as the Devil's drum. Anatole put down the telephone.

Rosalie's gaze wandered to every corner of the room. Shadows blended into the furniture like mingling watercolors. Often when she grew wary, everything in her vision hemorrhaged.

"What is it?" Rosalie asked, meek.

"I don't know, too dark outside. Police will be here shortly." Anatole sucked in a deep breath. Marcy opened her door, rubbing her eyes, dressed in a simple white gown.

"Marcy, are you well?" Anatole said.

"I—um, yes, only I don't know what to do. The noises."

Rosalie said, "Go back inside your room. Keep the door locked."

Marcy did. A relentless noise like a siren pierced the air. Pierced her. A noise as morbid as a baby's coffin.

"Screaming." Rosalie lifted her hands to her ears. "Someone's screaming." She willed herself to believe it was an animal, but she couldn't. The knocking, the—so high-pitched. She removed her hands. "Anatole, the police." They needed the police, the Sûreté Nationale. Why weren't they already here?

The sound of flesh (flesh?) on wood died.

A caterwaul like that of a wounded Chartreux broke the silence. How it soured the air, so close, so close Rosalie tasted the threat. Rosalie remembered a Bierce story she once read about a jaguar bursting through a window and stealing away a catatonic woman's body. She imagined a shadow leaping in, stealing Marcy.

Was Marcy still here? She had to, to, yes, she heard Marcy's breathing through the door, had to be Marcy, had to . . .

A jest, that was what this ordeal had to be. Boys not in the war, with nothing else to do than frighten others as their older brothers sacrificed their lives. That was it. It must've been.

Anatole looked out the curtains again for what seemed longer than a minute. "I still can't see anything."

Touching, they both settled in front of Marcy's door.

They had the same goal: keep any threat away from their daughter at the risk of injury or death.

"Don't go outside," Rosalie said, afraid Anatole would have a heroic moment. Her thoughts slapped the air before she could halt them. "Don't open the door. No matter what, don't open the door."

"I won't."

Jolie paced and drooled, her body heaving. Rosalie rested her cheek on Marcy's door. She felt and heard her daughter slumping with a tired, muffled sigh against the wood.

"Poupée, are you all right?" Anatole asked.

Marcy replied, "Yes, Papa."

Rosalie wanted to request that Marcy not leave the door. The quick breathing on the other side assured her that her daughter was alive.

Scratching on the window. Rosalie saw a glint out of the corner of her eye and shuddered, but nothing was within the house.

It could be a trick. She'd heard stories of people who'd cry and feign injuries so a sympathetic person would open the door and expose themselves to an attack and looting. Jolie paced in the living room and grumbled under her breath. Anatole laid a hand over Rosalie's shoulder. She didn't budge, didn't lean into his warm touch.

Rosalie's senses narrowed. Both she and Anatole paused as they waited for any footsteps, any scratching.

Anatole looked to her. She nodded to ensure him she was as well as she could be.

Rosalie worked to calm her heart. This was their home, theirs. They shouldn't be frightened to exist in it.

They stood. Marcy opened her door. Rosalie was so close that they almost bumped into each other.

Marcy came closer. "What happened? Who was screaming?"

Rosalie rubbed her chapped lips together. "I don't know."

Even as the officers came with their reassurances and though she worked to push the night away, the sounds haunted Rosalie's dreams. She was at the dinner table in her old home, and Juliette, lined with gold from head to toe, sat in front of her with an open palm and furrowed brow, but the screams came, and Rosalie knew Marcy was gone. As she left her sister and fled deep into the hungry thickets of briars and dying leaves, she swore Marcy called out to her, but she couldn't find her.

8

Marcy

Last night, the blue men spoke to Marcy, and she confirmed there was indeed a disturbance, but she couldn't say more than what she heard. When the officers asked for the appearance of the attempted intruder, she couldn't give them anything of value. They scoured the surrounding woods, but the perpetrators were long gone, it appeared. When the police arrived to investigate the call, they stated the cause of the disturbance was likely some boys joking, boys about Marcy's age, and they saw nothing that indicated a more pressing matter. The scare they had had made her impatient to go somewhere else, at least for an impermanent time.

The only evidence of the disturbance came with clumps of dirt and a thin, black smear on the porch, which could have been mud, paint, or blood.

Marcy sat on the couch and, instead of distracting herself, she kicked her feet and pressed her teeth to her bottom lip. What had happened the night before shook her, and she wanted to speak about it, but talking about bad experiences, even just after they had happened, wasn't in Maman or Papa's natures.

If only André were here; Marcy hoped he didn't hate her, but she couldn't find out without asking him. He could be helpful to speak to in his own André way. Yesterday, she had heard Maman and André's raised voices, and André disappeared with only a slammed door in his wake. They were arguing about her, she knew it, and it stewed inside her, simmering to a tented, foamy crescent of white.

It wasn't until she heard her name that she realized Maman was standing in the opening leading to the kitchen.

Blinking, Marcy crossed her arms over her stomach. "What is it?" Maman's features straightened like prison bars.

"André told me you proposed to him."

Her heart jumped. "I did." That was all she could say.

"Why?"

"Because, at the time, I thought it sounded like a fun thing to do, and it'd be the only time I could think of when I could try to have my first kiss. And if we did marry, we could have our own place, and I'd be able to leave the house all the time without permission."

"Is that what you want? To leave this house?" Of course Maman latched on to that.

"Yes."

"Ah."

Marcy glowered at her bare feet. She should go to her room and occupy herself, not continue this conversation. She didn't want to hurt Maman's feelings, didn't want to look up and confirm that she was too late with that wish.

"You won't even come near me. You hate looking at me." Marcy inhaled, held it in her for five long seconds.

When Marcy braved her head up, the lines in Maman's face were pinched in confusion, and Maman had the nerve to soften, cross the distance, and sit close, but they still didn't touch. That wouldn't help cure Marcy's righteous anger, not at all, and she needed all the help she could get.

"Why would you say that?" Maman asked. "I'm looking at you right now, aren't I?"

Marcy steeled herself, and a sharp pain pricked her eyes. "Why did you say you'd rather have me dead?"

With that, Maman leaned back, as if struck. Her lips worked without noise. If she loathed looking at her daughter, she made up for it now, more present than she'd been in their last heated talk. When Maman finally responded, it took Marcy what felt like a skittering minute to realize she'd spoken.

Hushed, meek. "I didn't know you heard me."

"What else do you say when you think I can't hear?"

"I didn't mean I want you dead. I only meant I want what's best for you."

"That's not what you said, though. Those are your choices for me, marrying André or death? Is death what's best? Is that what you want?"

Maman's eyes were bright like she'd cry, but her cheeks remained dry. "I'd rather neither of those be choices. I worded what I meant poorly. It seems to be a talent of mine." Marcy couldn't understand. Maman treated her like she either wanted a rotting foot or a flogged back. Marriage wasn't the same as death, wasn't a close option, and Maman and Papa loved each other, so the comparison further baffled her. Their marriage wasn't worse than death, Marcy had thought.

Could it be as simple as Maman's words not reflecting her mind? Marcy wanted to understand, and wanted Maman to understand in return, but that tower crumbled long ago, and it left old skeletons in its wake.

The unearthed desert bones poked Marcy enough for her to spout out, "Was I just a consolation after all that happened to you? Is that all I am? Is that all I'm good for?" If so, Marcy had done a terrible job consoling Maman with her existence. She shouldn't have let that crawl out. "I understand, I understand you lost your sister and your maman and him—but I can't live up to that. I can't fix—I can't heal anything. I can't be more, and I should be."

"I don't—I didn't mean—"

The mosaic shattered. All those cracked, pretty colors and lights Marcy kept in place to make herself happy. "I don't have anyone like me."

"I—I—of course you do." Maman opened her mouth like she would add something else, but closed it soon after.

"All I want is another girl like me. Some connection, something more. And you think I'd be better off dead." If only Jehanne were here. Marcy sniffed. More tears came. "Maman, I'm sorry, but I . . ." Her eyes stung so much she couldn't open them, and the more she rubbed them, the more the prickling worsened.

"I can bring you water, and we can discuss this—"

"I can't be here anymore."

"What? Where would you go?" God, Maman was trying, she was, and it was earnest, her hands seeking direction.

This was honest, but still they couldn't talk without a barrier.

"I met a girl, Jehanne, at the park, and she lives not that far, and I want to stay with her."

"That doesn't sound safe. I'm not sure. I don't know this girl, or her parents."

Marcy sniffed. "She only has her papa."

"That's terrible."

"Well, if one of them's dead, it's one less person for you to be paranoid about."

"Paranoid?" Maman's voice was wounded. "Is that all I am to you?"

Marcy struggled to speak over her tears, but what spilled out of her mouth was fully undammed. "I can't be here anymore, at least not today. I can't talk anymore. Please leave. I'm sorry. I can't." Maman backed off with a hand on her mouth. Marcy's anger wound down, replaced by tremors of guilt and regret. Her home was orderly and smelled good, and she was never without food when she needed it. But she couldn't stop what had built up over the years.

Jehanne. Marcy wanted, needed Jehanne. Someone to laugh with her. If she asked Papa if she could stay with Jehanne, he'd say yes.

He always did.

Her world narrowed to the ticking of the clock, like a venomous dripping, and Maman murmuring to herself over and over, "What have I done?"

And suddenly, Papa was there. Marcy hadn't heard the tap of his shoes, only his words: "What is it? What happened?"

Too far away, must've been talking to Maman, who replied, "I don't want to speak about it." Though she didn't hear Papa's entrance, she did hear Maman's footsteps fade.

A set of determined steps, another body came next to her, and she thought Maman had returned to make the situation more uncomfortable, until she saw Papa over her fallen hair.

"What is it?" he asked, his hand warm but firm on her shoulder. Marcy couldn't think of anything to say that

97

didn't sound petty. Seemingly able to understand her without prodding, Papa rubbed her back as she wept.

9

Jehanne

Jehanne started the day with blood smearing her pillow, a ruddy crescent from her nose. She frantically tapped Clair's shoulder, and when the servant rolled over with squinted eyes, her first words were, "Good God." Jehanne sat on the bed's edge until Clair handed her a washroom towel and said, "Tilt your head down. I'll tell your father." When Jehanne tilted her head up because it made more sense for the blood to go back where it came from, and the taste of a rusted copper coin wasn't really that awful, Clair arched back and rolled her eyes to the ceiling in exasperation. "Dear God, girl, don't fight me on this."

"Why would I have blood go all over me?" Clair spoke like she was much older, when Jehanne would bet they weren't even a decade apart in age. Girl, indeed.

"So you don't choke, and it won't 'go all over' you if you put the towel under your nose, quite obviously."

Jehanne postured the towel like a sword. "I won't choke. I'm not dumb enough to drown in my own nose blood."

Clair elected not to respond, and Jehanne stuck her tongue out when the servant turned her back, since it didn't count as immature if nobody saw. Tasting quite enough blood soon after, Jehanne decided to obey, but she did so grumbling to make it harder on her uptight servant.

When Father arrived and inspected the pillow, he remarked, "Pup, it looks like a pagan sacrificed a small rodent in here." She supposed with all his books on Rome and post-Rome Europe, that was a mix of what he knew and an attempted joke. "I'll take you to Moreau so he can strengthen your tea."

Jehanne panicked. "Am I becoming sick again?"

Father sat by her and patted her hand. Her breathing slowed. She felt guilty, letting her frail father see her bleed. "It's the cold, dry air," he said, "nothing more. It makes thin skin crack and bleed, darling—pup. Don't fret."

"But what if I start bleeding from other places too, like out my ears and eyes? What then?" And Father reached around her shoulders and pulled her to him. He sniffed, but didn't burst into tears, and Jehanne chewed the inside of her cheek. It wouldn't do to worsen his stress, but she couldn't help but spill out her worries to the person she trusted the most.

He exhaled. "Pup, Moreau will make you better, I swear it."

"And what if he doesn't?"

Father's lips met her temple. "He doesn't have a choice."

The dining room had a gold shine to it, and the dish cabinets looked like they were made to be brazenly displayed, with their shiny, gnarled edges like polished branches.

Both the back of the chair and the cushion were stiff. Surely Father could afford comfier furniture. Moreau sat across from Jehanne and grounded gray-blue and purple herbs together in a porcelain bowl. He dressed far more conservatively than Father today, with fewer plume-like colors. His tunic sported a dull maroon.

She asked, "What are those, the plants?"

Sweat stippled his hairline. His response was curt. "Sage and valerian, with poppy seeds."

Jehanne twisted a hand in her tunic. "We don't speak much, do we?" She knew little about him besides the fact that he devotedly tended to Father, and that he and Clair patrolled the grounds and ordered around the other servants Jehanne rarely saw.

"I suppose we don't." Something was wrong with him, not anything fatal, she didn't think, but some kind of cold, maybe a fever. "Is your throat hurting?"

"A little."

"Then I'll put honey in the tea as well." His smile didn't reach his clouded eyes. "That should help with the taste too, I think."

Jehanne shuddered. Tea-drinking had to be one of her least favorite activities.

Moreau dumped the bowl of ground herbs in a cup, and he left to place hot water in the mix. When he returned, Jehanne accepted the cup and said, "Do you make this for Father?"

He seemed surprised she asked that question, or at least that she kept speaking to him at all. "Yes. It's one of my many specialties."

"What else can you do?" Jehanne wondered if her tone was offensive, but didn't bother to ask.

"Like your father and Clair, I excel at giving orders."

"I noticed. With Clair, at least. She's bossy."

Moreau's countenance darkened. "She finds control where she can. But anyhow, it's time to drink the tea." He noticed her amount of enthusiasm, so he added, "It should lessen the bleeding, the dried skin."

"Thank you."

"Don't thank me unless it works."

Forcing herself to go ahead and drink and swallow the tea, Jehanne's face crinkled. It didn't taste as awful as the honeyed metal of the premenstrual remedy she had taken after her nosebleed stopped. Once one pain went, another would soon come.

If Moreau was offended by Jehanne's tacit critique of his concoction, he said nothing. He might've not noticed, since his gaze darted back and forth, his eyelids fluttering.

Once the aftertaste faded enough to make speech bearable, Jehanne said, "Are you all right?"

"Yes, why do you ask?" His face darkened like he was annoyed, but he nevertheless suppressed it swiftly.

"You look paler than usual."

"Hmm, the cold does that to me." He grinned, and it would've been charming if it wasn't so fatigued. "And the sun."

"Why the sun? Isn't that warm? Wouldn't that help with the cold?"

"If I stay out too long, it makes me weak and gives me purple blisters."

Jehanne frowned. "Were you born with this condition?"

"It's a fairly new occurrence, I'm afraid. It's not deadly, I don't think, but it hurts like the Devil."

"Is there anything I can do to help?"

They exchanged a curious look. Moreau's eyes were tender, and Jehanne wondered if she imagined a glint of fright. "No, I can manage alone."

"Did you go out more before this, to learn about plants?"

"Yes, my papa was an herbalist, someone who uses plants for medicine, and I helped him collect what he needed." Moreau's cloudy eyes had a storm to them, a brief strike of lightning, of enthusiasm, yet Jehanne still felt a chasm she couldn't cross.

What a strange, strange man.

When she heard the ringing, and realized it wasn't coming from her head, she rushed from the study to the telephone room to try out the oddly knobbed alien thing. With a nod, Father stayed behind where he'd been arranging the bookshelf and trying to find something, *The Duchess of Malfi*, he said, in one hand and some strange German text in the other.

When Jehanne put the little corded telephone piece to her ear, she waited as silence greeted her. Did she have to say something special to make the weird thing work? Maybe Father would've been better at this.

Wet, ragged breathing came from the other end.

"Is someone there?" Jehanne asked. She hoped so, because she'd call for Father if the telephone did this on its own.

"'Allô?" The voice was high and tentative.

Jehanne startled, pulling the telephone away. What an eerie little device. It was like a spirit in a shell. She set the telephone back against her ear. "Marcy?"

"'Allô, sorry—my, my voice's a bit off." It was raw like she'd been crying, which made Jehanne want to reach through the telephone and hold her.

"What happened?"

A sniff. "I—I'm having trouble with my maman. It's nothing serious."

"You're crying, or you were." Might've been impolite to point that out, but, well, too late. "That means it's serious, doesn't it?"

"We just—we talked. I don't know where to start."

"That's all right. Breathe for a minute. I can wait."

Marcy did as Jehanne said until her breaths evened out. "Before I met you, I heard her say she'd rather me be dead—"

A fiery wetness shot from Jehanne's belly to her tongue. "What? How dare she? You should've cuffed her!" The line went quiet, and Jehanne remembered herself, relaxed herself when she felt her nails biting into her palm.

Soft words, softer than anything Marcy had said at the park. "I—no, we don't do that."

With haste and a lick of fire, Jehanne replied, "You don't deserve what she said. You don't deserve to die. Did you tell her that?"

Marcy coughed and cleared her throat. "She—I just need time away from home. Uh, will your papa be okay with me staying with you two for a few days?"

Jehanne hadn't the slightest. "I'm sure it won't be a problem."

"That's good. When would I be able to visit? I want to come as soon as I can, but I also know it's hard to make arrangements—"

"You can come over today." Father would forgive her. Jehanne reasoned it was easier to do something she liked and repent later than ask for permission first and risk rejection.

She hoped.

"Really?" Marcy's voice brightened. "You're really sure?" The hesitance crept back in, but Jehanne wouldn't stand for it. She wanted the let's-climb-a-tree Marcy safe and comfortable.

"Yes."

"Thank you! This means so much, really. I've never done something like this, so I wasn't sure exactly how to go about it, but you made it easy."

"Of course, I'm glad to've helped."

"What's your address? I'll write it down for Papa. He'll know where to go. He'll likely want to drive me there to make sure I'm safe."

Jehanne told Marcy the address and said, "Will he want to meet Father?"

"I don't know. He and Maman don't meet with many people because of his work."

"What does he do? Cut up meat?"

Marcy paused, then coughed. "He cuts people's heads off." Swiftly, she added, "Legally, though. He's the executioner."

"Oh." Jehanne wasn't certain what she had expected. "But he . . ."

In a rush, Marcy said, "Papa's the greatest man alive."

Because of her own love for Father despite his flaws, Jehanne beamed. Though, to her knowledge, Father had never been an executioner, war meant death, and he and Marcy's papa could suffer from similar wounds. Even if Marcy's papa didn't meet with Father today, it could do them well to speak in the future.

"So long as it's legal."

Hopefully, Marcy asked, "I'll see you soon, then?"

"Yes, yes. Goodbye, until later, then?"

"Goodbye."

Bothering her lip, Jehanne rotated the candlestick telephone to see if anything had changed with it and, given no answers, she rested it on its cradle.

Now to go explain things to Father. Sure, he wouldn't approve of Jehanne inviting her new friend over without his permission, but she could convince him, let him decide to give her happiness.

When she re-entered the study, Father looked up from a thick book she recognized, a book he had condemned aloud because it was about Satan and the author was a papacy-hating cretin, yet he still read it.

"Who was it?" he asked. The firelight made him glow.

Jehanne swallowed. "Hold on. First, I have a question." It was partly a diversion tactic so she could formulate her words, and part genuine. This question, among others, had lurked in her mind for a long while.

Father's forehead wrinkled, but he waved his hand. "Go on."

"When is my birthday?" Jehanne held her hands behind herself.

She expected Father to say he didn't know, but he answered with enthusiasm, "The sixth of January."

Guilt stirred in her belly. Of course he'd know when she was born, of all things. *Even if he won't tell me anything else.*

Don't provoke him. You can't break him.

"How do we celebrate?"

He smoothed his palm over a creased page. "We can do whatever you like."

"What do we usually do?"

Father fidgeted with his sleeve. "It's normally a quiet affair, a small dinner. I don't have the staff to accommodate many guests."

"That's good. I'm okay with it being just the two of us," Jehanne said, more for her sake than his. "I wondered if we could travel one day. Maybe on my birthday?"

"One day. But I don't want to chance losing you."

"There's nothing that could happen that'd separate us."

"That heartens me." Father cleared his throat. "We'll make do, I'm sure. I'd never leave you unhappy, especially on a celebratory day."

Going on what Father had said about his inability to accommodate many guests, Jehanne said, "It must be lonely."

He half-smiled. "I've adjusted. The quiet helps calm my nerves, keeps me grounded."

Something Marcy asked at the park crept into Jehanne's head. "Do I have any brothers or sisters?"

"A strange segue." He tilted his head. "None now."

What a curious way to phrase it. As if she could one day. "Will I ever have any?"

Father turned a page of the book still teetering on his lap. "Why? Siblings are not always a blessing."

"Why do you say that? Do you have any?"

With that, Father looked up from his book, his eyes shadowed. "I did, a younger brother."

"What happened to him?"

His eyes pierced the floor. "René died, like everyone does. We were raised by my mother's father, your great-grandfather, after our father and mother died the same year, our father from a boar hunt gone awry, our mother from a broken heart. I doubt the typhus helped. Can't quite remember my reaction, only that I was informed during a tutoring session, and I'd just listened to a choir at breakfast." He added quickly, "On the gramophone, of course, which was new. You know, there's nothing more peaceful than a child singing."

"You were informed that they both died at the same time?"

Father shook his head. "Forgive me, my words are scrambled. I was informed of my father's death as I was being tutored. My mother, well, I saw her die."

Father frowned, and Jehanne pitied him. "I'm sorry."

Father snapped out of whatever meandering thought occupied his glassy eyes. "Anyhow, Grandfather always preferred my brother. It's as if there's an animal instinct to choose one sibling over all the others. Be glad I only have you to dote on."

"Did you love him, your brother?" She didn't know how she'd feel about someone who was the preferred child in the family.

"I'm not sure how to answer that. I hardly remember him." Father's demeanor gave Jehanne reason to relish being an only child; it was a good life to be the sole proprietor of his affection. "What made you ask about this?"

"It just jumped into my head, I suppose." Father didn't look entirely satisfied. "I wanted to ask you something— something besides that."

Father gave her a tired smile and rubbed his face. "I suspected as much. Is it about the telephone call?"

"Mlle Clair told you I met a girl in the park, yes?" Jehanne knew, she was there. She said it to refresh his memory.

"Yes, she said you were on a tree with another girl. I meant to discuss it, but I've been distracted. I supposed that was who that was, since I never receive calls."

"Her name is Marcy Deibler."

"That's not a very French name," Father muttered.

"'Marcy'? What does it matter?" Granted, if Father thought the French were the best at everything, well, he must be right, but there was no shame in acknowledging that people from other places existed. Though Jehanne could hardly read any of his books, based on her slow-going reading and writing lessons with Clair, it wasn't as if Father's extensive book collection consisted of only French literature.

"No, her family name. In fact—Deibler, do you mean like the executioner?"

Day-blair. Sounded French to Jehanne. "She's the executioner's daughter."

"You've made an interesting choice in companionship."

"I didn't know."

"I'm not judging. Go on. What have you told her?"

"Not much, really. We just speak about girl things." She swallowed. "She'll be safe, won't she, if she were to visit me and stay the night?"

"I don't see why she wouldn't be, with my protection. And Moreau's, of course."

And Clair. With her knife. "She'll be here today."

Father cocked a brow. "When?"

"I don't know, an hour?"

He blinked. She'd seen him cry and panic, but never had he looked this thoroughly stunned. "That's rather short notice, don't you think?"

"I'm sorry, Father, but she was crying about something. She's having trouble at home, and I wanted her to feel less lonely."

"She can't go to her parents, her mother? I imagine her mother would be better at gauging a feminine temperament."

"She relates to me more because we're close in age." Give or take five, possibly six years. *How old is Marcy, again?*

Father tilted his chin in thought, his eyes losing focus for a handful of seconds. "If it makes you happy, pup, I'll do what I can. I'm sure I'll arrange something. It would do if the servants prepared some food."

Jehanne rushed and embraced him. "Thank you!" She went to him so swiftly the half-empty glass by the armchair swished.

He patted her head. "Of course."

"You won't regret it." Perhaps having someone else here would help him out of his gloomier moods.

"I'm sure I won't."

"I think you might even like her company."

His smile was tired. "I may indeed."

"I just want to help Marcy as best I can."

Father kissed her cheek, but when he broke away, his expression saddened. "And that's what I love about you, pup, that fiercely gentle heart."

"Among other things, I'm sure." Jehanne stopped beaming. "But if Marcy's here, will that be too much work for Clair?"

He squeezed her shoulder. "Oh, pup, you're still worried over that? Don't fret. She's a paid servant. You can make her do whatever you want."

"Are you sure?"

Father insisted, his grip steady, "I'm absolutely certain."

Jehanne hoped for a peaceful evening, and with Marcy here soon, her sleep should be better.

It had to be.

10

Marcy

The late afternoon wind tugged on her coat as Papa drove away and Jehanne ran to her. Marcy and Papa hadn't spoken much; he had a knack for knowing not only what to say, but also when not to speak. Before Marcy left the lurching, sputtering auto, Papa kissed her and pulled her to him, and she smelled his cologne and sighed against his coat. In that brief moment of bliss, her mind drifted to a trip her family had made back when they took trips, the glass-green, hazy time when they went to Deauville and played by the sea. André and Marcy chased one another, and her parents stood knee-deep in the water. Both then and now, Marcy imagined she and her family (Papa, actually, just Papa) were some of the last people in the world on an island of magic and safe isolation.

Maman managed the money, kept a close eye on what was needed, what they could afford, and what desires they couldn't indulge. As such, the family never returned to the sea, but so long as the memory lingered, Marcy could find comfort in the old taste of salt-sweat and the cat-tongue burn of sand beneath her toes.

She wished they could return there.

The high, black metal gate before her looked like two giant spiders, and the path led to a stout structure of white stone. At least, Marcy suspected the manor had been white until the green crept between its teeth.

She carried the beaten valise, heavier than it had any right to be, the bag Maman had used when their family went to the sea. Besides the phlegm from crying, Marcy swore salt settled on her lips when Jehanne raced down the manor steps and flung both arms around her. Marcy could only offer an arm in return, her gaze on the leering, lichen-stained beast before her. A long, vined trellis crawled up to the yawning, half-caged mouth of a balcony.

Marcy laughed when they separated. "How long have you been waiting there?"

"A little while. Is it too soon to do something like that? I'm not sure how this works after, you know." Jehanne pointed to her own head.

"What do you mean? Embracing?"

"Yes, is it too soon to give an embrace?" Jehanne lowered her voice and leaned closer. She smelled of old pages and autumn musk. "Because you looked like you needed one."

Marcy was sheepish, a strange thing for her. If she weren't trying to keep composure, she'd shuffle her feet. "No, no, I really liked that." Embracing like this wasn't really done in her town, but if doing this the American way meant closer contact with her new friend, she was okay with it.

Jehanne leaned forward, and Marcy couldn't help but be drawn by her musty old book smell. "Are you feeling okay now?"

"I will feel okay, I think."

Jehanne cocked her head. "If you need to talk, let me know. You did let me spew off about my own problems, after all." She nodded back at the front door. "Anyhow, Father's in the main hall, at least that's where I left him." Rolling her eyes, she added, "Had to talk him out of chaperoning me out here. He made the servants prepare an early supper. The food's not ready yet, but it'll make you feel better."

With an aching grin, Marcy rubbed her cramping belly. And panicked a little. She had a pad in, but in her hurry, she forgot to put more in the valise. Oh no. "I hope so." She wished she could spur up the same energy she had at the park. She didn't have experience with friendships, and she didn't want to mire Jehanne in her muddy little mood puddles.

"I'll carry your bag."

"You don't have to." But Jehanne leaned to grip the handle, and Marcy let go, her fingers tingling when her friend's skin brushed hers.

"Don't worry over it. Mlle Clair should carry it up to your room." Jehanne strode toward the front door, and Marcy followed up the age split stone.

On each side of the vast main hall, perfectly symmetrical and angular, were two sets of stairs, but below the landing, there was a short stint of wall between the banister and the hall. The area was cold.

"You have an open balcony," Marcy said. She'd noticed the outside mouth of the thing, sure, but hadn't looked beyond the teeth. Jehanne's warm, enticing body had blurred her line of thought.

The space between Jehanne's brow dented. "Hmm, you're right."

"You didn't notice?"

"I did. I suppose I never thought about it much."

Before they could continue the conversation, the servant, the one who had dragged Jehanne away at the park, came out of one of the many openings in the hall. Clair looked as she did before, so much like Maman, but somehow more withdrawn, more severe.

The servant craned her neck and pointed to the valise. "I'm assuming this is yours?"

Marcy beamed. "I sure hope so."

Clair grunted, picked up the valise, and climbed the stairs.

Gazing back at the balcony, Marcy asked, "What about when it rains? Or birds fly in?" Marcy recalled Jaune, Papa's old canary who died two years back. Maybe Jehanne's father didn't mind birds in his home.

117

"There's a curtain, see? It's mostly for the sun, but it's thick enough to keep rain out. Father says it needs to be replaced because it mildews, though."

Skeptically, Marcy said, "I don't think a curtain can keep a bird out." The room was chilly, and she swore she felt a draft. "But it's a swell thing to look at." She could see whoever constructed the manor, with all the baroque paintings, the swords, and the tapestries mounting the walls, was someone who cared more about aesthetics than practicality. Or keeping warm and dry.

"Didn't you say your papa would be here?"

Jehanne *hmm*ed and rubbed the unscarred side of her neck. "I've no idea where he went."

"Well." Marcy spun in a little circle. "You have so much. This room—it's like something out of a different time."

"You really think so?"

"Have you ever been inside anyone else's home?"

"No."

Marcy poked Jehanne's shoulder. "We'll fix that! I'll make sure you can visit me one day, and you could—I'm sure André wouldn't mind sleeping on the couch." Good thing André wasn't here to contest that. "And you could meet Papa and Jolie."

"Who's Jolie?"

"She's my dog." Jehanne stared. "You do know what a dog is, don't you?"

Her friend gave her a lopsided grin. "Yes, I'm not quite *that* distant from reality."

"Have you ever been around one before?"

"I've seen pictures in books. That counts, doesn't it?"

That made Marcy sad, actually. "You don't know what petting a dog feels like?"

Jehanne shook her head and joked, "Is that something that needs fixing?"

For Marcy, this wasn't a laughing matter. "Yes! You can't just *never* pet a dog." Jolie was older than Marcy, so Marcy'd had a pet her entire life, and she didn't like seeing Jolie limp when her hip struck an odd angle or groan as she stood up. She didn't like the odd bumps hanging from her oldest friend's belly. She tried to distance herself from Jolie's waning years, but Marcy at least wanted Jehanne to meet Jolie before the end.

"How does it feel, then?" Jehanne asked. "Petting a dog?"

"Jolie has this wavy fur that's sleek like people hair. It's practically silk. Okay, that settles it, you have to meet her soon. Everyone should pet a dog before they die."

A man's voice said, "What's this about a dog?" Marcy whipped about. The man's face was long and blue-shadowed like Maman's, but that was where the resemblance ended; he was both wolfish and like a fatigued cherub—face rosy-cheeked, eyes egg-blue, hair curly-gold, where Maman was porcelain-wan, dark-eyed, and black-haired.

A cherub with teeth to him when he smiled. What an odd thought. Would Marcy rather he not have teeth?

He smoothed his hair and spoke to Jehanne first. "Sweet pup, you really should've given me more notice."

Jehanne shrugged one shoulder. "Yes, well."

119

"Oh, I understand. If this makes you happy, think no more of it." His hand settled on the crown of Jehanne's head like a sparrow swallowing a little moth. A gentle smile and open hands. Jealousy festered, because even though she had Papa, Maman and she still had a wound, and it'd spoil everything if she didn't clean and wrap it up.

"And you're Marcy, I suspect?" Well, they'd be in dire straits if she wasn't.

Jehanne's father wouldn't stop beaming, and what once unsettled Marcy called to her because she needed that sweetness, that absence of tense arms and eyes lingering for minutes on the tablecloth.

Marcy offered, "It's good to meet you, monsieur." She shook his hand, and it was hot, but she welcomed his friendliness all the same.

She expected to be shown around, though maybe the issue was that she wasn't asking questions, but she didn't think it was polite to ask, "What made you think having an open balcony was a good idea?" or "Does your furnace work? Where did you go to make your hand so warm?" She wondered if the manor had a new heater or one of those steam ones in the books that looked like these muscled half-octopus, half-dragon monsters.

Jehanne's father said, "There's a bit of a delay in the meal." He caressed his daughter's face and lingered in a way Papa wouldn't with Marcy, a second or three too long. Jehanne accepted the gesture with a tilt of her head and a smile as fleeting as running water, as if it was what a daughter would do, but not what she wanted. "Jehanne, darling, why don't you go on ahead?"

Marcy took a step to follow her friend, but halted when Jehanne's father didn't budge. He stared at a fixed point in the distance. Following his gaze, Marcy found nothing of interest.

He blinked. "Ah, look at this. The family coat of arms." The tapestry was shield-shaped, patches of gold-petaled fleurs-de-lis stippling an azure ground, a yellow shield dismembered by a black cross. In Marcy's eyes, the design was a tad garish.

"What . . ." What would her own family coat of arms look like? The Widow and a decapitated dove, since her medieval ancestors took care of doves before they tended to the gallows and changed their religion out of necessity.

She decided not to think of the subject again.

The monsieur answered, "It originates from an ancestor who fought for our country many years ago."

Unable to hold back her curiosity, Marcy asked, "Which war?"

The monsieur shrank a little, all his limbs retreating close to his heart. "The one that lasted over one hundred years."

Below the crest, there was an elaborate weapon on display. Hesitant but too curious to quell herself, Marcy lifted a finger. "What sort of sword is this?"

"A braquemard," Jehanne's father answered promptly. "Does that name mean anything to you?"

"No." It was pointy, as Marcy supposed most swords were.

His eyes lost their luster as he stared at the weapon. "I suspected not." Marcy tried not to ruffle like an indignant cat. By God, she knew many things! She thought it best to let the matter die and not risk the monsieur withdrawing into himself because of unpleasant memories. "Good for beheadings."

Marcy sputtered, "I—what?"

"The sword. At least, I suspect that's what it's good for." He added, "Your family name is German, isn't it?"

Marcy didn't expect the change in topic. She felt as if something bit off part of the conversation. "How did you know?"

"I'm fond of languages, but I could've assumed you have German in you without knowing your name."

"Oh. How?"

"I've read that you can do more than guess one's ancestry by their face; you can see their soul too. That's a science, and I can see the German in your bones." Her bones? She had hoped her skin covered them well enough. "To your credit, you do look bright, despite your heritage."

Marcy's jaw twitched. "Pardon?" She calmed her voice. No need to make a bad impression. "My maman and her family are from here, and Papa grew up here."

Jehanne's father pressed his finger into his collar as if he itched there. "Good, that dilutes any other influences." Marcy focused on a blotty shoreside painting and the ache from biting her bottom lip. Papa was good, he really was.

Even so, given the war, she didn't know how apt it was to defend his German heritage.

When Jehanne's father strode forth with a sweeping gesture of his left hand, Marcy straightened her dress and followed. He probably didn't mean to be offensive. Because of her relationship with Maman, she wondered if adults spoke this secret, cryptic language Marcy wouldn't understand until she grew up. Even André suddenly became blurry and weird after a time. But Papa made sense; maybe he was the exception.

She was being ridiculous. Best not to overthink when she wanted this visit to calm her.

The dining room smelled of lemons and roses, and it could've been beautiful before time strangled it with both hands. Lime and mildew framed where the floor met the walls, making the goldish corner tiles look like a child's rotten teeth after too many cream sweets. The silver fleurs-de-lis on the rain-stained, peeling wallpaper crept toward the browning ceiling. The space was as clean as it could be.

They sat down at a shiny table that looked too big for a two-person family. Marcy counted twelve chairs with legs curved at the bottom like question marks. She settled across from Jehanne, with Jehanne's father at the head. The plates and glasses before them were woefully empty.

A clock ticked like an inebriated woodpecker. Before another word was said, Marcy jumped when the manor groaned.

"Oh, never mind that," Jehanne's father said with a wave of his hand. "The manor likes to tell its stories. If these halls had secrets and a single mouth, they'd be as traitorous as an Englishman."

Jehanne straightened. "The English are with us, aren't they? The paper said—you would've fought with them."

Given her host's taut posture, Marcy wondered if she'd regret speaking, but spoke anyway. "Great Britain is our friend." She garnered that from the newspapers. "At least, as far as I know. I don't leave the house much. My parents don't like it." She decided not to specify Maman. If she kept her comments broad enough, she wouldn't need to dive too deep into the past.

Jehanne's father smoothed out his beard, though the wrinkled ire over the English hadn't smoothed out. "Why do your parents keep you so close? Are you their only child?"

Marcy's skin prickled, and she scratched her elbow. "Yes."

"Ah, I can't blame them then. Have you read the paper? These are terrible times for children, and you're their only one. It makes all the sense in the world, in fact, for them to hide you away."

Marcy shifted in her seat, tugging at her skirt. "The people hate my family because my papa, he—you know." She flattened her palms in the crease of her thighs.

"The headsman, yes. More humane than a rope, as odd as it sounds. Cuts clean through the spine. You and your family are too conscientious. The people who demean you are worth the cost of horses. Then, I suppose not, since a horse can be ridden longer." Marcy didn't understand his point. One wouldn't ride another per—

Oh.

Heat flooded her cheeks, and she fiddled with her embroidered napkin.

Silverware clinked against porcelain. "Father."

"Pup, who builds the theaters, the cathedrals? Who disposes of society's evil? These brutes, they hate the aristocracy, the law, but they're willing to roam the streets, to reap the benefits."

Marcy asked, "Who are the 'brutes'? The Germans?"

"No, everyone who'd judge your father and your family, the ones who'd make you hide and feel shame. They'll spit on war heroes, men recognized by the highest in power as noble and courageous. They make men do the work they're too cowardly to commit, then discard them. You give a pig its slop, and does it thank you?"

Marcy said, "Pigs are killed for us to eat. I wouldn't feel grateful if I was one, a pig, that is." She stared at the webbed cloth beneath her silverware and pursed her lips.

Before Jehanne or her father could respond, Marcy startled when a man appeared in the corner of her eye. When she looked, she guessed he was a servant because even though his clothes were nice, purple and red and accented with gold, he balanced a large, full moon tray in each flat hand.

Jehanne's father smiled, which made Marcy's heart flutter, but not in the same way as when she thought of André or Jehanne.

He said, clearing his throat and rapping his knuckles on the table, "Thank you."

Marcy forgot all about pigs and did a double take at the servant. He looked like he could be the monsieur's brother, but the way the monsieur brushed his wrist wasn't brotherly, not at all. The man stood behind his master like a pampered Dobermann. She couldn't help but notice the servant was dashing, but his presence put her off. He had purple rings under his eyes like he hadn't slept in a week, and his pallor reminded her of when she or anyone in her family caught a long-suffering cold.

Marcy's mouth watered as she peered at the plates of food, the smells filling her nose, the tastes flooding her mouth before she took the first bite.

There was a pastry-wrapped chicken stuffed with bacon and smelling of what she thought was sage. Custard tarts with saffron. Studying Papa's cooking did her well here. Marcy tasted the dark wine—spiced, biting her throat. It made her cough. Papa sometimes let her drink from his cup, small sips, and she hadn't yet acquired a taste for wine. There was also a pitcher of tea, but when Marcy sipped it, it had a funny, bitter aftertaste.

Despite eating nothing, Jehanne's father dabbed his lips with a folded cloth napkin, while Marcy set a curled hand to her lips to cover up a belch. She ate as if she hadn't done so in days. She believed her greediness was likely shameful to those around her, but nobody commented on her behavior, if they paid attention. By the time Marcy finished, she was the sated kind of full, that type of ended hunger that ached, but only a little.

"Father, why don't you eat with us? You shouldn't just *not* eat." Jehanne's tone was light, but the skin around her knuckles tightened when she laid her hands flat on both sides of her plate.

"Ah, my appetite has left me again, pup." He stood.

"Did it ever come back?" Jehanne asked.

"I'll pick at what's left later. If you don't mind, I think I'll retire early. You'll escort your friend to her room, won't you, pup?" Marcy wondered why he alternated between "darling" and "pup."

"Of course, Father. Please feel better. And eat." Jehanne kissed her father's cheek and said to Marcy, "Your room's in the same hall as mine."

"Moreau, come." The servant, Moreau, followed her father.

Once the monsieur and Moreau left, Jehanne complained a little loudly, "He never eats with me. If he's self-conscious about people watching him eat, he should just say so."

Marcy muttered, "Do they sleep in the same room?"

Jehanne didn't lower her voice. "Yes, why wouldn't they? Moreau might need to tend to Father in the night." While Jehanne didn't seem to catch the innuendo in her voice, she must've taken notice of Marcy's expression because of her next question. "Is it really that odd? Clair does it with me in case I need help."

Marcy ground her teeth, unsure how to word what she meant. "I don't want to say odd, just not, not something you really see." Marcy didn't know Jehanne's beliefs about that sort of intimacy, or what she believed God would do about it.

It, it. Such a small word for a big weight. How Jehanne stirred Marcy's stomach in ways similar to André, but deeper. But she couldn't dwell because if she let herself down that path, she'd end up like Wilde, not even allowed religion and sick in Berneval-le-Grand, except if she had to leave France, where else could she go to die?

So, she stuffed her feelings away like a well-sucked childhood blanket.

"Is your papa normally so—animated about certain things?" He had captivated her attention, despite her misgivings, and anything that distracted from what happened at home was good.

"No, he doesn't often joke about—horses. Or rant about pigs. I think it's good because it means he trusts you. He's probably like me, excited to meet someone new."

Marcy yawned and rubbed her eyes. "Is it all right if I go ahead and sleep early too? I'd like to talk to you more, and maybe explore some, if that's fine, but I'm just so tired."

Jehanne patted her elbow. "Yeah, you must be tired from what you've told me. Follow me."

By the time Jehanne showed her the bedroom, which was bigger than Marcy's room at home, André's room, and the kitchen combined, Marcy yawned and stretched, taking note of the valise sagging in the pawed chair near a horned bookcase. It was opened. Jehanne went to her own room, across from Marcy's.

Desperate for a bath, Marcy went to the washroom adjacent to her room. By God, the room was big enough for five tubs, but it held only one that winked at her.

Beside the sink lay a nightgown and undergarment taken from Maman's valise, but that wasn't the strangest thing. It didn't bother her that a female servant prepared those.

What scratched at her was the gaping, cream-colored purse squatted next to the linen gown. Marcy peeked inside and frowned. It was littered with white cloth pads.

Her head spun. She hadn't said she'd forgotten to bring menstrual pads. How did anyone know she had started bleeding today? Was it that obvious? Was she that bloated? Had she stained the back of her dress? The smell couldn't be that terrible. Her cheeks flooded with prickling heat.

Marcy postured with her back to the mirror and strained her neck. No stain, yet.

Odd. Maybe the pads were just in case, a coincidental act of consideration. She searched for possible ill intent, but she couldn't find any.

After she took her bath, Marcy dressed and lined herself. She stumbled across the hall to the guest bedroom, which was lined with gold and silver. She had no idea a bed could hold so many pillows. With few thoughts on anything else, she burrowed under the covers and drifted into a deep slumber within a minute. Only a faint creaking and rustling vibrated against her bones before her release.

11

Rosalie

What had she done to her family?

What the hell had she done?

Yesterday, after taking Marcy to her friend's home, Anatole stepped inside, took off his coat, saw Rosalie on the couch, and said nothing. That night, he retired first, and they slept with their backs to one another. Now, Rosalie sat on the couch with her head in her hands. She wouldn't cry. That'd do no good. She straightened when the stairs leading to the top floor creaked. Anatole approached her with Jolie following, and he beamed when he saw her, though he grew somber when her attempted smile hurt and broke.

Anatole asked, "What happened? Why was Marcy crying? Why did André leave?"

He had waited this long to ask, and Rosalie still wasn't prepared. She muttered to herself, "It's my fault. It's always my fault, isn't it?"

"What's your fault?" Anatole knelt and touched her knee. "Please tell me what's the matter, just for your own sake. If nobody else, let me in, trust me." His eyes scorched her—blue, bright, terrifying in their vulnerability.

Abruptly, Rosalie stood without planning where to go. She strode over to a small table set between two bookshelves. She adjusted the curved lampshade.

"Marcy proposed to André," she answered. "They kissed, and I confronted him. That's the start of it, I think." She looked to Anatole; he had stood. He stared, hauntingly silent. "You aren't disturbed?" *Do you already know? Is this another thing you thought you'd keep from me?*

"I don't know how to feel. She's young, and whether she marries André or—"

Rosalie wrapped her arms close to keep her heart inside her. "She won't. She can't. I won't allow it. She's a child."

"Of course. I don't mean now."

"It'll never happen, not so long as I'm alive."

"Why? What if it's what she truly wants, what'll make her happier than anything else?"

"Marcy shouldn't marry somebody who wants to be an executioner." She wouldn't let Marcy be her. If that happened, Rosalie would crumble like a pillar of salt, crumble to dust like the thousands of skeletons already

131

tombed in the earth that Anatole fashioned into a garden of roses.

"Like your mother? Like you?" Rosalie froze at his tone. His body was stiff, and his eyes shone in a way that was neither warm nor cold. The air between them swelled. "Do you regret marrying me?"

Rosalie stumbled over her words, and she couldn't look at his face, so she stared at his right shoulder, the white of the fabric. "I love you."

"That's not what I asked."

"Isn't it?" Her voice rose. "We wouldn't be married if I didn't love you."

It hadn't been only pity that brought them together. At first, yes, she pitied the lonely man who lived in a house of shuttered windows, but when they had their first long conversation at the cycling club, he offered to cook for her, and he did so with a bashful tilt of his head. They raced as equals through both the winter slush and summer blaze.

Anatole stepped forward. "It is my duty. It's all I know to do to give us a good home."

He gave her so much, too much.

"I know, and I'm not trying to be ungrateful."

"I understand. I only want to know if you regret our marriage. If Marcy and André married out of love, if they were like us, if they were like your parents, or my own, why would it be so terrible, so unthinkable? What is it about André doing my work that would be any different from how things are now?"

"I don't want that life for them."

"'That life'? Our life?" His mouth stayed open, and Rosalie crossed her arms and looked away and stared at the burgundy lampshade. "I'm content. We're content, I thought." She wished he'd leave this be. If he continued pushing, she didn't know how closed she could continue to be. "Rosie, please speak to me." She exhaled once. "Have I hurt you? Do you hate what I do?" He choked. "Do you blame me for what happened?"

A shock rippled through Rosalie, and like a child resting a hand on a hot stove, she recoiled. Juliette, Maman, the other unspeakable thing that ruined them both.

Thing, such a bitter word.

Rosalie couldn't even think it, and Anatole couldn't say it. It, there she went again. Married for two decades, and this was what they could share with each other.

Reluctantly, Rosalie answered, "It isn't that; it's everything else." So odd, how the least offensive thing about the guillotine was that her husband sheared gentlemen's heads with it.

"What do you mean?"

Rosalie bore her eyes into the space beyond Anatole's shoulder. "It's this whole bloody world. Have you ever thought that a loved one of those condemned would come and take out their grief and hatred on you? A vengeful father, son, mother?"

"Of course I have."

"They could come to our home, and even if they don't hurt Marcy or André, they could kill you out of spite. Even when you aren't the one who prosecuted or sentenced the men. It's just the same as the looks you'd get, the looks I'd get when we'd go to the circus or theater." Even before André was born, all the sneers and remarks made Rosalie fear one day someone would be so driven with disgust and loathing that Anatole would die. "And Marcy and André would need to hide even more, because even if they're isolated now, it'll be worse for André when he takes your place, and if he marries Marcy, women are often the victims when men want to destroy other men."

She hadn't meant for all that to come out, but there it was, strewn out like carrion for the crows.

Anatole lowered his gaze, presumably in thought. "In all the years I've worked, you've never told me you fear for our lives."

"Why would I, when this job is all we have because I can't do anything?"

He snapped his attention back to her. "You do more than enough."

"I do more harm than good."

Fidgeting, she tilted her head and bore her attention into the lamp until the burgundy darkened.

Anatole pleaded, "Please look at me."

She struggled to pierce the quiet, the swelling sore under her ribs. "When we married, you were always alone, and I was alone. And I loved you, and I couldn't stop. I can't stop. What you do, it's not that that's the issue, not the justice. It's how everyone else reacts, how we're shunned. I had hoped—I hope Marcy and André can escape that loneliness, this blood we have."

"Haven't they stayed with us, cut off from the rest of the world?"

"The world is cruel. We've both seen that. André— André has been in it."

"And he's lived."

"He's made terrible decisions that completely changed a woman's life. And the child, their child, what will she do when she was already born without any marriage or planning?" Anatole took pause, and Rosalie pounced. "Why didn't you tell me about André's child the first you heard of it? Why did I need to open a letter from his lover to know?"

Rather than deny the knowledge, Anatole said, "I'm sorry. I didn't know what to say."

Rosalie worked to conceal the hurt by shifting her face to the side. "You hide—you hid the truth from me about André. How can you expect me to be forthright when you aren't?"

"I know," he said softly. Damn him with the tone that made it difficult to kindle her grudge. "I'm sorry, but he's lived, despite his mistakes, and that's the most important thing, I think. We'll find a way to help the mother and the child, if we can. We always find a way. And I'll do whatever it takes to earn your trust again."

"What of Marcy? I thought we could keep her safe, but she's gone, and she hates me, and I'm not sure it's unwarranted."

"She adores you. I've told you."

"She can't even look at me, can't even stay in this house. Neither can André. They're gone. What's wrong with me, Anatole?"

Gently, he said, "What's wrong with *us*, you mean. Why haven't we spoken about this before?"

"Don't blame yourself."

"Haven't I kept quiet too? Haven't I suppressed my thoughts and cried alone to keep everyone else comfortable? Just like you have?"

"I suppose, as one might guess, though it's hard to know what hasn't been said." They shared the faintest of smiles. "And about what happened." Rosalie's ribs ached with how fast her heart hammered against them. "I—no, it was my fault."

I had a dove and the sweet dove died; and I have thought it died of grieving. O, what could it grieve for? She raised her clasped hands to her lips. *Its feet were tied, with a silken thread of my own hand's weaving.*

"What do you mean?" Anatole inhaled so deeply that when his chest expanded, it looked like it hurt. "Oh, Rosie, love, no. No, it wasn't." Of course he'd say that; they were killers, the two of them.

"But it was. I should've known somehow the dosage was wrong."

Anatole's forehead crumpled, his temple tightening and trembling. "Don't tell yourself that. Please don't."

As his eyes brightened with wetness, Rosalie tasted blood from how hard her teeth kneaded her tongue. *Please don't cry. If you break, I'll fall with you.*

"I've blamed myself, yes, and I did blame you sometimes." Rosalie bit her lip, rubbed her nose, and exhaled shakily. "I think there were times I hated you, and I hated myself more for those moments."

Rosalie dared another look and regretted it when the hurt in his eyes threatened to spill over more than before. She shouldn't have spoken, shouldn't have hurt him and ruined everything. There were some feelings best left neglected and unspoken, hoarded like a sack of feathers and stones. Anatole hadn't needed to know her worst thoughts all those years ago.

No blood in the bed, no death in the bed.

Anatole said, "How could either of us have known we'd lose so much that winter? And you lost the most."

Rosalie swallowed blood and worried loose hair with two fingers. "I don't want to compare our grief."

"You know I don't blame you for any of it, don't you? I never did."

"That makes you better than me."

"Stop, please, no, it doesn't."

"It does. I've been hateful and angry. Even in secret, it's still there. I don't want Marcy to be like me. God, what have I done to this family?" Her demons had needled inside her until they had torn the fabric of the household. At times, she would release them for a second, only to regret what was prickling vulnerability.

"Why do you still blame anyone at all? Why do you blame yourself? Isn't this my doing too?"

"Anatole, no. Don't listen to what I said. I'm sick."

"How else should you be expected to act after what you lost? Damn the world if they'd judge you." To be fair, Rosalie thought with bitterness, the world couldn't possibly hate her as much as she hated herself. So why did she fear it? "Haven't I been closed up too?"

"Not to the same degree."

"Does it matter? Haven't I tried to make us perfectly domestic at the expense of letting things fester? I'd cry alone on walks after I thought I shouldn't cry anymore. Because what would anyone think of a man who provides for his family, yet can't stop himself from fits?" His next breath sounded as if it rattled deep. "But damn those expectations."

"You've always been strong to me."

"And you to me. There's no reason Marcy shouldn't look up to you. You're strong, brilliant, resilient."

Rosalie snorted. "I've ruined everything without trying."

"It's not ruined if we can mend it."

"Marcy and André will come back, won't they? Please say they will."

"What happened? Is there something else that went on that I didn't see?"

Ah, so she proved herself a hypocrite with her own secrets. Rosalie blurted, "Marcy heard me say that I'd rather she be dead than marry an executioner."

She refused to see his reaction; she couldn't bear his disappointment.

It wasn't until her tongue bled that Anatole said, voice careful, "Did you mean it?"

"I only meant I would want her to be in any position but mine, but I'd been frustrated at André and—it's no excuse. My words were wrong, and it seems with Marcy, I only let her hear those wrong words."

"Dead. Would that really be better? Would you rather be dead than here with me?"

"No, God, that's just—we have this, and Marcy has what we give her, but I want her to have more options than hiding away."

"Isn't she already hidden? For her own protection?"

"Yes, until she's old enough to know how to elude the cameras." Those weighty, wood-and-nickel things. "And those eyes, all those damn eyes." Rosalie's mind soured, turned inward again. "God, Marcy. I always say the wrong words. I'm always her enemy when you tell her 'yes' and I have to tell her 'no.' Do you understand what sort of position that puts me in?"

Anatole said softly, that shade of soft only Rosalie could detect over the past two decades, "Why should we tell her what she can't do? Us, of all people? Won't the world do enough of that?"

The world, the sick world, with its weaselly denizens. "Because we keep her safe, like you said."

"The world isn't safe, and our house is a part of the world."

Rosalie wanted to yank at her hair. "But we've said for so long that it isn't." *No blood in the bed, no death past the threshold. No war, no world.*

Keep blood out of the bed, out of the house. Keep the dead where they rest.

"I know, but we, especially I, have lied to her. It's a lie to think what I do out there won't influence us here. And the world, it'll tell Marcy what she can't do because of her blood or my work or because of what she wants or how she looks. It's just like when you were told you couldn't ride a cycle, and what did you do? You were France's first woman to race on a cycle. And you won, again and again."

Rosalie couldn't help her sadness. If life was a cycle race, one hundred wins couldn't reverse one knee-breaking fall. "And you loved me for it."

"I loved you before that, and I love you after."

"But Marcy isn't us, and this isn't that decade, that century. I don't want her to be us."

"Are we really that terribly off?"

"Are you truly happy with a madwoman for a wife who shuts herself in and a duty you were forced to do despite all your attempts to escape it?"

"You aren't mad."

Yet there had been a time when they agreed to consult a doctor, a doctor Rosalie could only think of as Dr. _____, a shrew-eyed man who diagnosed her with "the American disease."

Dr. _____ ordered her to rest in bed for months at a time, and she and Anatole had hoped her head-moths would lessen. It made no sense, given her constant stays in bed anyhow, but the doctor said if she committed to isolation and stayed in bed alone every day, her mind would clear.

After six months, everything was yellow like the fuzzy center of a wildflower. After a year, it still made little sense, but she smelled yellow, the yellow of old books and rain-ruined wallpaper. Dr. _____ instructed Anatole to not be with her at night, an order that gave him as visible an agony as the sticky, black bile inside her, the bile that spilled over the walls.

Anatole delivered her food at the door until the silence spoke too much. Rosalie called for him, and he was at her side. Against the doctor's orders, he was there, smelling of his cigars and roses and newspaper comics.

The muscles in her right arm spasmed when she sat up, and her legs were numb. Her fingers tingled. Sweat prickled her brow. She was sick with a tuberculosis of the mind, and it consumed her, killed her. "I'm going insane. I'm insane."

She was dead.

"You aren't insane." Anatole's gaze had lingered on her nail-worried palm, and he clasped her hand to his lips. When the only thing between them was breath, she leaned against his shoulder.

She needed to go, she needed to be . . . "Not here, not here in this bed. Not where he . . ."

"I know."

"I can't go outside, not for long, but I can't stay in this room forever. Not anymore. I'm afraid I'll die. Please call Dr. _____." Rosalie did her best not to cry, but it was hard. "He won't believe me. He'll tell me I'm paranoid, manic, stubborn, but he'll do what you say." Despite being the only soul to live in her own mind, Rosalie's opinions about her psyche wouldn't be trusted more than those of her husband. Dr. _____ likened her mind to a compass always pointing south. In a terrible way, she was fortunate Anatole would listen to her, that he had. That was, in that moment, the only way she could seize control.

Until she lost everything, Rosalie hadn't realized she'd been happy. She wanted to be normal—like Anatole was desperately normal. She needed to recapture herself, the bright girl who loved cycling and feeling the breeze on her neck more than anything. But that image was like snow on hot fingers, gone as soon as she caught it.

Anatole had said. "Would you like to go cycling while André rests?" That was how they fell in love, after all.

"No." Rosalie didn't move her gaze away from the ceiling and its wooden ribs.

"Would you like to go to the garden?" She had pitied Anatole. Though he wouldn't say as much, he needed a regular, pleasant home life to offset his work. He needed a regular, pleasant wife.

Still not shifting, Rosalie whispered, "I can't move. I don't think I can move." The pain in her lungs had a weight to it, and it was insurmountable. Even if she did move, she couldn't absolve what she lost. She hated the world outside, hated the people who would gladly have lunch with an esteemed judge who ordered death sentences, but not the man who carried them out, the man denied another path in life because of his father's occupation.

She hated the quiet house, and she hated the tense seconds before peering into André's crib when she did bring herself to leave the bed to feed him. She'd snap if she left now, even when she wanted to. Even if she stayed still, she'd die because of the constant ache in her chest. The silence curled into her back.

She wanted to move, wanted to follow the Vilaine where it met the Atlantic and allow the restless water to drift her away as if she were a trembling and soggy plank of deadwood.

Anatole had set a hand on her forehead. When Rosalie finally looked at him, he was struggling to speak without crying. He said, "Would you like me to carry you, or hold your hand?"

Rosalie swallowed. How weak was she that she needed her husband to guide and carry her? But then, it took momentous effort to accept help at all. It took every bit of strength left in her bones and muscles.

Several minutes passed before she reached for his hand, and when she rose and went to the stairs, Anatole didn't lead her, but rather followed as she stepped down at her own pace.

Despite being aware, she was a husk of herself as, on the hot, tickling ground, she rested her head in Anatole's lap, and he smoothed his hand down her back.

Blinking away the memory, Rosalie asked, "But are you happy?"

Without hesitation, Anatole said, "Yes." Oh, how she hated and loved that incorrigibility. She had to be silent and normal, painfully normal. Not too much blood or bile, no hysteria, no infectious words haunting the air like chanting flies, yet she couldn't oblige

"Are you truly happy with Marcy gone? Or André?"

"Marcy will come back, and André will come around. There's a bond there."

"With you, perhaps. I don't begrudge you his fondness, but he outgrew me."

"I know he didn't receive his sense of humor from me. He loves you, Rosie. You raised him since he was not even a year old."

"What else could I do, leave the poor boy on his own?"

"He's the son we lost—"

Rosalie cut him off. "Stop, now. Don't say that. No, he's not. He's our nephew. He's Juliette's son, not ours. Don't take that from her."

Anatole asked with that soul-reaching stare of his, "Why have you never considered him to be like a son to us?"

Shouldn't Rosalie treasure her sister's only baby? Didn't she? She didn't hate André, of course not, and she didn't hate Marcy, yet they both left. As they grew up, Rosalie kept away as much as she could, so she wouldn't poison them, yet she managed to do it anyway.

Just what she had tried to avoid. It wasn't fair for André to think of himself as a replacement for Ro—her son. It seemed obvious that a boy—her nephew, the son of her sister and dearest friend—would be like the son she lost, but it was cruel. Not just toward her son's memory, but to

André. He didn't deserve to be the stand-in with the same shoes and crib.

But if André wasn't a replacement, what was he? A nephew, yes, short-tempered and hot-tongued, but always with a hint of concern and this keen need to please. So like Juliette and her way with people, but with a bitter undercurrent.

How terrible was it that even when he fed from Rosalie, she trembled, yet she felt nothing toward him because she was mired in memory? From her, André drank the dead like gods drank ambrosia. No wonder something curdled in him. It was a mistake, feeding André and Marcy from herself, but it was the only closeness and selfish fulfillment Rosalie could afford. Besides, a milk bottle too could seethe with unclean, infectious things, so even that wasn't a safe alternative.

Why have you never considered him to be like a son to us?

Rosalie said, "I did it for André's sake, so he wouldn't think he was only meant to be a replacement, a consolation. That burden, that empty pit—André was just a baby. It wasn't his responsibility to be that for us, to exist to fill another's place. It still isn't. Only our—only Roger could fill Roger's place, which he . . ." Rosalie's voice broke, and she cleared her throat. "I wouldn't think it fair for Roger to fill André's place, if it'd been Juliette who lost a sister and son."

"I suppose you're right." Anatole wiped his cheek, and Rosalie shook to the point her teeth rattled. "I still think of him every day, you know."

Rosalie fully faced her husband so they were trembling and exposed together. "Don't tell me that, don't . . ." If she pulled away now, bolted away and locked herself in the washroom, she could maybe keep her resolve. Stiffen, inhale, hide herself away. If she hid and continued running, grief couldn't find her. Despite stewing in concern after concern, she told herself if she didn't wear mourning colors, she'd mourn less. Her insides would match the outside. That wasn't a rational thought, but if she believed it enough, it could be, one distant day.

She said, swerving to another angle of the living room. "I killed him, Anatole." She stood as far away from her husband as she could manage. "I killed him."

12

Marcy

Before the next morning, Marcy slept, and she rose.

Her eyes opened, and white feathers snowed from the festooned bed canopy, as if the bed's wings relented their down. She lifted the sheets off and went to the door. As she stepped out, a pall of purple-gray dappled with feather-snow and silver lights draped both sides of the hall, the ground cold and soft beneath her.

Someone was crying; she measured distance in sobs. Her steps thundered in her ears like a train beating its tracks. A pitter-patter marked her ribs like ocean winds on white whale bones.

Eventually, she found a figure on the floor, and it took a moment for her focus to clear. Moreau slumped himself against the wall and wiped at his eyes. His palms attempted to iron his cheeks.

"I'm not ready," he murmured in a distraught, mucus-y way, over and over. His hair was disheveled like a disgruntled finch after an autumn rain. Was it raining? The sky hadn't unfrowned last she saw it, but Marcy didn't check the sky all that much. No, it wasn't raining, it was snowing, that made sense.

"What is it?" she asked. "What's wrong?"

Moreau startled, and he stared at her like she'd explode the moment he spoke. "You need to go back to bed. You need to leave before you're taken."

"By what?"

He buried his nose in his cupped hands. "I'm hungry." That didn't answer her question, but it was okay because she forgot what she had asked.

"Then why don't you eat? You know where the kitchen is, don't you?" If he didn't, it was bad because Marcy had no idea where it was. She would've guided him if she did, though.

Her questions made Moreau cry harder, which bemused Marcy. She meant to help.

She asked, "Do you need a touch or—something?" Maman would have a nervous fit if she knew her only living child went around offering strange men embraces, but it was all she could suggest.

He stared at her like she'd sprouted horns and wings, and Marcy noticed him more. More colors came to her. As well as that, with half his tunic unbuttoned and collar in disarray, Marcy saw Moreau's flesh better than when they had met, and he had reddish pink and purple marks like segmented moons on his neck and left shoulder.

Marcy pointed at the marks. "What are those from?"

Marcy's attention trailed down to his splayed hands, his ghost-white fingers, because his answer came in twitches. Three rings, that was what caught her fancy, and they looked like a little sapphire-ruby-opal centipede close to his creamy knuckles. He unlodged the sapphire ring with a thumb and forefinger, and it left a pink, depressed circle. He skated it up and down his marriage finger.

Before Moreau could answer, the door before them gave light and angled open. The monsieur of the manor stood in a robe.

"There you are," he said to Moreau. "Have you recovered?" He wasn't confused when he locked eyes with Marcy. His countenance dimpled in concern. "Dear, are you awake?"

Her brain tickled. "I think so." She played with her hair like she twirled the pig-tailed telephone cord around the creases of her fingers as she talked to Jehanne.

The monsieur's eyes grazed her body where her nightgown hung like hoary moss. His look made her scalp crawl, and his lips fluttered for a moment, as if deciding the answer of an arithmetic problem. "If you don't mind my saying so, your eyes are like glass."

"I don't mind," Marcy replied, and he laughed under his breath. She saw moving shadows around his neck, the skin there pebbled and red, but when she blinked, the darkness disappeared.

He continued, voice gentle like a parent comforting a colicky infant, "Do you need help finding your way back to your room?"

"No, I'll go. I'm sorry I interrupted."

Jehanne's father asked, "Interrupted what?"

"Your night."

"Oh, you have nothing to apologize for. Are you quite sure you can find your way back? I don't want you to have an accident. It's a terrible thing for girls to wander alone in strange places."

Parents were so worrisome. "Yes, monsieur. I know the way."

"In that case, have a restful night, my dear."

Moreau stood, and as Marcy pivoted around, a soft click came after her sixth step.

After her thirtieth step, Marcy snapped awake.

Where—all she had were the small wall lights. A hall, all right, the manor, so she hadn't gone far.

It'd been years since she'd sleepwalked, since Papa or Maman had guided her to bed and, when they told her what happened in the night, she remembered none of it. Before the war, she'd have night terrors where she screamed, *Oh God, Oh God, Oh God,* and it bothered everyone but her because she never remembered whatever she panicked about as she slept.

In that regard, she'd been blessed. Horror kept a respectable distance from her.

She should keep it that way and go back to bed, but curiosity gnawed at her like a jackal with a meaty bone. She wracked her brain for what she'd seen as she glided through the dark halls, and she inched back from where she must've come. With any luck, this path would lead back to her room, but all the halls looked the same, and when she happened upon an impressively large bedroom door, she realized she was lost, no doubt about it. Lost and alone.

All except for a noise, a noise she mistook for dripping water, and when she crept closer and froze, she leaned against the door.

Slurping, that was what it was, the slurp and smack of a feeding mouth.

She dared a look in the near-dark, and a guttered nightstand candle gave her half a picture. A figure on its knees, head moving as it gripped something like fingers— an uncurled fist. It was chewing on someone's wrist.

It paused and slanted its head toward her.

Marcy ran. She flung herself as far as she could until her legs spasmed and the hall became more familiar. When she recognized the door Jehanne had gone through, Marcy didn't even knock as she swerved inside. Her ankles protested the swiftness, but with no stopping, no hesitance, she threw herself on the bed and shook the closest leg.

That drew a shout, and someone clicked a lamp on so swiftly it was almost knocked off the nightstand.

Clair stared at Marcy with a tangled rat's nest perched like a rook on her head. So did Jehanne, her eyelids slitted.

Marcy said, "There's something wrong."

Jehanne sat up and rubbed her eyes. "What?"

"Something's wrong in your papa's bedroom." To Clair, the most adult of them, Marcy begged, "Please go check. Please. There's something in his room."

"What is it?" Jehanne asked.

"I couldn't tell. It was too dark."

Her friend asked, the skin around her eyes pinched, "Are you sure you didn't imagine it?"

Clair slipped a gossamer-thin robe over her cream-colored shift. "What were you doing in his room?"

Marcy straightened. "I was outside the door! I woke up from sleepwalking, and when I tried to return to the bed, I got lost. I don't—I don't exactly know what I saw."

Jehanne reached out to her servant. "Let me go with you."

Clair replied, "Please, stay here. I'll return shortly."

"He's my father," Jehanne persisted, following Clair step-by-step. "I should be allowed to go see him!"

"I'm begging you, stay here. Your friend needs you." Clair rushed out, the thud of the door leaving a swell of quiet.

Jehanne huffed at the wood and twisted around to look at Marcy. "You really didn't see it all, what really was happening?"

"No, it was so dark. I didn't know what else to do." Marcy bothered her fingers together and hoped she didn't send Clair into harm's way.

Jehanne sucked in a cheek. "We should've gone with her."

"She told you, us, to stay."

Ambling to Marcy's side, Jehanne scoffed and flopped face-first on the bed. When she lifted her chin up, she blew away strands of crinkled, darker gold. "I hate her orders and her rules. If I wanted a big sister, I would've asked for one."

"Typically, you only ask for a younger sister," Marcy joked. She only knew her older brother's name. Roger, who never grew older. It would've been nice, having him around, but thinking about it was like listening to a sullen violin on a gramophone, except a thousand fold, so she put those thoughts away. Growing somber, she said, "It was strange. I sleepwalked, and when I snapped awake, I heard the chewing sound. I saw . . . maybe it was this waking dream, but I don't know."

Jehanne held Marcy's hands, twining their fingers together while she hummed in thought. "I've never sleepwalked, but I've seen strange things in my dreams, the—what I told you about. But I can't imagine walking around while I did it. I can see why that'd bother you." The validation livened Marcy, this late-night female camaraderie. With their hands touching, like friends do, but different. "Do you think you need to go home?"

Jehanne's grip was twitchy, and she shifted her attention to the door.

Marcy considered this, considered how she had waded through oppressive darkness once she snapped awake, but there'd been lights, and nobody had hurt her, if she'd even met anyone along the way. It wasn't as if this was a new occurrence, though it was the first in a long while. And, at the same time, this was her first overnight stay in an unfamiliar place—at least, besides the oceanside trip.

When she was smaller, that overwhelming darkness crept in and woke her from her sleepwalking. The shadows would breathe, and she would always feel as if they'd grab her and take her to a place of eternal night.

Yet, the sun rose, the rose garden bloomed, and life continued.

Marcy beamed. "I think I'll live."

Jehanne tapped her elbow. "What is it?"

"What if I came across your father, or one of the male servants, and they saw me in this gown?" Marcy tugged on the nightgown where it had tucked into her panties, and she smoothed out the fabric.

Jehanne eyed Marcy's hands. "Does that mean something?"

The gown was white and showed nothing beneath the linen, but still, it felt thin over her. No men but Papa and André had ever seen her dressed like this. With her menstrual cycle on top of it, Marcy's angles rounded out and swelled in places they normally wouldn't.

"It's just that it's not proper." By God, she sounded like Maman. "I could've made them uncomfortable."

"Father is a good man, and he wouldn't think anything of it. Besides, maybe nobody saw you."

Marcy must've been as red as Papa's roses by now. "I didn't mean to imply your father is—"

Jehanne elbowed her and laughed. "I know."

They both startled when the door creaked open, and Jehanne shielded Marcy with an arm.

Clair stood in the doorway. After a pause, she staggered in. Her left cheek was red.

Pushing herself off the bed, Jehanne asked, "What happened?"

The woman straightened. "It is nothing, everything is as it should be."

"Did you speak with Father?"

"Yes, he was asleep, and he was quite displeased I woke him. Now, if you don't mind, he instructed me to return to him after I informed you that he's in good health."

"Was anyone else there?" Marcy asked.

"No."

Marcy persisted, "There was more than one person—er, thing in there, and I know what I heard."

Clair tilted her head, holding back the ghost of a sneer. "And what was that? Snoring?"

Marcy bristled. She wouldn't be mean to the woman, but she wouldn't be insulted either. "No! Noises like someone eating. Or drinking."

"Indeed, well." To Jehanne, Clair said, "Your father asked me to return to him, and I likely won't be back tonight."

Jehanne leaned forward, the balls of her feet touching the floor. "I want to go with you."

Clair hung her head as she hunched in the doorway, supporting herself on the frame. "Of course you do." None of the servants Marcy met (all two of them so far) looked like they slept well, but Clair embodied this fatigue as if her soul were hundreds of years old and withered.

"Please just tell me Father's okay."

Clair said curtly, "As I said, he's perfectly well." She left in the same way she did before, disappearing as swiftly as a ghost. Jehanne groaned, turned, and reapplied her face to the bed.

Marcy hesitated until she dredged up enough words to string together. "Is there something wrong here?"

"No," Jehanne said, muffled.

"Are you sure? What about Mlle Clair? She didn't look well."

Jehanne shrugged and crossed her legs, sitting by Marcy so their knees grazed. "She always looks worried." Worried and sad, yes, Marcy had that impression.

Jehanne looked to the side, squeezed her hands together, and pursed her lips.

"But what about her cheek?" Marcy persisted. "It was red."

Jehanne frowned, brows working in thought, lips tighter together. She rubbed her palms over her eyelids. "Maybe it was just heat rushing to her face. She did have to walk a long distance." Jehanne leaned into Marcy's shoulder, which made breathing hard. "Everything is fine, trust me. Tell me one of your stories."

Can you be this dense? No, no conflict. She went away from home because of that.

Marcy obliged, but not without a wiggling doubt that wouldn't leave, like a cockroach skittering into a crack whenever she put her foot down.

She awoke the next day with Jehanne's cheek on her shoulder. Lifting her head, Marcy couldn't help but admire how peaceful her friend looked. It was good knowing if she sleepwalked again, someone would watch over her. It was with reluctance she returned to her room, careful not to disturb her friend. As she crossed the hall, silence pattered the walls like a heartbeat. The thudding rhythm burdened her bones, but no voices called to her.

She dressed and decided to go to the dining room, hoping for company and, most of all, food. Comforting herself with food worked at home after she batted her lashes at Papa. She wouldn't mind any room she found, so long as there was food.

Traveling down the hall, she found herself distracted by all the religious paintings, and the silence broke.

Raised voices. She flashed back to Maman and André before her cousin had run off.

When she found a half-opened door and peeked in, she recognized Moreau and Clair, their profiles a harsh chiaroscuro with the angry fireplace behind them.

Though eavesdropping was wrong, of course, Marcy knelt behind the door and looked in.

Moreau finished whatever he started, "—climbed on the others' backs and escaped. I can't believe it ran so far, and the little devil's tongue . . ." It was all incomprehensible to Marcy.

Clair crossed her arms. "I don't want to hear anymore."

"But this'll all be over soon. After this, I'll be free, and you could be free." Moreau's expression knotted. "Don't you see? This is all a new beginning, a better one."

Clair shook her head. "I couldn't."

"Be free?"

"Do what you've done." That piqued Marcy's curiosity, and she instinctively leaned forward.

Moreau clasped his hands together, and Marcy realized he was shaking. "Milla, do you think I enjoy it?"

"Enjoy what?" Clair's eyes widened like sauce bowls. Her hair was like a disrupted briar patch, and her clothes were rumpled, as if she had slept in them, or as if they had rested wrinkled on the floor and then were re-worn. Maybe she enjoyed sleeping nude. Marcy wouldn't pass judgment, regardless. "Hurting—Christ, Tristan, do you actually touch them?"

Touch them? Touch what? Touch whom?

158

Moreau's fingers were still threaded together, and he took great interest in them. As far as appearances were concerned, he looked about the same, though finding a point of reference was difficult, since Marcy had only known him for less than a day. "I . . ."

"Damn you, look at me. Tell me, do you touch them?"

Moreau stuttered for what seemed like a minute. Sweat pooled under Marcy's dress. "The master makes me. Do you think I want to? That I want to feel unclean and unholy every single second of the day?"

Clair snapped, "It seems to me you do!" Her tone could split a tree. Marcy wished she knew what "them" was. It could range from monsters, which was outlandish, to feral cats, which was more likely, but boring.

Moreau snarled. "Aren't you the same?"

"You bastard. I'd never—"

Moreau broke and flailed his arms. "But you don't stop all the evil, do you? But by God, you'll judge me for trying to find some sort of salvation from it, for doing what I have to, so I can live!"

Clair shrank and stepped back. "Do you see what you're becoming? You're dying. You're letting yourself become tainted."

"*Letting* myself?" Moreau's voice was strained. "I don't tell you what you've endured is your fault, but should I? Should I tell you that if only you were sweeter to the master, he'd give you more?"

"This is what he gives me." Clair pushed her sleeve up, but Marcy couldn't see why. She could only see the blue shadows playing on Moreau.

He said, softer, "You don't think he hurts me too?"

Marcy's blood turned to ice, and Moreau stepped toward Clair with open arms.

She exploded like a cornered cat. "Don't touch me, you beast! You're filthy!"

"Milla, please, I—I'm begging you—"

"Leave! We're both disgusting, ruined." Clair paced and tugged at her hair so hard Marcy winced. "We're damned filth, filth." Like her legs were two crumbling wax pillars, Clair collapsed by the hearth, heaving with sobs. She muttered *Nonononono* until it became a hoarse *Whywhywhywhywhy.*

Failing to start a sentence despite multiple tries, Moreau rushed to leave.

Marcy hurried away from the cracked door and squatted behind an empty decorative table. Her heart thundered in her ears.

Moreau stormed out and, thankfully, went in the opposite direction. After his back shrank enough, Marcy found the courage to breathe and lift herself up.

She needed Jehanne.

13

Rosalie

Anatole stared at her as if she had caught fire from a stroke of lightning on a cloudless day. "Love, my heart, how could you've known the dosage was wrong? The medicine was supposed to help. You did as the chemist instructed."

But it was poison, like Rosalie. She poisoned Roger, then she poisoned all else. A goddamn cough, that was all his sickness was, a tiny cough, but he'd been hungry and squirming and alive and hers. If she hadn't gone to the pharmacist, if the pharmacist hadn't made the error, if she hadn't listened to his instructions and hadn't done just as the paper said . . .

When Rosalie snapped back to reality, Anatole approached, and it should've been comical, the way they circled around the living room. She stared at the lamp table, the couch, the curtains, anything but Anatole. He stepped close, and she swiveled away so she didn't have to see what she'd done to him. They'd avoided speaking like this for so long. Maybe, just maybe, she could preserve herself. Lock herself away. Lock Roger away and preserve him as he had been before that winter morning—when she woke up with him dead beside her and screamed.

And yet, it was almost a relief to tell Anatole her doubts and worries, but not relief enough. Enough, that elusive bird.

Anatole was saying, "It wasn't your fault, remember? I told you, I said, that day." The strain in his voice broke whatever he wanted to tell her, but Rosalie understood and lost herself in another unwanted memory.

Still sore from birth, Rosalie couldn't bring herself to leave the bed most days. The bed, the marriage bed, Roger's grave. *He was born in our bed, and he died there.* Both she and Anatole neglected the house's cleanliness. He would try to hang his coats, they would fall, and he didn't bother to pick them up, so when Rosalie went downstairs once a week, black puddles of cloth marked the floor.

She and Anatole had both stunk and, when he thought she was asleep, Anatole paced, tapped his pen against his diary, sat on the edge of their bed, smoked his pipe, and wept to himself. Her husband never smoked too close to her, and Rosalie feigned sleep, though despair paralyzed her enough. They should've been clasping one another, but Rosalie couldn't speak to let Anatole know she was awake, so she mourned the abyssal depth that yawned between them, that hopeless stretch of bed that reached on and on like a lightless canyon.

After, Rosalie had watched her sister give a last heave of breath, and Rosalie was the one who called Maman, despite Anatole's offer to do it. André became theirs. During their nearly mirrored pregnancies, Juliette had fretted that André would be stillborn like her daughter, Albertine, two years before, when she was still in her late adolescence. When Juliette had conceived again, her husband Jean Baptiste died of sickness, leaving her a frightened widow. Still, Rosalie and Juliette were pregnant at the same time, so they carried each other along.

Rosie, I can't take it if this one dies. Juliette cried into her sister's sleeve, their swollen bellies pressing together. *It'll end me. I need another pretty girl so our little ones can play together.* Rosalie caught her tears; she always did.

After watching Juliette die, after hearing her mother sob on the telephone for an hour about the funeral and how Juliette loved roses and carnations, the truth didn't register in Rosalie's mind until she set the telephone down. Her sister was dead. The consumption had gotten her. She had had a funeral. Rosalie had seen her body.

Her sister was dead.

Juliette loved roses because they reminded her of you.

When Anatole had moved to her side, his fingers brushing her back, she fled to the bathroom they shared and sat on the commode. With her head in her hands, she couldn't bring herself to cry. She wanted to because Juliette was her sister, and crying would mean Rosalie was alive, that she was normal.

But no, she was dead in all but body. God had killed her; Anatole had killed her. Blame came easy and hot like bile. Instead of unmoving despair or nothingness, rage bubbled inside her and threatened to overwhelm her sight. She dug her nails into her palm, and she wanted to hurt someone, hurt herself. She hated the pendulum of emotions from crushing melancholy to numb resignation to overpowering fury.

Nightmares assaulted the pale hours she slept. At Rosalie's request, Anatole suckled her after Roger's death and before André's arrival. It was a bizarre state of grief they were in, the odd sort of aching, joyless intimacy they shared. When they wouldn't speak, that was all they had. His drinking from her relieved, though only a little, the strain of carrying milk. Still, the more Anatole obliged Rosalie, the longer she'd keep her breasts full, which seemed contrary to moving on, but she wasn't ready to be empty.

While grieving Juliette, Rosalie held André with milk still in her. That was bitter luck, her ability to feed him. She was surprised she could have milk in her at all, with how dead she was.

Maman had visited one afternoon, sitting with her mapped, spindly hands primly in her lap. Rosalie spoke to her in the living room, herself strewn across the couch, sinking down into the cushions, head on a pillow. Maman had had a miscarriage once, awoke to a sea of blood in her marital bed, her new widow's bed, and this was her attempt to breach the distance between her and her surviving daughter. To say she understood, but in their grief, they were lost to one another.

Rosalie sat up to make room for Maman. André, heavy yet little in her arms, sucked on an unbrushed length of hair.

She said to Maman, "Isn't this what you wanted? You once told me you'd rather see me dead than married to Anatole." Here it was. Anatole had killed her. So Maman could rejoice now. Everything in this life was posthumous, the postscript of an all-too-drawn-out letter.

André sniffled, and Rosalie stiffened. No, he couldn't be sick, not like Juliette or Roger. Could God be crueler than He was already?

Maman had replied, "I should've never spoken to you that way."

Rosalie found all her grievances with Maman had no stopper. "I'd rather you never speak to me at all."

André wailed.

In tears, Maman said, "Juliette wouldn't want you to be so lost."

Rosalie sneered. "She can't want anymore, can she?" Her voice cracked. "She can't want, and Roger—he was too young to want for anything but milk and love. And what happened? Before he could talk, or hobble, the hospital cut into him." A more bitter thought consumed her: No son of theirs would ever find happiness.

Instead of calming herself or weeping, Rosalie lashed out until Maman sobbed, "I can't bear this."

Maman had been right. She couldn't. *You were supposed to be the one comforting me.* It was all a succession Rosalie couldn't keep up with at the time. Rosalie birthed Roger, Juliette grew ill, Roger died, and Juliette died. Maman succumbed to a heart attack a few days after Roger's death. Because Juliette was gone, Rosalie and Anatole took in André. Maman had touched Rosalie, and Maman had died, and Anatole clung to their nephew as they discussed preparing the nursery. (It had all been Rosalie's fault.)

Her insides weighed like marble. Each blow crippled her. God stuck a dirk under her ribs, and with each loss He pushed it an inch deeper. There was no name for that grief, the person she was after Roger. If Anatole died, Rosalie would be a widow, but she had no name for herself.

In nineteen days, she mourned a son, a sister, and a mother, and she simply didn't know how to act with a baby who so reminded her of her sister in the face and in his smile. She smelled Roger like he was at her breast.

Nineteen days.

Nineteen days—Roger, Juliette, Maman. It all gave Rosalie a new skin, this iron-latticed, unfamiliar one.

Yet, iron rusted, and when it did, it became something new and broken.

On the twenty-third day after Roger's death, Rosalie had brought herself to the cold latrine, leaned down in front of the sink to apply water to her face, and noticed something

During her rest, milk had leaked and stained her gown.

An ink blot in her mind: Need to go feed Roger. When reality sank into her marrow, she slung across the washroom the bottle containing Roger's medicine, and it shattered when it hit the wall.

I'd like to die here. She had slapped a palm against the mirror. The impact stung—she may've screamed, but not from physical pain. An overdose crossed her mind, an overdose like Roger's because of the pharmacist's mistake, that too-big prescription for a minor cold, the drops Rosalie gave her son before she fed him, before she unknowingly killed him.

Or she could use a blade, to be poetic.

She would be able to die. Take a kitchen knife and drain herself in the tub so her death could be as clean as possible. So the world could be relieved of her blood and mucus and even the white pus from every blemish, because she was still but a girl masquerading as a grown woman.

But Rosalie had Anatole and André, who'd grieve for her.

André, no, André would be too little to remember her if she ended her life, but Anatole was another matter. His life had been tragic from the start, doomed because of his father. How long would it take for the smell of Rosalie's hair to disappear from the pillows? But Anatole could marry again, couldn't he? An executioner's life was lonely, and most women wouldn't want a headsman for a husband, but Anatole was a gentle, quiet man. Surely he'd find someone else to take her mantle.

But no, he wouldn't. He couldn't because of his profession. Damn him. Damn him for killing men, killing her, and not letting her die.

Rosalie scratched her cheeks, and whether she meant to bleed didn't matter, because she did.

Sickly glowing in the daylight, swollen as a chilled melon, she wished she'd died in birth so that she had never met her son, that she could bathe in the Lethe. She wondered why unbaptized babies went to Limbo, Hell's cinder-colored hem, and who'd hold and carry her son, if anyone would, if he wasn't lonely and squalling on a sooty bank.

If Roger fell into Hell's river, would his dormant sins burden him like an anchor? Did souls there become hungry; if so, who would feed him? Christ sacrificed Himself and suffered, granted mercy, and said, "Let the children come to me, do not hinder them." Unbaptized infants were then cast into the valley of the shadow of death. Grace was a sparse currency for children.

Bitterness twisted into gnarled thorns. Both she and Anatole carried the headsman's legacy like a rat-borne plague. Both their fathers' curses braiding together like knitted bone—Louis Deibler, as well as her father buried in Algeria. Black blood ran in their veins, scourged them all.

She couldn't move beyond that spot, beyond the laughing mirror. How fitting that an executioner's wife should die young. It was like the start of a grotesque fairy tale. The nameless mothers and wives always died; it was all they were good for.

Before she knew it, warmth encircled her; Anatole clasped her from behind like she was his heart and like he'd die if he released her.

His heart, her heart. Too many hearts, too many, she couldn't keep them all.

They both trembled, standing there over the running sink, and they slid to the floor together, bowed on the tiles and wracked with sobs. Sense fled Rosalie, all except the texture of his untrimmed beard against her neck.

After the milk, mucus, and tears had dried, and a sticky redness blotched their faces, Rosalie undressed Anatole. They didn't make love. Rosalie was unsure if she'd want to do that ever again, and she was still healing from Roger's birth.

She led Anatole to the bath, where he gently cast her sullied gown aside, and they sat together in the soapsud-glistening water, her cheek on his shoulder, their fingers wrinkled.

It had been the closest Anatole had held her since she awoke to Roger unmoving beside her; even Rosalie asking Anatole to feed from her held an air of detachment.

Rosalie's mouth tasted of mucus, and she fantasized that the hand rubbing her shoulder gripped her hair and plunged her head in the water. She'd release a long scream, water burning her lungs, and she'd die.

They stayed that way until André warbled for attention from his crib, a new crib, because Rosalie didn't want André to be in the shadow of another baby's dreams.

Later, while preparing for bed, Rosalie had turned to Anatole. "I was the one," she said, voice as thin as a reed. "I killed him. I didn't know—didn't think—I was the one who gave . . ."

Anatole closed the distance between them and massaged her shoulders, leaning his forehead to hers. He whispered to her, only capable of a single coherent word: "No."

And that was the last they spoke of Roger—with his hands and his smile and his coffin, a devilish gleam, no bigger than a breadbox.

In the now, Rosalie drew a shaky breath. "Anatole." She reached for him, he crossed the distance, and they received each other, collapsing to the floor. Returning Anatole's embrace, she pressed her nose to his neck and tasted him and the salt of tears with only a breath.

They cried together, and Anatole murmured against her hair, "I'm here, I'm here." A soft litany. A candle flame, small, but a candle was a light in the dark nonetheless. A soft plod on the floor, and Rosalie moved so her cheek was pressed against Anatole's shirt. Jolie sniffed them both before sitting on her haunches and tilting her head.

Rosalie mumbled, "I made Marcy think I hate her."

Anatole squeezed her. "But you don't."

"How do I let her know? I'll have to talk to her, won't I?" Rosalie would have to talk to her only living child with only scattered words at her disposal. It could only end poorly. "But I don't know what to say without making everything worse."

"She'll understand. Speak to her like you have with me."

"I hurt you."

Anatole set his lips on her brow. "No, I can't help you if I don't know what your worries are, and they're legitimate worries. And I did keep something important from you. Even if we don't know how to change now, we can not know together, can't we?" The smell of his shirt, his thumb rubbing the base of her scalp. "I'm here. I'll always be."

"Don't promise me that. I may resent you if you don't keep your word." She laughed under her breath. "When you asked if I regret our marriage . . ." Rosalie inhaled his scent, kept him by her heart as long as she could. "I don't regret you. I just wish we could bring back . . ." No, she couldn't say it, even now. "I'm weak, pathetic."

He trembled. "Please don't think of yourself like that."

"It's true."

"You've made it this far, despite everything." Shoulders sagging, Anatole murmured, "I'm sorry." Sorries and love threaded through her hair like yellow wildflowers.

Rosalie abruptly broke their embrace, bones quivering as she stood. "For what? I'm the one who needs to be sorry." Her back touched the wall. "Did you ever blame me for what happened to him?"

"I said I didn't." Anatole stood.

"But really, truly?"

"What good does this do?" His jaw twitched, and he laid a hand on the leaved end table.

"Answer me."

He opened his mouth once, only to make a soft rattle, and closed it again. Whatever he saw in the wallpaper, she couldn't say. "At times, I did. It wasn't your fault, but I did think that at the start. When I remembered you giving our boy the medicine."

She crossed her arms and shrank. "See? Even you thought—"

Anatole's visage contorted. "It was the pain! I couldn't think outside of this fog, this episode where I could only see Roger's corpse in my mind again and again, when I'd dream of holding him, of watching him grow, and wake up to that cold space between us. I was weak."

"But you had André."

"We *have* André. You don't think of him as a son, and we're the only parents he has."

"I told you. I can't see him as a replacement. It isn't fair."

His mouth tightened. "Is that what you think? That I see him as our second Roger? Do you think I'm that apathetic, that callous? That we lost one son, so we can never have another? Is this where we stand? Is it because I stopped crying? Is what we've done the wrong way to grieve? Is there a wrong way when you've been told all your life that a strong, steady person cannot falter and endanger his family?"

"You can falter with me." When he didn't respond, she scoffed. "We're both inept at helping each other, it seems." Rosalie fidgeted with her hair. "And our daughter feels better with a near-stranger than here with us. It's my fault. I'm not normal."

"I don't know what to say to that."

"You know it too, and you need someone normal. Someone who can go cycling with you or spend a day without loathing herself."

"What does that mean? What is 'normal' for us, for me? Over two decades ago, my normal was an eccentric drunkard for a father and dissecting sparrows and squirrels at his bidding and seething with bitterness I couldn't show. Before we met each other at the cycling club. Before I knew I could be loved despite everything."

"I don't want Marcy to be like Roger." Because of her. Because she was poison and ruined all she surveyed. She'd sooner leave forever.

"I understand."

"You've said that, you say that, you always say that, but do you? You've killed men, but do you know what it's like to kill someone that grew inside you? Someone that is you, yet so much more? To have your son leave you empty when he's born, to spill everything for him, and then be empty again?"

He broke eye contact. "No, I can't say I do."

"You only cried a few times, and I stopped because I thought I would've moved past it."

"Move past it like you thought I did?"

"You deserve better than a miserable woman. You need a new wife, a better wife. Is that what you want? Do you regret our marriage? Do you regret me?"

He didn't answer, which was answer enough. Her throat swelled. She needed to sleep.

Just as she went to leave for bed, Anatole spoke.

"It—it hurts to feel like I need to help you, but I'm useless no matter what, whether I'm silent or doing something. Every treatment causes you pain, and I've caused you pain, and God, Rosie, I don't know how the hell to do anything outside of using the blade."

"That isn't—"

"And though that hurts, it hurts more to know you think so little of me after all we've survived together. You believe I'd abandon you without a second thought."

"I won't martyr you for my sake, won't keep you caged with me."

"Caged?"

"You've stayed through the worst. And is that only because I was your second option for a wife? Because there were and are no good choices left?"

He rapped his knuckles once against the table, mouth bending inward. "Do you want *me* to go? Is that really what this is? Would it help you if I left?"

God, even now, he didn't comprehend. "No, I told you it isn't your job."

"It is, isn't it, if I make us unsafe?"

Rosalie steamed over his reply. "But maybe it'd be best for you and the children if I left. Perhaps they'd stand a chance. Perhaps all they need is the one who isn't sick, the one who always says 'yes.'"

"God damn it all. You truly think none of us would care if you left? That we'd be better? That we'd throw you out and never miss you? That I care more for someone who left me because of my job than someone who's stayed and cared, even when I'd have nightmares or bury myself in minutiae?" He dragged his hand down his face and beard, his knuckles white as classroom chalk. "That, Rosie, is the worst insult I've ever been given."

"You asked for my feelings, and I told you." It was Anatole who faced away from her now, and coldness was all Rosalie knew. "Tell me what I should do to make amends. To be a better person, a better wife and mother."

"That's just it. You are enough now, yet you won't believe it."

In resignation, Rosalie offered a bitter smile he couldn't see. "I'm always to blame, aren't I?"

"That's not what I meant."

"God, this is just like you to say things like that. That I'm enough, that I haven't done anything wrong when we both know you're lying. When your daughter and nephew left because of me."

"A liar. You won't believe anything I say because you think I'm lying with each word." His forehead rumpled like old parchment. "Maybe I very well am, with all my little roses and comics, all my unconvincing normalities, but if we can't trust each other's words, then what else is there?"

"I'm sorry I ruined our home for Marcy and André."

"Rosie—"

She put her face in her hands. "I'm sorry I made everyone loathe me." Her vision narrowed until all she knew were the dark shadows of her palms.

Her husband pulled her close. It was a perfunctory, hollow gesture, done before and done now out of tired desperation. Despite their closeness in this inane American gesture, Rosalie earned no peace, yet all the same, numbness thrummed in her veins like hundreds of vibrating needles. She heard the thunder of seawater in her ears. The wintry finality, that black trench. He was her sunrise, but twilight was here in the walls.

She opened her mouth—

Rapid, hard knocks on the front door.

Not again.

The knocking was insistent, and a hot tension coiled in her heart.

Rosalie squeezed Anatole's wrist when he started toward the door. "Who do you think it is? André took his key, didn't he?" She worked to calm herself. She had guns if anything terrible happened, and it was like André to lose his house key.

That comforted little.

Anatole pulled away. When he opened the front door, they were both met with the grim scowls of two policemen.

14

Jehanne

She traced her nails along the spine of her Arthurian book when Marcy opened the door.

"Jehanne?"

"Good morning."

"G'morning."

Jehanne settled her hands in her lap. "Did you not sleep well? You look bothered."

"I saw Mlle Clair," Marcy replied, guarded.

"Really? Good, I've decided I need her for my reading lesson." It was a tad early, but Clair would have to cope.

"She was arguing with Moreau in the study, and—and I think something's wrong with her. That she's hurt. I don't know how. She's on the floor crying."

Panic. "I'll go to her. Stay in your room."

"Okay," Marcy replied, her brow knit. "When do you plan on coming back?"

"As soon as I've checked on her." Marcy opened her mouth, but Jehanne swung out of the room and flew to the study.

When she stopped at the doorway, she heard Clair before she saw her in the near-dark. It sounded like she was struggling to breathe.

Jehanne cleared her throat. Clair snapped her head up and hastily wiped her cheeks with open hands. When the girl stepped close, she noticed Clair's sleeve was up, exposing more than usual. Clair followed Jehanne's sight, but before she could yank the fabric down, Jehanne saw scores of bruises and burns, knelt, and gently gripped Clair's elbow. "Was this a demon?"

"Don't be stupid." Clair's voice had no force in it. "Don't worry about it."

"*You* don't be stupid. I'll worry if I want. Are they back, the devils?"

Clair sputtered, "I-I can't." Jehanne wanted to recoil because she didn't understand how to speak to a distraught Clair when she was never meant to be distraught. She was meant to be fixed like one leg of a drawing compass.

"Are there still demons here? There are, aren't there?"

"I don't know."

Jehanne pushed, her hands hovering. "What happened to you? Did a demon do this?"

"Quiet down, please. I beg you."

Jehanne lowered her voice, not wanting to frighten the woman any more than she already was. It was disquieting, seeing Clair unraveled. Exposed in the heavy light, fragile yet weighted from being crushed between a king's fingers and turned to gold. Her swollen cheek now had a bruise forming in the corner. Jehanne hadn't thought to notice before now, which bothered her. "Were you attacked, did a demon do this? Did you see a demon in Father's room?"

Had the demon harmed Father, despite what Clair had said? Jehanne needed to see him.

"No."

"You're sure?"

Clair gave a wet sniff, visage downcast. "Quite."

"Did a *person* hurt you?" Somehow, that was worse than a demon. The furious red on Clair's cheek last night, molded like a hand. Jehanne had tried to ignore it as a trick of the light, but now she sucked in a loud breath. A chill scored her back. A creeping dread settled like worms, squirming and writhing at the base of her stomach. "Did Father do this?" No, he wouldn't; she felt guilty asking it. Father was a good Christian man. Tormented, but kind. Not him, of all people, not the man who prayed and wept for her.

But then, she drifted back to his nonchalance when he mentioned Clair was compensated well, and therefore she'd do whatever Jehanne asked. Her mind whirled and her throat constricted. The whisper came out as more of a squeak: "Does he hurt you? I'll ask him. I'll make him tell me. Whatever made this happen, I'll stop it."

Clair scratched angry sigils into the pale knob of her elbow. "I don't want you to compromise your love for your father for someone like me."

Jehanne couldn't breathe for a minute. The dying hearth mocked her. "Why? Why do you think you're not worth compromising anything? Why won't you tell me? Why won't you say it? What'll happen if you do?"

Mucus and spit poured from Clair's nose and mouth, and she buried half her face in a handkerchief stippled with a little blood. Her knuckles were death-white. "I can't."

"Please. I want to help. Did Father do this?"

Clair gulped, cupped her mouth, and exhaled wetly. "Yes."

The word smacked the wind out of Jehanne.

"Does he—does he do this often?" As if it mattered. As if once wasn't too much.

"Yes." Clair heaved, as if shedding off an iron weight. Jehanne needed her to be lying; Jehanne needed that more than her own heartbeat, but it'd damage Clair if the first person she spoke to about this called her a liar. "Please don't tell him I told you. Please don't bother him. Please. He's worked so hard to keep you safe, and I can't ruin that. I don't deserve your regard."

"Why? What do you mean? How could you ruin something when you're the victim?"

Clair laughed, and it was the least joyful noise Jehanne had ever heard. "No one cares for the weak till they're dead, and you're just a child. You can't help me."

"I'm not a child," Jehanne insisted. "At least in body. You should know. You're really not that much older than I am."

The attempt at levity failed, as it should've. All Jehanne knew was rage.

Blinding rage.

She should've gone with Clair to protect her, but she failed, and Father, he—

"It shouldn't be your burden. Please don't worry about it." As Clair pleaded, Jehanne stood and extended a hand. The woman leaned on Jehanne until she secured her stance, and though she hated to, Jehanne left Clair alone and stormed to Father's bedroom.

Anyone with a deep-seated regard for decorum would go to a quiet place and dwell on a shocking revelation before responding, but to Hell with them.

Without knocking, Jehanne flung open Father's door.

Father sat dressed, buttons half-done, on the bed with his feet on the floor. Moreau was standing before him, and they both bore their stares into her.

Father said, "Pup, what do you need?" Moreau looked ready to faint. There were shadows under his eyes, like the Sandman had pressed his fingers to the skin too hard without gifting any of his grit.

As softly as she could manage, which wasn't all that much, Jehanne said to Moreau, "I'd like to speak to my father alone."

Father waved a dismissive hand. "Leave us." Something akin to annoyance flashed over Moreau's face, but he bowed his head and obeyed.

As soon as the door closed with a thump, Jehanne strode closer to Father, who remained sitting on the edge of the bed.

Jehanne said, "There are some things I want to ask you."

"What is it?"

She juggled between subtlety and forthrightness. "Please, let me know you, know more about the past. Talk to me about Mother."

"Is that what's so urgent? You really can be quite dramatic. Why? Won't it only hurt? Wouldn't you like to do something less strenuous?"

She refused to budge. "I'm stronger than you think. I need to know who she was to know who I am. You're always so vague. I love you no matter what, no matter what you've gone through, no matter what you've done. Please talk to me about Mother and your past."

If he suspected her of any subterfuge, he didn't falter. "You swear you'll love me?"

"Yes, of course. Tell me what's hurting you. That's what love is, caring for each other despite our pain. Forgiving each other as Christ would." She'd make him admit his sins; she only needed the right honeyed words.

"Father, tell me, please. If you can't tell me about how she died, it's okay. I just want to know how she lived. Let me carry your burden too."

I want to know what kind of man you were, are. I want to know if you're the sort of person who'd hurt Clair in such a way, any way, and how I can fight it.

"You truly won't think less of me?"

"No, I would never," Jehanne lied.

He rasped, eyes falling to his knees, "I treated her badly, pup."

"What do you mean? Did you . . . beat her?"

"No, I would never," Father answered, an eerie echo. He leaned back, as if stunned. "But the ways I hurt her." His voice broke. "I hurt her, and I've carried it with me with no one to comfort me." He leaned forward and averted his eyes, seemed as if he'd speak no longer. Just as Jehanne opened her mouth, he opened his. "In one of our quarrels, I upset her until she miscarried. Before that— we'd been married for years when that happened—she didn't want to marry me, but no other man could have her after I . . ." He trailed off.

Jehanne persisted, "Why wouldn't anyone marry her? What did you do?"

Father winced. "Pup, that was another time. I did as my grandfather instructed to ensure an heir to the estate." He squeezed the fabric of his trousers, twisted it above his knees. "It seems so—perhaps this wasn't the best idea. Look at us, we have one another. Isn't it enough?"

"What did you do to her?" she pressed, and she'd keep pressing.

He wouldn't look at Jehanne. "It's not important." His fingers clenched hard into his palm.

No other man could have her.

"You—you raped her." Jehanne was going to vomit. She pressed her knuckles to her lips. "Oh, oh, God." She waited for him to contradict her, but the silence slapped all her senses awake. She stood by the bed, waiting for an answer before she realized the stinging nothing was his answer. "You raped her, so everyone would see her as tainted." Spoiled, like a piece of fruit. It took all her strength not to crumple to the carpet. "Please—please tell me I'm wrong."

"It wasn't seen as that." He still avoided her, his eyes gleaming dead like glass.

"Seen as that by who, you or her?"

Flatly, as if reckoning his checkbook, Father said, "I needed a wife so I could have a child to possess my property after my death."

"And that makes it okay?"

"I'm sorry you've reacted like this. I did respect her. She was calm and obedient, as a good woman should be." His words were quiet and measured. "She kept to her bed, and I kept to mine. I tried to make amends. After all, about a decade in, I gave her a daughter to entertain herself with." By God, Father was trying to appease her; he thought this was enough. He didn't see an issue speaking to her about this because so long as he apologized and diminished the pain he caused, it wasn't a heartbreaking revelation.

"'Like a good woman should be'? I'm not always calm and obedient. Am *I* not to your liking? 'Quiet and kind'— that's what you told me I had to be to keep safe, but I'm not. I'm too much like you."

"I wish that were true." Damn it, he could at least not be a coward and meet her eyes.

"Wish what were true? That I was more like you, after what you've said?"

"No, actually, I wish I could be more like you. You're different from any other person, any other woman. You've always been."

"No, I'm not. I'm not any better than Mother or Mlle Clair."

That troubled the dark lines above his brow. "But you are, you are!"

"Why would you think that? What is it about me that'd make you say that?"

"I can't tell you."

"But why? After all you've already told me, why not tell me why you think me better than any other woman? Because I'm not. You should treat us all the same."

He had the audacity to shush her. "Calm down."

Her fingers burned by her sides. "I won't!"

Father stood, his gaze sharp on her. "Your tone is too much. You told me you wouldn't judge."

Her *tone*? He raped Mother, but it was Jehanne's tone that ruined it all? She stewed.

"I expected you'd killed a soldier in desperation or something, something terrible you truly felt sorry for, something you hadn't wanted to do. Not that you hurt those who don't fight back."

"Do you think God has forgiven me?" Father blurted, and he softened like sense broke through. She hoped it was sense. Jehanne didn't answer, couldn't without crying. No matter what he said, she still had the figments in her head—resting against her faceless mother's arm as she drifted to sleep, the smoky satisfaction deep in her breast. With his hands squeezed together, Father murmured, "Here on this lowly ground, teach me how to repent."

He wasn't low on the ground, but he deserved to be.

Jehanne simmered about being alone because of Father's actions, but even if her mother had never miscarried, he had no right to treat her or anyone that way.

She asked, "Was this before or after I was born, Mother losing the child?"

He looked at her as if she'd changed into another person right before him. "I'm not sure how to answer that."

Jehanne slammed her fist on the end table, and the lamp squatting there shook. "How can you not know? Did it happen more than once?"

"Please," Father croaked, raising his hands as if surrendering a battle. "I didn't know it'd upset you so."

"How could it not upset me? How did it not upset you until you noticed how I felt?"

Father murmured, "I really haven't given it much thought. I already asked for forgiveness, and I assumed it was enough." He met her gaze, and then averted his eyes. "You've never . . ."

"Gotten angry at you?"

"Never spoken to me quite like this." His voice shook, and for the first time, Jehanne couldn't bring herself to pity him. "I should've expected this wasn't the best truth, but I believed you when you said you'd love me regardless. I still believe it. You've always been exceptional, and, for me, it's better to have a bitter truth than a secret. Less of a burden on me."

Jehanne pursed her lips. "Enough about you. What did Mother love to do? What did she do when she wasn't hurting because of you?"

Father pulled a handkerchief out of his breast pocket and dabbed his dry cheeks. "She was a reader, but after our wedding, she didn't seem to enjoy much of anything anymore, even with an entire library on her side of the home." He still worked to console Jehanne, it seemed, but bitterness laced his words like he was indignant about his wife not reading the books he had lent her between the rapes. "Jehanne, pup, I was alone for so long. I didn't know how to treat your mother, how to treat you, but what matters most is that you and I are here now."

"Did you ever love her? Even once?"

"I owe you the truth." His frown deepened. "No, not for a moment. I thought that, when you search everywhere and try everything in your power, you're bound to strike silver one day. I hoped we could love each other one day. I never struck her, and I allowed her safe passage in our home."

Jehanne's hackles rose. "And you think that's enough for love? Shouldn't that already be how you act?"

"I believed it was enough." Father spread his arms. "But look at what we have, the two of us. The past doesn't matter. The rest of the world doesn't matter. And your mother, God rest her heart, is at peace now, and there's nothing I can do to tell her I'm sorry, to tell her I appreciated that she was a good, obedient wife in her warmer moments. She was what women should aspire to be."

For all Father's attempts to appease her with his honesty, Jehanne's vision bordered on scarlet.

"What was her name?"

He looked at her like she'd spoken German. "Does it matter?"

"Yes, yes! It matters. Of course it does. It matters more than anything to me."

"I—Catherine. She was Catherine." Jehanne started. The name sank in her like a bag of stones. Familiar, so familiar, one of the few truths she had, and tears came to her eyes as furiously as ever. He took her in, and his gaze made her feel dirty. "Oh, darling, I knew that wouldn't help you."

"Father, listen to me." She rubbed her nose on her sleeve, but she wouldn't be cowed. "Eve came from Adam's side—not his foot or the air above him. Because they were equals. They were meant to stand together on the same ground. I don't understand how you'd think—if a man treated me like you treated Mother, what would you think? Wouldn't you want to kill him?"

Father shook his head. "I can't change the past. I can only repent, or try to as best I can."

"And you think that's enough? You think your tears are all it takes?"

"Isn't it? With God, isn't there always that new chance? God always forgives those who repent." His voice rose, a hopeful lilt.

"Do you treat all women like this? Father, you came from a woman's womb. The Lord was born from a chosen woman. He met, saved, and listened to women, and then it was a woman sent by another woman who saw the Resurrection. The saints—women have died for God's will."

Father gave her an odd, bitter look. "Yes, I know the stories. I don't need to be lectured about women who've been sacrificed to the wolves for God. I've seen what happens to women who try to act outside what they're meant to do. It can be endearing, admirable, but it leads to ruin when they aren't watched carefully enough."

"Aren't men hurt and killed too? How is it any different? How are some women's deaths proof that all women are incapable, or even that *they* were incapable?

190

That's insulting, don't you think? How could you be so hateful?"

"It's not out of hate, but love."

"What you did to Mother wasn't close to love. You said it yourself." Jehanne grunted in frustration, and the catalyst for this came to the forefront of her mind. Clair and her rules and walls, her eyes downcast or blank. Her injuries. "Have you been hurting Mlle Clair?" She thought of Moreau too with his ghostly pallor.

"I compensate her exceedingly well for her services."

"And that excuses it? You really don't understand."

"There's nothing to excuse. Clair receives food, shelter, money—endless compensation for meager tasks. If she fails, that's the sole time I punish her. I don't go out of my way to hurt her, and I don't beat her or any of the other servants." The others, those in the shadows, those Father never named. "That is reasonable enough treatment."

Jehanne's feet twinged like she needed to pace, but she needed to make her point. "Punishment. What sort of punishment? Father, no, Father, please, please tell me you're not that man anymore. What do you do to her? Why does she look sad all the time?" She wanted to corner him on the burns and bruises, but he'd suspect Clair showed them to Jehanne to force this confrontation, and he might—she didn't know.

"Please don't be so upset, pup. I don't want you to grow tired and ill again. The winter could be so difficult for you."

A diversion. She scoffed. "Mlle Clair needs help, not me."

"You're too kind for the likes of her."

"You aren't kind enough!"

Lowly, Father said with a scowl, "That's a terrible assumption to make. Do you know what her life was like before I found her?"

"How could it be any worse than having a master who hurts you?"

Father puffed out his chest. "I bought her from the brothel her father had sold her to for a modest sum. He had debts, and she had her uses."

"You *bought* her?" Jehanne's blood froze.

Some fathers sell their daughters, you know.

"I purchased her and Moreau's services—for the manor, that is. I saved them and gave them a new life."

Saved, what a word.

"They were both there?"

"I know you may wonder why I was in a brothel, but—"

When he stepped closer, Jehanne lurched away and spat, "That? No, I'd rather not know. Though compared to you raping my mother, that's nothing. Unless you would rape those women too?" Not waiting for an answer, she continued, "You used her after she was betrayed. You use her still, don't you?" Use, as if Clair were a tissue. To say she wanted to slap him was an understatement. Whatever she wanted to do, it was violent. "Do you 'take' her? Have you learned nothing? Please say you at least don't do that anymore."

Father laughed as though she were an infant trying to eat her own toes. "Darling, don't fret so much." She noticed he kept switching between "pup" and "darling," and for reasons she couldn't say, it made her skin crawl. "You can't rape someone in that profession. It's in their nature to acquiesce. I assure you all our private matters are just."

Jehanne swallowed down bile. "How can you say that?" She narrowed her eyes. "Is that how you excuse it? You *do* hurt her like you did Mother, don't you? It's against God."

"I told you it's in the past—"

"Mlle Clair is here and alive *now.*"

"—and that I'm sorry, but I'll excuse your tone. You have a soft heart, and I love you for it."

"How can you dismiss what you've done and say you feel remorse all at once? And I don't have a soft heart."

"That's not an insult."

"I want to hear you say it. Do you rape Mlle Clair like you raped Mother? Say you're a filthy rapist to me."

"It's hardly the same predicament." She couldn't understand his callousness, how he could talk fondly of her soft heart and speak of hurting women like it should be nothing to either of them. How he could hold her and bruise someone else. How he seemed regretful in the beginning, hoarse and tearful, but the minutes scraped that warmth away to reveal a rotting, squirming core. By Mary, he expected her to simper and comfort *him* and let this go.

"Do you hurt her? What do you do?"

"Enough." Stiffly, Father said, "I've said my sorries."

"To Mother or Clair, or only to God when you're by yourself?"

"We will act as if this conversation never occurred because it is utterly pointless."

"For all your talk of demons and behaving . . ." Jehanne sneered. "It's no wonder demons would live here after how you've acted, and yet I'm the one who's supposed to be quiet and kind."

His lips thinned. "Don't."

"You don't think your actions are a threat, that you could make evil return? Do you think force makes you strong, when it's made you weak?"

Father reached to touch Jehanne, maybe on the cheek, maybe on the shoulder. Any other time, she'd accept, but her world was scarlet with a white, blinding center. Before her mind could meet her body, she stormed forth and shoved him so hard he stumbled back, knocking against the bed.

15

Rosalie

Jolie growled under her breath, but when Rosalie gave her a pointed look, the old girl, bless her soul, had the politeness to bow her head.

The two officers were aged, perhaps closer to Anatole's age than Rosalie's. They each removed their hats, the tops of their heads an unimpressive silver. With a brief glance, the only discernible difference between them was that one was taller. Anatole shook the men's hands.

The taller one faced her. "Rosalie, I am—"

Rattled, Rosalie said brusquely, "*Madame* Deibler, and I couldn't care less who you are. Why are you here?"

The shorter one said, an edge in his voice, "Why was there a severed tongue in the woods by here?"

Anatole started, "I—"

The taller one added, "Our companions didn't find it when we first looked through the woods after your night call."

Anatole's visage knitted. "I haven't the slightest, gentlemen."

Rosalie raked her hands through her hair. "How should we know? This is ridiculous."

Anatole only killed those who deserved to die, and yet the townspeople who shunned him whispered around and followed him around too—she shouldn't hate people she'd never met, but really, they made it difficult.

"May we search the house?" the taller one asked.

Anatole said, "If you must." He and Rosalie followed because it was better than waiting. The stains on the porch were gone. The four of them went into the barn with the Widow, the blade clean and sleepy. The search was uneventful, all except for the guillotine, and Anatole's desk when the shorter officer jiggled the handle of the top drawer.

He said, "It's locked."

Anatole replied, "There's nothing inside."

"Are you certain of that?"

Rosalie choked. "Please, I can't. My . . ." The taller officer looked to her, and without him saying anything, she answered, "No."

Anatole started, "Monsieurs, please."

The shorter one said, voice surprisingly softer, "Get the key for this, please."

Swallowing and forcing her face into cold resignation, Rosalie replied, "Oh, indeed, monsieur, since you ordered it so kindly." Anatole offered her the ghostliest of smiles, and she didn't know if it was pride, or consolation as she slipped her hand under the mattress and retrieved a small key.

With a blank visage, she handed it to the shorter officer, and she thought for a second she could keep her peace, but when he bent down, opened the drawer, and held what was in the desk, she averted her gaze and worked to control her breathing. Anatole was by her side, and she leaned into his shoulder while neither of the officers inspected them.

Apparently satisfied, the officers returned the mementos to their rightful place and locked the drawer. The shorter officer returned the key to her with an ashen look, and Rosalie shook and placed it back under the mattress, a little haphazardly.

After a stifling minute of silence, the taller officer motioned for everyone to leave the room.

Because of that distraction, neither of the officers bothered to look in the bedroom chest where she and Anatole kept the guns, nor did they find anything of interest in the other rooms.

Back in the living room, the squat officer said, "Isn't it odd that all the disappearances occur in this part of town, and what sort of man would be so dead to killing that he'd go after children? Why, one who kills for a living."

Anatole replied, focusing on nothing in particular, "Monsieur, with all due respect, who orders the deaths?"

Pointedly, Rosalie added, "What of the judges and lawyers you dine with, the ones who condemn and sentence the men?"

"I would never hurt a child," her husband offered, "and there is no indication the missing children have been killed."

The shorter officer stroked his pathetic beard. "And why not?"

"Why not hurt children?" Rosalie said. "Are you mad?"

He replied, "I've always wondered if a man like you broke, who'd execute the executioner?"

Grimly, the taller officer said, "M. Deibler, I assure you. I don't want to do this."

Anatole broke a little with that. "I—I didn't do anything to a child. I wouldn't."

The taller officer said, "I don't disbelieve either of you, but we need to explore all our options."

Rosalie crossed her arms. "I can't believe you lot." This sort of thing shouldn't reach the home, shouldn't reach them or Marcy or André.

Her husband, her dear husband, conceded, "I understand, and it's terrible, what's happened. But I can't abandon my home for long. Surely you can understand that." Anatole was Anatole, open to appease and compromise, calm and not eager to raise his voice, and while Rosalie was the same, she found the strength to steel herself when she had to defend him.

"Isn't this what you people have always wanted?" Rosalie spat. The threat eclipsed her discomfort. These men wouldn't, couldn't steal him from her. Anatole endured not only his work, but nearly four centuries of unappreciated family service, yet he maintained kindness.

"Have courage," he'd say to the condemned, a friend to all manner of traitors, rapists, and murderers.

He was too good for this town, for this world, and this was his thanks.

The taller officer, with the audacity to look affronted, said, "You don't think I respect those who help us with justice?"

Rosalie's fists stung where nails pierced flesh. "Monsieur, we have a daughter and nephew who need him here. My husband is a good man. He helps us survive with what our country and the law ask of him."

"Madame, it's only for questions. Your closest neighbors have said there have been suspicious sounds coming from here."

Rosalie scoffed. "Rumors! Unless they mean the sounds. My husband called you lot about them, need I remind you. It seems contrary to good sense, doesn't it, for a killer to call the police?" The fire stroked, licked, flashed with Rosalie hard and cold between the police and Anatole, as if, even with her stinging eyes and trembling ankles, she could be that wall.

The taller officer said, "Is there another man here?"

Anatole said, "No, it's only been us."

"And your nephew, the one who helps you?"

"He's likely with a friend," Anatole said.

"But you don't know?"

The shorter one whispered to his partner, "What about her?"

"The woman looks too frail to leave the house."

"Perhaps if you continue to speak directly to me, you'd see how frail I am." She added with a bow of her head, "Monsieurs."

The taller officer's eyes were haunted, and despite Rosalie's indignation, his reluctance made it worse. It'd be easier to fight if she could hate him more, hate him into abstraction. To Anatole, he said, "If you come quietly, we can be finished with this soon." That would've been a good time to refuse to be silent or gentle, but Anatole wouldn't do that. Always having to bend, appease, sacrifice for the people's sake. Always the honest public servant.

How could they do this to him?

Anatole squeezed her shoulder, but she barely felt it. "I love you. I'll be back."

In an instant, she was cold. "Just like that?" If only those who loathed Anatole knew how little he fought; if anything, Rosalie needed him to fight more, more bones, more teeth.

"I've no choice," he said, quiet. "It'll only hurt us more to put up a fight."

Ignoring the two other men in the room, and ignoring all the decorum she had learned from Maman and school, Rosalie said, "But I—we need you here, Marcy and

André." She exhaled. "If you aren't here when they return, they won't survive without you. Is that not enough for you to fight more? Are your daughter and nephew not important enough?"

"They'll have you, and I've more faith in you than God, my heart." His thumb brushed her cheek.

Rosalie scoffed. "Don't go to Hell on my account."

"And I'll return, I swear it."

"There you go again with your promises." Unable to restrain herself, Rosalie flung her arms around him, nuzzling her cheek into his firm shoulder. "God, I love you too." It hurt her throat. Defeat trickled through, a leak widening into a flood. She rubbed apologies into his shirt, but her nails couldn't reach deep enough, couldn't find warmth.

When they separated, Anatole turned to the shorter officer, set a hand on his shoulder, and leaning close, whispered, "Hugo, I'm sure you'll find Addie."

The man's jowls quivered, and the taller one took Anatole by the arm, and her husband showed no resistance. The officer called Hugo, who had a talcy smell, tried to comfort Rosalie with a touch on the arm.

She lost her grip on the moment like it was water, and only when the door closed and no words came, she realized herself and shuddered.

No one here, gone, all gone.

Not a soul besides her and the dog.

She collapsed on the living room rug, which burned her palm when it hit the coarse threads. Bent like a splintered willow stuck in post-storm fog, her sobs broached screams, and the house echoed back to her.

Heaving, Rosalie whispered, "God help him. God help us. God help me." Jolie padded over to her with a low whine, offering a single paw.

With nothing left to do but mourn, she buried herself in Jolie's coat.

16

Jehanne

The room froze, the bookshelves gaping down like mouths with crooked, discolored teeth.

The air fractured, and Jehanne's mind stuttered like a broken gramophone. Father made no move to get up, hands splayed by his sides, legs strewn as he sat and stared with wide eyes. Fear, that was what that was.

Her fury scared him.

When he broke his gaze and pinched the bridge of his nose, Jehanne ran, swinging the door behind her. Her world was a damp flurry of light as she fled away from Father. Going, going until she collapsed by a hall window, gray light, the burgundy curtain spilling under her.

Jehanne tried to conjure the portrait of her poor mother, her mother grasping the satin crushed in her fist, grasping for her sanity as her belly cramped and blood ran down her legs. But nothing came, it was only Jehanne there alone, utterly alone, while she swallowed her sick and felt her menstrual bleeding start.

She contemplated running away before she rotted away like the walls, before she became lost in wondering what leered in each corner. The logistics didn't matter in this maddening daydream, only the thought of new, fresh wind in her hair. A bustling green country with no war and no demons, with no blood or ashes in its rivers.

Jehanne released sob after sob. She'd ordered around Clair like Father had, asserted her power when she could. That meant she was his shade, a monster like him.

God, maybe literally, but that was ridiculous, wasn't it?

It'd explain her feeling of new skin. Jehanne could be afflicted with a witch's curse; she could be a loup-garou, a wolf-person. Oh, Father would hate that she was taking stock in fanciful little myths. A wolf-person—that'd explain the scars, wouldn't it? It'd explain why she was found naked on the riverbank with no memory of what had happened before. Maybe the special teas didn't just heal Jehanne; they suppressed whatever needed to be locked away.

Bitterness flooded her mouth. Why couldn't Father just tell her what had happened that made her sick? If Jehanne knew more about what was wrong, if Father could move past secrets, she could be more knowledgeable about controlling herself before she hurt someone.

But she could no longer face him.

Maybe she should be thrown behind one of the many locked doors. Doors with dust and darkness behind them. Dust, books, doves? Which door had doves behind it? Part of Jehanne wondered, a little shamefully, whether the doves existed at all, or if they were little fancies in Father's head to calm his stormier moods.

What good *that* did.

Worst of all, if they did exist, she wondered if this hollow madness in her would make her tear their wings off to spite him.

No, she couldn't let the burgeoning resentment win, couldn't be like Father, couldn't give in to the molten roil in her belly. She had a choice.

Vision blurring, Jehanne shuffled to the kitchen, hips and legs knocking against hallway corners. The kitchen smelled of ammonia, and the dim lights flickered. A glass tray of tarts rested on the counter. Raspberry or strawberry, she couldn't tell.

She wrapped one in a cloth napkin, and the filling smeared a bit. What a sad little treat, she thought, putting it in her pants pocket.

When she returned to her room, climbing the stairs and treading forth with mounting dread, she was hopeful to return to sleep, but her bed was undressed. Jehanne set the tart on the nightstand. She opened the drawer and reached for a pad and pen. She couldn't write much, so she strung together wobbly letters as best she could manage.

mlle,

sorry I rude to you few many times. heal.
jehanne

When she read over it, she huffed. How asinine it was to ask Clair to heal when she still served Father.

Her throat burned. She stumbled to the washroom and vomited. How funny it was, the relief, that brief weightlessness before her heart hardened to iron. When she finished, she stared dully into the commode and laid her cheek on the porcelain. Emptiness filled her; she shuddered. She was vile, vile and lonely.

From there on the bumpy tiles, she heard faint shuffling in her room, the rustling of sheets. When she gained the courage to face another person, and placed a pad where it needed to be, Jehanne ambled into her room. The bed was fully made with sheets that looked no different than the old ones. That was a godsend, but her heart lurched when she saw Clair adjusting a pillowcase.

Clair paused and clasped her hands when she noticed Jehanne. On the nightstand, the note and treat were unbothered.

"Are you ill?" Clair asked. Neither of them must've looked well then, since Clair's cheeks were blotched, her countenance a shade whiter, the darkness under her brow the sort from a sleepless night.

"I think so." It wasn't a complete lie. "Please, if you can, if you want, I need tea to sleep, and I don't know how to make it myself."

"It's not night. It's not even noon."

206

Jehanne sniffed and crawled into bed. "I know."

"Did you speak to your father?"

Jehanne couldn't trust herself to speak without crying, so she nodded.

Clair took great interest in her own simple black shoes. "I don't know what you learned, but I'm sorry."

"So am I." Her eyes leaked, and she made no effort to wipe at them.

"I'll go get your tea. I'm sure Moreau has already prepared some. If not, I can try my hand at it."

Jehanne curled into a ball. "Thanks. Take your tart."

Clair's forehead crinkled. As she accepted the gift and read the paper, she sucked in her bottom lip, and Jehanne couldn't tell if it was because the words were powerful or indecipherable.

Swallowing, Clair covered her mouth as if to hold in a sob before rolling the napkin up and setting the tart in her apron pocket. She took great care to place the uncreased note there as well. Jehanne wondered how long it had been since anyone had gifted Clair anything without expecting a service in return.

"You really shouldn't have done this," Clair said. "Why would you do this for me, of all people?"

Jehanne whispered, "Why wouldn't I?"

Instead of giving warmth, the new understanding between them ached like a broken arm set back into place.

Sore and cold, Jehanne whispered, "God, God forgive me."

"Forgive you for what?"

"Father abused my mother, hurt her because he thought it meant no other man would want her." Her arms spasmed from tremendous weight. Was Father possessed by a demon? "He's my father, and I shouldn't hate him, but I do. What must God think of me?" Was Jehanne possessed? Was that why her mind was so broken?

Clair, with her frazzled hair and anxious-but-composed scent of sweat and chamomile, flexed her hands. She sat on the bed so that her arm was the closest thing to Jehanne. Given that Clair was a wisp of a person, the mattress didn't so much groan as grunt. "That's not your fault." With her fingers and spine curled, Clair looked like she was struggling to be as taut and closed as before. "Our fathers aren't our fault, unless we choose them before we're born."

Jehanne folded deeper into herself. "I never thought he'd be capable of that. Was it the war trauma that made him do these things? No, this must've been before. The war hasn't gone on that long."

"For your sake, you should try to make it work. He's sacrificed so much for you. There are some things not worth compromising for that little piece of joy in this awful world." What a terrible burden for Clair to not see herself and her abuse worth ruining a relationship for, as if her pain cost others more than it cost herself.

"What does it matter? How can I love someone who abused Maman so badly she miscarried? How can I love him when he hurts you?"

Clair slouched more and sniffed. "He's your father. I'm only your servant."

"You don't deserve this. Whatever happened in the past, you didn't deserve that either."

Clair shuddered, her breath a long, wet sigh, and she rubbed her face with both palms. "What would you know about my past?"

"Father told me he bought you."

Clair scoffed and, through the woman's hands, Jehanne saw her deep scowl. "Of course he did. Not even my story is safe from the likes of him." She shook her head, exhaling sharply and straightening. "I shouldn't speak like that. I'd rather be here than where I was."

"The brothel?"

Clair peered foggily ahead. "Home."

"Do you—you can say no if it's . . ."

"What do you mean?"

"Can you tell me what happened?"

The woman's lips thinned. "It's not important."

Jehanne shook her head and forced strength up her throat, or perhaps it was more vomit. At this point, she could no longer tell. "It's your choice. It's your story, not Father's, not your father's." Clair's story was her; it was in the blue shadows under her eyes and the defeated curve of her back.

For several minutes, they stayed frozen like a caterpillar interrupted and contorted in a chrysalis, forever a half-winged, soupy creature.

"When I was a girl, my mother died. I believe it was 1896. Father would cry every night and drink himself to sleep, as one does. I raised myself in those years. I was a gawky, scared little thing, and I was never taught how I should feel about all that happened. I spent the time reading alone in my bed until, after a time, Father would tell me how much I looked like Mother, and I enjoyed the attention, enjoyed him loving me again." Clair laughed bitterly. "I suppose you can imagine what happened." Jehanne didn't want to answer. Clair balled her apron in her fists. "When he'd visit me at night, he'd tell me it was supposed to hurt, I was supposed to hurt, that he was trying to teach me to be less frightened of my body. He was teaching me, and so long as I pleased him, he was well and happy, and I thought it'd hurt less with time. He'd joke, and he was kind, like your father can be. He could be good if I didn't provoke him." She pinched her nose, and Jehanne swallowed the sour taste in her mouth.

Something should be said, but she didn't know how to comfort anyone besides giving out food she didn't make or offering to hit a man she'd never met. Instead, she asked, "Is that why you don't leave, because you can't go anywhere else? Because you can't go back to your father?"

Clair pursed her lips. "We sometimes have to accept our lots in life."

"No, you don't. You don't have to. You didn't deserve any of that. We could—I don't know what we can do, but I'll protect you."

Huffing through her nose, Clair replied, "I want one of us to have a father. No matter his faults, he's never hurt you. He's always loved you, I think, since before you were born."

Jehanne's belly turned as she thought of her poor mother stumbling around, heavy with the child from her rape. "If being with him means letting people be hurt, letting you be hurt, I can't do that. I can't allow it." *And I've allowed so much. Stupid.* "Why don't you think you're worth saving?"

"Who could care for a cold, cowardly, broken woman?"

Jehanne trembled, failing the war with her tears. "Me."

Clair shifted and shook her head. "The only people who cared about me were my sisters and brothers at the brothel."

Brothers? "Moreau?"

Clair glowered at the floor, knuckles the whitest they'd ever been. "He trained me in . . . and if I ever were to try to go back and get help, the master would find me, and he'd have help. I'd be one sad, forgotten wretch against somebody with enough wealth to turn away everyone's eyes."

Jehanne lifted herself up with an elbow and buried her head against Clair's shoulder. The woman winced. Right, that wasn't smart, but when Jehanne thought to pull away, Clair shifted to pat her back, so Jehanne found herself wool-eyed against the woman's collarbone.

As she returned Clair's gentle pats, Jehanne wept in deep, stinging bursts. She whispered, "It's not your fault, what they did." *What I did, how I spoke to you.* "You're not alone. I won't let you be. I'll fight for you. I'm sorry. I'm so sorry for how I've treated you." Clair gripped her tighter, a strong hold. Jehanne was wrong. Clair wasn't a sad wisp; she was steel, blood, fire, because she had survived horror and still allowed some obnoxious girl she worked for to cry on her. It was the least Jehanne could do, to comfort her through the spit and mucus. She figured she was doing a poor job of it. She wanted to hold Clair, whisper to her, kiss her, and she couldn't make sense of all her thoughts.

Eventually, cold sank into Jehanne's bones and dragged her to the pillows. Ever since she had woken from her sickness, with a dull needle and frayed, tattered linen, she worked to sew the scraps of mostly forgotten dreams and half-memories together. But now all she wanted was to sleep and forget. It was safer that way, she realized too late, to let the past lie.

Somewhere above her, Clair said, "I'll go get the tea."

"I don't think I need it anymore." The sheets smelled like lavender. "Thank you for the clean sheets."

Clair replied something quiet and brushed Jehanne's hair from her eyes. Right, Jehanne had forgotten something, but her eyes were fat sandbags. She should—Marcy, Jehanne should be with her now. She'd promised; she couldn't give up so swiftly, and Marcy could comfort her with a story.

But Marcy, a red and blue fog in her head, drifted away from her thoughts, and Jehanne forgot the feeling of claws scratching under her skin.

17

Marcy

Marcy didn't swear much, but damn it all, Jehanne had chosen the worst time to sleep. She really needed to know if all was right. When she walked into Jehanne's room after thirty-one minutes had passed without a word, she found Clair brushing her friend's hair behind her ear. Clair didn't notice Marcy's presence until she stood up and made her way to the door. She regarded Marcy with disinterest, and her cheeks were splotchy.

"Is Jehanne okay?"

Clair answered, the edges of both eyes pink and swollen, "She will be."

"All right, then." Marcy wanted to ask more, but Clair looked ready to fall apart.

They left the room together, though Clair kept walking down the hall, the soft tap of her black pumps the only beat for a time. Curiosity squirmed as the quiet swelled. Marcy would find out what had happened when Jehanne awoke, but for now—the study, something told her that was where she needed to go. If nothing else, to pass the time with books, new stories to digest and retell as her own. Good stories, not the ones where all the mothers and wives always died. It might take some searching. Jehanne's father seemed like the sort of man who read old tales.

The wallpaper followed her steps as she went to the study. Nobody was there anymore. It was dark, so Marcy flicked the light switch, and the room became suitably bright after a small sputter. She examined each shelf. A book on Roman emperors, a book on feudalism, and a two-part story by a German man.

"Gurt," she mumbled, tracing the author's engraved surname. *Goethe.* Funny, this one, given the master of the manor's thoughts on Germans.

She discovered a string of English plays too, by Marlowe and Jonson and Webster, whoever the last one was. (Didn't the monsieur hate the English too?) Marcy took the beaten *The Duchess of Malfi*, perused a page or ten before deciding that, though it was like many other morbid stories she read, it was maybe best to leave this one alone. Given her cycle, she wasn't in the mood for blood today. She then opened a random page of a well-worn text called *Justine, ou Les Malheurs de la Vertu* by

Donatien Alphonse François de Sade, but, upon reading a sentence, realized her mistake and shelved it.

Eager to move along in her search, she found a book of Greek myths, and when she cracked it open, she looked at the spiked letters scribbled at the top of the first page.

Never regret thy fall, O Icarus of the fearless flight. For the greatest tragedy of them all is never to feel the burning light.

Marcy beamed. Wilde was a good choice. She put it back and then knelt when she noticed some books bulging out in an odd wave on the lowest shelf, like something was behind them. She pulled out three dense texts before she found purchase: A black book with the spine almost broken.

Tenderly, she propped it in her hands and opened it like it had a snake inside. After a moment of staring at the first page, she blinked. Marcy could tell the words were French, yet she couldn't understand many of them, as if they were a combination of French and another antiquated language.

As she curled back pages upon pages, she snapped her head up at the slightest creak or moan. The book looked like a personal diary, but none of the entries had dates, and many pages were incomprehensible. God, was this Latin? Good for the writer; they were more of an aspiring

Catholic than she'd ever be. Eventually, she found a sentence simple enough for her to decipher.

Light has left my life. I wish this damned war never happened.

War. This was the monsieur of the manor's diary. It made sense. Papa kept his own black book, though she hadn't the slightest if Papa's diary possessed as many peculiar gaps and odd hiccups in language. Then again, Jehanne's father was a strange one, for sure.

Her heart twinged at this passage. The thin paper smelled like wet churchyard grass and regret. The next few pages were blank, except for a number succeeded by dried ink blots.

140

As she kept perusing, the handwriting grew more slanted, but the French, where there was French, grew more recognizable. Some strange symbols caught her eye, their meaning lost on her. Marcy read another entry:

I miss François so much it hurts to breathe. His hair, his voice, his eyelids when he slept. Yet when I remember harder, it saddens me to think of him and only conjure this delightful, but insubstantial, mimicry of

Faust. All I have left is his spell book, and all my attempted rites have granted me nothing. But there's nothing left but this; all I have left is to try.

It is times like these I wonder, with these sacrifices I've made, if I should bring him back so we can get on like we did before. Still, if he is in Hell, it'd be less of an offense to God to bring him here. There have been enough demons conjured beneath these floors, anyhow. So why not take from Heaven instead, if such a feat can be done? Long is the way and hard, that out of Hell leads up to light, but all is not lost, the unconquerable Will, and study of revenge, immortal hate, and courage never to submit or yield.

If my soul would be the only casualty, I've nothing to lose. Oh, Jehanne.

Marcy couldn't make sense of the words beyond the fact that a male lover had died. Maybe this was a story, but from what she gathered about the manor's master, there seemed to be some truth. Spell book, rites—indeed, she knew the man had been shaken by the war, but not enough to find solace in tricks.

And demons? His shell shock had gotten the best of him. That, or his penchant for vivid, dramatic metaphors came through here. With all the crucifixes in the manor, though, "demon" didn't immediately cross her mind. Far stranger, she realized, was the number at the bottom of the entry. At first, she skimmed over the numbers, too immersed in the words. But the diary was small, and *743*, smudged in the curled corner, was too big a number to correlate with the page. No matter how she tried to make sense of it, all she could think was maybe for a wary soldier, shadows had faces, and he counted each one. Marcy turned the page to find part of a poem torn from another book.

> *And there I lived amid voluptuous calms,*
> *In splendours of blue sky and wandering wave,*
> *Tended by many a naked, perfumed slave,*
>
> *Who fanned my languid brow with waving palms.*
> *They were my slaves—the only care they had*
> *To know what secret grief had made me sad.*

The monsieur, for all his oddities, had good taste in poetry, Marcy decided. At least, insomuch that it rhymed, so it looked good to her. The page had an odor to it like talc on a lily, a smell that stuck to her fingers when she pulled them to her nose. It made her bristle for a reason she couldn't discern. Marcy's eyes flitted to a number.

751

She flipped to another page.

These shall be my last words: She's awake and alive. I've done more than anyone ever could. I've fooled God. Against all, I've proven myself triumphant.

And on that day, the number remained unchanged. That wasn't the part that sent a hateful chill down Marcy's back. It was the signature:

Baron Gilles de Rais of the House of Montmorency-Laval, Hero, Marshal of France

Gilles de Rais.

Marcy flung the book off her lap. That name. That name she remembered from the morbid book she'd read about the man who—the man and the—

The monster in *Là-Bas*, that morbid little book with the phallic tree trunks, the one she'd refused to relay to Jehanne. She remembered one passage:

> Everywhere obscene forms rise from the ground and spring, disordered, into a firmament which satanizes. The clouds swell into breasts, divide into buttocks, bulge as if with fecundity, scattering a train of spawn through space. They accord with the sombre bulging of the foliage, in which now there are only images of giant or dwarf hips, feminine

triangles, great V's, mouths of Sodom, glowing cicatrices, humid vents. This landscape of abomination changes. Gilles now sees on the trunks frightful cancers and horrible wens. He observes exostoses and ulcers, membranous sores, tubercular chancres, atrocious caries. It is an arboreal lazaret, a venereal clinic.

Marcy shuddered, all her resolve leaking away like a drained cyst. God, Jesus, Mary. Gilles, Gilles de Rais, the terrible Breton knight. She didn't know at least ten of the words in that passage, and it wasn't exactly like remembering a Bible verse. By God, it shook her, the greedy, pitiful, war-beaten criminal staring at the blue, venereal growths he created from the blood of innocents. Those bulging sores that were unearthed from the dirt and leaves as all he thought about was what he could molest and destroy next.

God, no, she couldn't make assumptions. Maybe it was a coincidence. People could have the same name. But not this one, especially not with the exact same house name and military title. It wasn't possible—it was, it was now, and all the worries in the town, all the stories in the newspaper. The missing—Gilles de Rais. God. He hadn't even tried an anagram to hide his identity.

Was the monsieur mad? Was *she* mad? She remembered, God, she remembered reading how he'd allegedly saved himself with prayer and La Pucelle's spirit came to embrace her old war companion and take him to

Heaven as he wept. And he had hanged and burned; he was supposed to be dead for centuries. Yet, the old French words, the spell book, the listing of titles after his name for personal affirmation—hero, marshal. The only living marshal Marcy knew of was Ferdinand Foch.

This couldn't be real. Marcy needed to wake Jehanne, and they needed to leave this place. A telephone. Where was the telephone? Did the manor even have one? Yes, it had to, of course, because she had called Jehanne. In a flurry, she ran to find it. Before she woke Jehanne, she needed to call the police.

Police. Papa.

Call Papa.

18

Rosalie

The world is on fire.

Eventually, Rosalie found the strength to rise off the floor without the dog's courteous assistance. She breathed deep and slow, and the air scratched every hole in her.

Everything's burning.

She checked all the doors and windows and wished Anatole would return unscathed, but she had the solace that Marcy and André were away and safe. She worked to calm herself and failed. Going upstairs, she went to the desk beside their bed, rattled that certain drawer knob once, and left it.

Some memories were best left alone.

Yet, God, she'd lost her wits today.

She thought of the time after she and Anatole lost Roger. She remembered she'd been in the wet garden when, after many years, she craved Anatole again. Rain thundered down like it had during Rosalie and Anatole's first cycle ride after they married and entangled themselves under the oaks without care. There in the garden, her body shook like the rosebushes disturbed by the rain. Moisture trickled down her nose, chin, neck, thigh, trickled like the silver veins on the church windows when she married Anatole and morning rain had sleeted the roads.

It had been too long since she had let Anatole inside her.

The wind had lashed against her, but she didn't break. She was rain-soaked when she walked into the living room to her husband reading. Anatole questioned her health, thought a cold would strike her down, but she was forged of lightning that day. She removed her coat, her dress sticking to her skin like a second flesh. She kissed him like the rain had renewed her fire. They joined in the armchair beside the kindling hearth, and it was the first time Rosalie eclipsed him since they'd lost Roger. He smelled of earth, tobacco, and wet newspaper sheets. She smelled of old books, that mingling of almonds and damp grass. She felt their souls entwined. They wiped the tears and rain from each other and, in the following days, they acted like they had the weeks following their wedding. He pressed his lips to her hair, and she moved his cheek so she could taste the ash in his mouth.

One night, when they were naked in bed, Anatole had bent between her, his lips on her knee. She had tilted her head, sadness pinching her brow. She wanted to say, *How can we be happy without forgetting?* He clasped her chin, rubbed a thumb across her tearless cheek. *I don't want to forget, I don't think, but I don't know how to honor him. Would he've enjoyed cycling?* It would've sounded like nonsense, but it made complete sense to her. She hid those thoughts; no need to make Anatole's body a lithograph of her pain.

As time passed, though she stayed inside, she beamed more and listened to the songbirds. She would tease Anatole, and they'd dance to the gramophone's tune; they even took in a stray puppy. When Rosalie suspected she was pregnant and called a doctor to confirm from her symptoms, she told Anatole the same way she'd told him about Roger: no telling at all, only taking one of his hands and letting it linger on her belly. He embraced her, rubbed her back. They stayed like that for a minute. The obstinate sun shone, and she laughed, a talent she'd regained.

It had been a frosty November morning, and Anatole wore far more black than usual in private because his father, who had gone from jackal-like to sad, drunken, and quiet, had succumbed to cancer after his body and spirit tired. Anatole had openly cried once and wore mourning colors out of decorum. Perhaps Anatole mourned the father Louis could've been, the one he was in snippets. Louis' only posthumous gift to his son was the dead, once-scarlet orchid he'd kept in his coat buttonhole.

A Parisian newspaper had claimed Louis owned five hundred and two rings made of iron from blood he'd extracted from his clients, which was an impressive feat for a man who'd killed only one hundred and sixty clients and had hid his blood-crafting ability exceptionally well. Rosalie knew little about Louis beyond Anatole's stories. Of Anatole's mother, Zoé, even less so. The madame, whose father preceded Rosalie's as the Algerian executioner, would dress as a man and attend executions, and Rosalie pondered if she watched and assisted for her husband's sake, or her own.

Given these details, Anatole was a blessing, though Rosalie wouldn't be surprised if the newspapers reports stated that, in his spare time, he drank the blood of children. For Anatole, executions were not entertainment as they'd been for Louis before he deteriorated. Before Anatole took over, his father had executed a woman, a bad omen, saw faces in the corner of his bedroom, witnessed gaunt sneers on the heads of apples hanging from orchard trees, and wept daily. A year before his death, he had called Anatole and spent an hour gulping down sobs and whispering, "I've seen so many." Many what, he never answered. Shortly before his death, Louis, with his watery dream-eyes and violinist hands, visited and mumbled about an incident when blood spurted onto his pants, and he suffered a severe paroxysm. Naturally, blood was nothing new to Louis; before his son turned thirteen, he forced Anatole to dismember small animals as preparation for seeing a dead man's insides.

Yet, that single incident at the guillotine had shattered Louis' resolve. For her husband's sake, Rosalie had kept her peace; she couldn't say she liked Louis. She pitied him, but she pitied Anatole more. Little Roger had died nineteen days before Anatole's birthday, and now his father was dead, but Rosalie discovered her pregnancy with Marcy a few days before his forty-first one, so for the first time in years, they celebrated.

And the dread returned.

It seemed no matter what, whether on the path of pins or the path of needles, her feet ended up bleeding. One night a little over five months into her pregnancy with Marcy, Rosalie dreamed she lost the baby inside her, that the bed blossomed red like an autumn tree under her, the black spots like clumps of robin eyes.

She couldn't lose this baby, couldn't let them bleed out of her. Rosalie dreamed of what her mother described to her when she'd lost a baby—tissue chunks, endless blood. Rosalie tried to push the pieces back inside her until she stained her hands and arms, and nobody answered when she called—no people, no ghosts. Not Anatole, not Maman, not Juliette. No Roger, pale, bloated. Drowned in the Styx. Wailing. *No blood in the bed.* She told Anatole they couldn't bring others' blood to the bed. The room was black, and all she saw were the ruined sheets, her fingers, and her thighs.

A searing ache had dragged her from sleep in a shivering sweat, Anatole present and snoring next to her, an urge to relieve herself, a stillborn scream on her lips. *How many times do I need to watch you die when you haven't been born yet?* When she went to the commode, her undergarments were clean. Rosalie reached between her legs, and her fingers remained unbloodied. She returned to bed, and the sheets were wet only where she'd perspired and cried.

I do *love you. I'm sorry, so sorry if you hear me crying and think otherwise.* She rubbed her belly, felt Marcy respond with forceful kicks. *No blood in the bed. Leave it at the threshold.* Rosalie was careful. *No blood, no death.* What if Anatole died, then the baby died, and there was no trace of him left?

She had asked him that evening on the couch, "Do you hope for a girl or a boy?"

He rubbed her hands, his eyes drifting away from her face. "I'll be happy regardless." Rosalie wanted a girl, but if she said as much and the opposite occurred, Anatole would suspect her disappointment, and he wouldn't be wrong. Raising a son, well, they tried, were trying, with André being the closest to a growing child with family blood, Juliette's blood.

A long pause punctuated the air. Rosalie touched her belly and could almost feel the skin giving way to reveal her child, a child she could have inside her longer than they'd have a name. The flesh around her eyes grew taut, but she didn't want to break, didn't want her child to feel her sadness, the stress pulsing inside like an engorged worm.

Rosalie didn't need to voice her fear, for Anatole released the first sob. With his trembling hands around hers, she rested her head on his shoulder.

"I don't think I can do this," she said. Her burgeoning child, too large to contain. The women in her family fared so poorly when carrying children that it was a wonder they had children at all. Anatole offered no solace like "We can have another one" or "At least we know you can conceive."

Which was good because she wanted the baby in her to come to life *now*.

Through his sobs, Anatole told her, "I'm here. I'll still be here. You know that, don't you?" Through his labored breaths, he added, "I am utterly useless." He took her hand and settled it against his chest, putting his other hand on her back.

Rosalie did her best to live, did her best counting the money and managing what affairs she could. She learned how to distill perfume, so she could sell it, and she could embroider purchasable items, yet she thought—no, she knew—she couldn't keep a baby inside long enough. A baby, the one under her hand, still alive. She was small and unworthy, less of an ideal young wife and more of a combustible pile of half-standing walls and well-beaten chair legs.

"You aren't useless. I need you because I—I can't do this by myself." The hand on her back traveled to her nape, and Anatole leaned his head against hers. With each minute, they had slumped deeper into the cushions.

Now, her thoughts settled like dust. She took interest in the damned holy painting on the wall—the Virgin with an open mouth, hands splotched with her son's blood, her horror a sacred fetish for poets and novelists to fawn over. Not even the bastard who seeded her womb saved their Son, saved what was also Himself.

But I did survive, and Marcy survived too, so why am I still worrying over the past?

Ah, Marcy. Rosalie lost herself again. Late in the pregnancy, Rosalie saw Marcy's outline in a way she hadn't with Roger, and it struck her with rapid gulps and shivers.

My baby's dying, and she called for Anatole. She went to a lying-in hospital and had birthed Marcy four days later after much distress. With a hand in Anatole's, André would visit her and choke back tears because he couldn't stay with her. He begged her to come back home, and she would cry whenever Anatole and her nephew needed to leave. As Anatole would guide the boy out, André's eyes were always the last thing she'd see.

Anatole was there with her when she birthed Marcy, who looked alien with blood and amniotic fluid and a dark-green substance the doctor identified as feces. Amusement struck Rosalie, then. *That impatient, are you?* She was too tired for embarrassment when she considered she, perhaps, had messed herself during the final push, staining her daughter with more than blood.

When cleaned, Marcy looked pink, scrunched, and angry. Oh, her girl.

Rosalie rubbed Marcy's head. "I don't want to ruin you," she whispered so only Marcy heard. When she had her son, she hadn't been as tired as she thought she'd be, but when looking at Marcy, weariness turned her feathery thoughts to lead. For the first time in years, she prayed, prayed to Mary that her spring baby would last longer than her autumn one.

I don't want to kill you.

On that day, Marcy's little head had errant tufts of near-white hair that would fall out and give way to a strawberry-wheat color that came alive in the sun. Red hair, Anatole's hair. Little Roger took after Rosalie. As young as he was, Roger had a mop of black hair wild like crow feathers. If he'd grown up, the black couldn't have become any bolder. Roger had been hers, and Marcy was Anatole's.

It was good, Rosalie thought, for Marcy to be as different from Roger in every way. When Anatole would rest on his back with Marcy swaddled and sleeping under his chin, Rosalie was an intruder. Even on Rosalie's birthday, when Marcy was five and smeared her face in whipped cream, it was Anatole she dozed with on the sofa, as Rosalie sat away from them.

Anatole was the one who—

Rosalie jumped when the telephone rang. She stood and let it ring again, but with the possibilities flurrying in her mind of who it could be, she sighed and picked it up.

"'Allô?" she said.

"Maman?" It was Marcy, panting like she'd sped across town and back. "There's something wrong."

"What is it?" Her heart hammered in her ribs, throat, head.

Marcy wheezed for breath. "I—the missing kids, I think—demons—"

Rosalie's face contorted. "Demons?"

"Can't explain. Called the police already, but can Papa come and pick me up?"

"Your papa isn't here."

"W-what, not there?"

"The police took him in for questioning because of the missing children. What was it you were going to say about them, and is there anywhere safe you can go?"

"I—" A loud thud and choking gasp.

Her heart seized, blood freezing. "Marcy? Marcy? Marcy, can you hear me?"

The telephone clicked.

Rosalie stiffened, despair besting her body again.

She knew where to go; Anatole had told her the address, and when she had cycled long ago, she often traveled down that street.

But she couldn't do it.

Her cycle had long gathered rust, so her only options were walking (too long) and the auto. Even if she found the key, she couldn't drive that mechanical abomination. It wasn't a matter of will; she had never learned how to navigate such as bulky thing after a few cursory tries.

She couldn't. She couldn't. She couldn't. She was old, useless. She was an accomplished cyclist, but anything with more than two wheels would kill her. If she drove, she'd crash, and if she crashed, she'd die. And, as expected of anyone, she'd be no help to Marcy dead.

But Rosalie was no help staying here. Marcy could die if she stayed idle, and though the police could help, the station wasn't that populated, and their numbers were already diminished by those dispatched to take Anatole from her.

Yet she couldn't leave, couldn't drive, couldn't save her daughter. If only André had never left. If only the police would return Anatole. She couldn't do anything, and she breathed deep.

I must do something.

Marcy couldn't be like the lost children, missing or otherwise. Today, there'd be no more blood or death, God help them. *God help us.*

She wished Anatole were here to touch her elbow and whisper, *Rosie, you can do it. I know you can.* Her fingers lingered on his coat, forgotten in the haste of his arrest.

Don't bend. Don't bow. Don't break.

Rosalie ran upstairs and retrieved her pistol from the chest, since a shotgun would be difficult to aim and burdensome when she needed to run, and she already had her body against her. *By Christ and Mary and every godforsaken saint, I won't bury Marcy. I won't.*

God, You can't have this one, not today. When she returned downstairs, the stairway longer than usual, Jolie stared up with an inquisitive tilt of her head.

Hand brushing the auto key in Anatole's coat pocket, Rosalie ordered, "Stay here, sweet one." The dog grumbled, but obeyed. "Good girl."

As she flung herself elbows-first out the door, Rosalie shivered from the wind. She heard the taunting of crows fat from chewing on the soured orange of the day. She staggered, the sun hitting her wrong.

God help us.

19

Jehanne

Jehanne brushed away her tangled hair and rubbed her eyelids. God, she wanted to keep sleeping, but the people outside the door talked too loud.

"That damned girl called the police on us!" Moreau. Girl? Police? Jehanne sat up, leaned forward, and looked over herself. She was still in her day clothes, the tunic and trousers Father said made her look like Mary Frith, whoever that was.

Father, smiling at her. Her heart hurt.

Next came Clair's voice. "Are the officers here? Shouldn't we hide? They'll find the pit with—"

"They'll be here soon! Come, the master wants us to help face them. He'll join us shortly."

"We shouldn't go! The police will hurt us if we fight."

"The master will hurt us if we don't! God, I'm so hungry. I've been waiting for a moment like this."

Clair's voice rose. "Are you mad?"

Jehanne strode toward her door. Moreau said, "Milla, I won't let anyone hurt you."

Bitingly, Clair asked, "Except the master."

Jehanne swung the door open and startled them both. "What's happening? Where's Marcy? Why are the police coming?"

Moreau said dryly to Clair, "I see your tea isn't as effective as mine." Jehanne had fallen asleep before Clair gave her the tea.

Clair scowled, then said to Jehanne, softer, "Stay here."

Jehanne placed her hands on her hips. "You know I won't."

The woman said, "But you must, you foolish girl, if you don't want to—"

Moreau scoffed. "Oh, she's survived centuries as ash, she can survive being an idiot now. Being an idiot has done her well so far."

Jehanne's eyes widened. "What did you say?"

Clair smacked Moreau's arm. "Don't listen to him. He's inebriated." Even if Jehanne knew what that meant, she wouldn't have been satisfied, and as Clair and Moreau hurried away, she followed them to the main stairs, where the few other servants Father lined the banisters and bothered their fingers.

Storming down the stairs to the landing, Jehanne cut through the damp anxiety like a sword through swamp water.

When Clair, standing beside Moreau, saw her, she hissed, "You need to go, damn it!"

For once, Jehanne took pause, never having seen Clair this hostile.

Moreau said to Jehanne, "Your friend called the police. They should be here shortly. For once, you should take Clair's advice before the master returns." Why would Marcy call the police? Even with Jehanne's discoveries about Father, Marcy couldn't have known what she found out. Father—

Was a rapist. *Don't be dense.* Even when she shook herself, tried to make herself remember their argument, a fog still blanketed her mind, as if forcing her to remain idle.

No. He hurt Clair. You can't forgive that.

I'm not, but he isn't a murderer. He wouldn't—he wouldn't let us die. Father had been ecstatic when he first embraced her after her sickness. The very same man who had hurt—was it possible to salvage the scared, gentle man and extinguish the monster? How could Father reconcile those two parts of himself? He thought her better than other women, but maybe all he needed was reason—

Don't be dense. Don't be dense. Don't be an idiot. Remember.

The fog was less pressing, as if her mind had changed, as if—

The tea, the tea she hadn't taken today. The supposedly innocent tea suppressing her nightmares and—

Memories, is that it? But I still don't remember. Her past rolled about her tongue like a word she could *feel* without knowing the meaning.

Remember.

Centuries as ash?

It didn't take long for Jehanne to regain herself. "Let me talk to Father," she insisted.

Moreau said, "Oh, I'm sure it'll do you good."

Jehanne glowered. While she understood more than many how sickness could barb one's tongue, she couldn't pity him now. "I'm staying, whether you like it or not. Why don't *you* leave?"

Moreau smirked, a shaky line that didn't reach his eyes, and waved a hand. He was like pretty wallpaper on crumbling wall. His cheeks were rosier. His sickness seemed to have disappeared within the day. "As far as I've been told, this hall is open to all of us."

Clair stood stiff like her feet were nailed to the floor. Jehanne wanted to punch a wall, but she needed her knuckles. "Where is Marcy?"

Clair pursed her lips. "Please stop asking questions."

How can I protect you if you hide things from me?

Moreau narrowed his eyes. "Oh, you know she won't."

"Why did Marcy call the police?" Jehanne asked.

Moreau scowled and, for once, became ugly. "This is all your friend's fault, you know."

Clair said foggily, "Please go to your room and lock the door."

Jehanne blinked. Something glinted in Clair's right hand, but she hid it behind her. "What—what do you have there?"

"It's not your concern," Clair replied.

Father appeared just then, coming down the stairs and joining them on the landing. His hair was in disarray, his shirt haphazardly buttoned. His expression fell when he saw Jehanne, and she bristled.

"Pup, it wasn't . . ." His voice was gruff and tearful. "I *tried* to keep you safe, darling. You can't fight. You need to go." He reeked of his spiced wine, the deep scarlet kind.

"Why?"

"Because you need to be safe."

Jehanne raised her chin. "Where is Marcy? The police, they can try to help us."

Father gripped her arm with such strength she winced. "I won't let them have you."

Jehanne pulled away. "I'm staying. If nothing else, the demons or whatever you've drawn here can take you, but I won't let you hurt anyone else." Even with the conviction behind her words, her heart darted about like a hummingbird, light and heavy at once. Somehow, Moreau seemed larger, closer.

Father turned to Clair and spat, "You are completely useless."

Clair winced and ducked her head. "I'm sorry."

He continued, "How difficult is it to keep your eye on a girl before she ruins us all? You've always been a waste, ever since I found you in that filthy establishment."

Clair met Jehanne's eyes, and something changed. The chilly air had an electricity to it. Her shoulders set.

"Why were you there if it was so filthy?" Clair's reply was meek, but took such a resolve that heat colored her cheeks pink. "Why employ me if I'm so useless?"

Jehanne shook with rage at Father. Why wasn't Moreau saying anything? Why wasn't *she*? This new Father—God, she still hadn't mourned the old Father.

Father said, "Because you're utterly forgettable, and if you happened to die then, who would've cried for you, hm? Certainly not your destitute drunkard of a father."

Clair replied, louder than Jehanne had ever heard, "You're one to speak of drunkenness!"

"You disgusting, deceptive, pitiful whore—"

Jehanne found her words. "Leave her alone! She's just as worthy as anyone God's made, and you've no right to judge her."

Father's eyes still held a baleful gleam. "This isn't your concern."

"Yes, it is!" Jehanne protested. "You can't speak to her like that."

"I employed her. I can treat her however I like, unless she'd like to retreat back to the diseased rat's nest she crawled out of." Father snapped his fingers. "Jehanne, go."

"No, you're completely mad! Do you think you can speak to others like this, and I'll let it stand? That you can speak to someone like they're nothing?"

Father broke. "You ungrateful—you're defending her, are you? Her, of all people? I've given everything for your life, and I won't see you—"

Ungrateful? Dear God. All she had wanted was to help him. Jehanne rested a hand to her collarbone. "It's mine, my life, my body, and I won't let her or Marcy or anyone else be hurt. Marcy—"

Before Jehanne could inquire about her friend, Clair revealed her hidden hand. It wielded a knife. When Father saw the weapon, rather than showing alarm, he sneered. "Did you enjoy twisting that into your father's neck?"

"I did," Clair answered, "and I'll do the same to you."

Before the woman could do anything, Father lashed out and clutched Clair's wrist. Jehanne reached forward and jerked his hand away. It almost hurt, how his skin burned. Eyes wide for a second, Father rose a hand to strike Clair, and Jehanne grabbed his sleeve—

A hot, biting jolt snapped across her cheek, and Jehanne wasn't meeting Father's gaze anymore. She clattered back, flesh yielding to knuckles, and pain surged from her head to her mouth. Aching and strewn on the hard floor, she twitched and snapped so suddenly it was as if something broke. Her head, she'd hit her head.

When she looked up, it was Clair she noticed first, Clair with her hands to her mouth, the knife gleaming like an unnatural smile. Jehanne blinked, rubbed the corner of her lips with the back of her hand, and locked her eyes on the blood. She was mist, devoid of soul. Not here. Sifting through the bitter syrup of her thoughts, she looked to Father. He was silent, mouth gaping, eyes wet, but she couldn't find a way to care.

Father said, all the menace and fury melting, "I'm sorry, darling—pup. I'll explain this later, just leave."

He offered his hand, but, still feeling its sting, Jehanne sat up, knelt, and looked at nothing but her lap. Her mind skewed and expanded like frozen water, adjusting and twisting in its bone prison. Splitting the bars.

Nobody could move her; not even God. More than anyone else, Jehanne wanted Marcy by her side because she was truly alone and wanted to be warm and safe again. Even that thought passed into the dying Lethe.

Pounding against locked doors. Father took a loud step and said, "Look at what you've done. This will be the last time you inconvenience me."

More pounding. Her head threatened to crack open.

Clair's voice was grave and steady amid the cacophony. "No, listen to me, you bastard, you swine. You can't have me, my body, not anymore." A squelch, a broken wheeze, and wetness, wetness on Jehanne's nape. Weight collapsed on her. Jehanne gave in to it, let it roll off her.

Gasps. Moreau cried out. A door opened somewhere, and there were shouts and curses thrown, an argument she couldn't care about because her mind had locked down.

Father left her side. Bullets on both sides flew and chipped at the banister, and there were at least four men in blue on the main floor.

As Jehanne followed Father's feet with her eyes, he disappeared over the banister beside her. He was then on the wall below, standing like it was the floor. Her world had slanted. Not sparing a look toward her, Father freed the braquemard, and before Jehanne could shout, could find her mouth, he was on the main floor; she couldn't tell if he jumped or ran down. He staggered a little when two officers buckled their feet and shot at him, but, because she must've been dreaming, he didn't stop until he raised his sword quickly. He didn't act hurt at all. Jehanne averted her eyes, but still heard squelching clatters amid her stunned uselessness.

As she forced herself to see the dream again, the hall rippled and became the blue-green of stormy seawater. An invisible hole must've been somewhere in the space, a depression making the world crumple.

Moreau—God, she had forgotten he existed—looked the same as Father: no wings, no glowing eyes, yet his feet barely touched the ground as he sauntered. Moreau had no gun, and like Father, he hardly flinched when the officers' bullets hit him like errant rosary beads. He was so swift, it was as if time skipped, like a shoddy gramophone needle, and he twisted an officer's head so while the man's back faced Jehanne, his eyes gleamed up at her in surprise. As Father wielded the sword with ease, a bizarre, practiced grace, and Jehanne couldn't bring herself to movemovemove, Moreau was at a poor man's neck, latching on, she thought absurdly, like a little pup nursing on its mother. The officer had too little time to properly panic or fight Moreau off. They splayed together on the ground like twisting swan necks breaking under the water's weight. Father stood over Moreau and beamed. When Jehanne's eyes followed the banister on each side of her, every person whose name she, in her arrogance, hadn't bothered to know lay on the blackened floor with their useless pistols. They had died by bullets, the way Father and Moreau should've, but didn't.

Jehanne was iron and crumbling wax all at once as she looked to see the weight that'd slumped off and fallen before her. Amid the fading cries, the truth in front of her took root: Clair, twitching and convulsing, her neck sliced neatly open, her hand still grasping her knife like a precious childhood token.

Jehanne muttered, "No, God, no no no no no." She reached forward and brought Clair to her lap, but the woman kept turning her head away whenever Jehanne tried to meet her eyes or cup her face. "Mother Mary, please be kind." Blood gushed from the woman's open neck and stained Jehanne, bled through to her skin. The world, once drenched in a lazy sea wash, dried with gun smoke and rust. Dried, all except the blood.

Though Clair couldn't speak anymore, she mouthed words. Jehanne could only catch a little. *Sorry, m'sorry.*

Oh, darling. What do you have to be sorry for? Jehanne stroked her hair. *Whatever it is, I forgive you. God forgives you.* Somehow, those words in her head weren't enough. Her mind moved again, splintering its barriers, flooding, Father's slap, her head, the blood—

Hay, Catherine, sewing needles, war, smoke, Christ—

Jehanne screamed, and she remembered everything.

20

Marcy

Marcy's head throbbed, and scurrying came close to her ear. For a long stretch of time, she was only conscious of pain and skittering. The black of her vision became as gray as a January morning.

With her eyes open, she couldn't see anything but scythes of light, the crackling of her mind focusing and falling aslant. Marcy rolled on her back and saw what she believed to be the hole her attackers had thrown her down. The "wall" of earth was steep, smooth, likely impossible to grab onto, ten feet, maybe. Or fifteen. Or twenty, no, maybe seventeen. If only she had something to stand on. If she tried, she might be able to climb up and back to—where, exactly? Did she really fall from there?

Did they carry her down? And who would "they" be? Only shadows clouded her memory.

She teetered, supporting herself with both aching elbows, and, once she stood, she felt a crusty residue on the back of her neck.

A cough bubbled up, and Marcy winced. When she trailed her fingers up to the crown of her head, they came away sticky. Her mouth was dry. The—dear God, whoever overcame her as she spoke to Maman, they had put her with the demons, or whatever was down here.

They: Rais, his servants, surely not Jehanne. Surely. Jehanne was good. There had to be another explanation for Marcy's circumstances besides a risen evil man and demons. Rais was the man from history, the Monster of Machecoul, but she couldn't prove Jehanne's father was him, though a part of her wanted to. Because a monster, a demon, a wolf-man, was easier to reconcile with, easier than a mortal man of flesh and blood and gentle longings who felt sorry for raping, maiming, and killing children for hours, yet he couldn't stop. She needed to think of him as a monster from an older, extinct time. If he were Rais, she preferred a devil over the likelier reality.

Her mind was fog, and she was stuck in a pit. Priorities. Escape first, and then logic. Marcy closed her eyes, willed away the headache dampening her thoughts. Yes, priorities. She released a slight groan before clamping her mouth shut. No more noises. Maybe the demons didn't exist at all, but regardless, each possible breath and step hardened in her bones.

She slowly progressed in the darkness, but hid in the pockets of that darkness at the slightest huff or drip. As she went forward, she encountered lanterns, these thorny, squat beasts of flickering light, caged. That was good because they made her remember herself and her family. Papa would say to her, "Turn the lights off, poupée. We aren't in Versailles." But those had been electric lights, not firelights, not lights so frail they'd die from anything as gentle as a breeze.

Her heart seized, though. Anything she could see would see her too. Shivering, Marcy fumbled, a ringing in her ears. The world swam, and she cloaked herself in a sea of slithering black. In the darkness, she swore there was movement, but nothing came. Then, she heard something, coughing and moaning, deep and ragged. She couldn't tell if she was dreaming, or if the sounds came from one source.

Monstrous gold light twined around her ankles like hair, so she shuffled deeper into the shadows. The blanketing darkness might not even protect her from the light. Hell was surprisingly well-lit, indeed, and demons could probably see her even in the darkest corners.

A procession of slow thuds like footsteps. Marcy stared at the blue-yellow earth until her eyes ached. Something, something breathed on her neck, she swore it did, but nothing was behind her when she looked.

A shout came from somewhere in the dark hollows, then another. Marcy's breath hitched. It sounded like a man, and the hairs on her nape rose. The shout was ragged, like whoever it was—was it a demon? Marcy didn't want to go on, couldn't move her head without it hurting.

Wailing. Guttural sobs carried through the taut emptiness. As she inched forward, Marcy encountered nothing but lanterns. She wished she could blend into the blacker nooks, turn invisible like a nineteenth-century science fiction hero. Her legs rattled to the point she struggled to stand, to walk, and her gums stung as she clenched her teeth. Moving was like wading through an icy river with no paddle or ferryman in sight. The tunnels she came across were like the Paris ossuaries she read about. Shouldn't think about that, though. Needed to think of a warmer feeling, like the sand between her toes on a spring day. Spring, or did they go to the sea in the summer? Either way, the beach air greened Papa's eyes, and she wanted that green back.

As Marcy's mind gained more ground, her attention focused again on the lanterns. It grew harder to make herself inconspicuous, if she could even hide, as she navigated the labyrinth, tunnel upon tunnel, expecting horns to impale her once she turned a corner. Lantern light rose like yellow sulfur. Yellow sulfur, sulfur over summer's corpse. No, no talk of corpses. How did anybody place them here? Rais must have had a ladder, the bastard. Or rope.

Another echoing shout. Marcy pressed her hands against her mouth.

Lumbering footsteps thudded through the curved rock. Labored breathing in the tunnel. Marcy crawled and crouched where the most darkness pooled, but in reality, she was likely visible enough for anything that would find her, for whatever lurked nearby. No matter how she twisted or made herself smaller, she couldn't escape the lights; the pocks in the earth walls were too shallow.

Could they smell her? Someone or something had known she was menstruating, must've smelled it. If so, truth be told, she had little hope of surviving, but she couldn't stagnate in that mire of thought. No matter how much it seemed her head would burst, no matter how helpless she was, she needed to believe God wouldn't let her die like this.

Whatever slinked about in the shadows halted, feet scuffling on the ground. Marcy cupped both hands over her nose and mouth. Nothing floated in her mind, nothing with a weight to it, nothing so strong it encompassed everything. Her nails dug into her cheeks. A rhythm rushed in her head. No epiphanies, no final wishes, no pleasant family memories. All she had were the noises on the other side of the craggy yellow where lantern light played against the black and brown and blue, the moment timed by the rapid drum battering her lungs. Soggy aches in her ribs, limbs, an acute point in her head pounding with blood.

Her own heartbeat and the void flooded her mind, distracted her from noticing if the presence, or presences, had moved on. Even when nothing disturbed Marcy for over a minute, when nothing alerted her of a close person or thing, she refused to budge. If she didn't keep going, though, something would find her. Bitterness filled the hollow of her heart, as did the need to blame someone for her predicament. People, people who thought they could do whatever they wished in the dim, unsupervised corridors of their decaying castles and manors. Rites, sacrifices, Rais' yellowed words.

A putrid taste flooded Marcy's mouth. Heat pulsed all the way to her fingertips, and she closed her sore eyes. Couldn't look. If she didn't look, it helped. Couldn't search, couldn't find.

Why hadn't anyone saved her yet? God, she wanted Jehanne.

Realizing she needed to be strong, Marcy tried to slow her breathing. She needed to be like the poised movie women in the newspaper ads, the ones across the ocean, like Helen or Pearl. Or Grace, Grace Darmond with her dark, soulful eyes and curly hair.

Marcy didn't release her grip on herself until her breathing slowed, and she registered the pain in her left hand. She'd bitten her palm. She'd never find her way back if she went farther. She possessed no golden yarn, so she remained close to the ground, close to a bulge, a boulder in the pit's almost perfect design. Stunned and unsure how to proceed, she waited to face a red-mouthed minotaur. A hulking, molten-skinned thing, that was what must be close to her, and she needed to run, run like the Devil nipping at a sinner's heels.

She didn't. Marcy stayed in the shadows, so whatever was there with her wouldn't see her. Breathing, breathing in her ears, might've been her own. Her mind emptied, leaked out the back of her skull, and hopelessness arrived, little tendrils. The blue shadows blurred with the lantern's glow. Her head kept throbbing. No matter how much she curled into herself, no matter how much she refused to look, the dark stared. The entire clan of shadows inspected her.

Though Marcy, given her age and sheltered life, had never been in perilous caverns, she knew it was unwise to venture toward the loud darkness. She bore all of herself into the dark wall of earth. If she picked a corner to hide in like when she was little, she would live. It was a game; she could only lose if she gave in to looking at the void.

If she died now, her life would mean nothing. She had people who loved her. She'd had them all along. There was that rift, and she'd done nothing to help her home, much less the world, become better in ways that had mattered. She couldn't face the darkness alone, but she did so right now, even when her heart thumped so hard and fast it came close to giving out.

The air stilled, tightened with loneliness, then a noise resounded, echoed to the point that Marcy couldn't tell where it originated.

A panicked voice called, "Help! Help! Anyone, someone, please!"

Marcy's blood froze; the moment stuck like a fly in sap. Her eyes snapped open. (When had they closed?) The voice was familiar, but it was a demon trick, a trap, a delusion. It had to be.

"Help, please, someone!" The coarse voice pierced her pounding heart, as exact as a doctor's scalpel. She didn't call back, even when a name wadded up in her throat. The voice was small, but it sounded like it was by her ear. How long had it called to the darkness before giving up and deciding to start again later? Or worse, had something answered it before slinking back to the tunnels?

A rank, half-earthy odor she couldn't explain overwhelmed her nose. She imagined the ground vomiting, but it was worse, yet nothing like a pastry left out too long, nothing like the rot she knew. As foolish as it sounded, that was the most experience she had with decay, with death, except for one morning not so long ago. With the singing and smell of fresh bread, the morning she couldn't think of.

Stumbling, gasping when a lantern fell over and the shouts continued, she followed the voice, followed, followed, and she blurrily saw there on the craggy, lit wall, a body in a "Y" like Christ, shackles like faint Christmas lights. Marcy squinted to make sense of everything, and her eyes grew large. Footsteps came behind her, but they didn't sway her attention away from the sight before her.

"André?"

21

Jehanne

Her memories surged.

Knee resting against Maman's, Jehanne mended a sleeve on their hay bed. Sewing was her favorite distraction from the day. Besides, if she didn't mend clothes, her family would be naked all the time, and she would rather avoid that. Her brothers laughed and joked outside the cottage, and confused roosters crowed in the pink of dusk.

Maman, her hair long, pale, and uncombed, tensely paused from sewing up Papa's drawers. Jehanne set down the shirt and gripped Maman's shoulder. "Maman, what is it? Is it about Catherine?" She missed her older sister every day. She didn't miss the cold cloths, the wheezing, the angry, rose-colored rashes. Roses, what a terrible way to describe those hateful marks.

The rattle of that last breath, the moment the Spirit rolled like a wave across Jehanne's shoulder, and she broke for Catherine. After that, Maman and Papa were more protective than ever about what water the children drank and what food they ate, when they had something to eat. Everyone washed their hands in the basin more. The grief hung close as they all huddled together at night in their only bed. When her breaths grew ragged as she thought about the English coming to hurt her family, Jehanne begged to God and the saints for help, hoping Catherine was happy now and that her family would be safe and live long.

Maman stared at the floor, shoulders low. "Your papa keeps having these dreams about you. Each night this month."

Jehanne prickled. She was no stranger to repeated dreams, but she couldn't tell a soul for fear of accusations that she was a witch committing some form of divination. "The same dream?"

Maman's mouth was thin and grave. They cast aside their needles and met each other's eyes. "Yes."

"What does he see?"

"He sees you running off with the soldiers in the war, and he thinks you'll be . . . one of the women in the camps." Maman drew a shaky breath, her mouth curling in contempt on *women*. "He told me he'd rather drown you than for you to be in that sort of unholy place. And if he dies, he wants your brothers to drown you if you try to make that come to pass."

Ice doused Jehanne. All the laughter and crowing died away. "He isn't serious, is he? He's Papa. You wouldn't let him do that, would you?"

"The Virgin as my witness, I'd do whatever I could to save you, even from yourself. Better dead than a whore, wouldn't you agree? Is that the life you'd want? Would you?" Maman was shaking her.

Jehanne eyes watered, avoiding Maman by staring at the meager hearth they slept by in the winter. "I don't know."

Maman shook her shoulders again. "Don't know? Why would you say that? How could you even think for a moment we'd accept that?"

"But death, Maman?" Jehanne squeaked. Maman only had two daughters, after all, and unless another was born, Jehanne was the only one left in this lifetime.

"You must stay pure. Even if you were to die young, my little dove, what is this life compared to what's to come?" Maman pulled her close when Jehanne sobbed. "Don't worry, shh. It won't come to that, so long as you stay good, indeed?" The last word was more of a question than Jehanne liked.

Did Maman want an answer? Jehanne appreciated her life of prayer and sewing. It had austere meaning; every night, before she slept, she felt accomplished because she could mend clothes and speak to the angels and saints. Yet, the same voices told her to go elsewhere, into places that would horrify Maman and Papa in different ways than those dreams.

You were born to do this, Michael had told her with a flaming sword he held, but he hadn't meant using her needles (which she never stopped loving) or cupping her hands in prayer before nestling beside Maman at night.

Then, just like that, Maman was gone, and blood, blood overcame Jehanne, the stink swelling in her nose and mouth. Jehanne smeared tears against the back of her hand like she was a girl again. Sick for home like Ruth after she was widowed, barley rows shuttering her crumpled, weeping body from view. If, back then, Jehanne had fled back home before she went to court and met the Dauphin, if she'd been in Maman's arms again, and they could apologize to each other, them and her entire laughing family, they could've—

Jehanne was in Gilles' arms, and she barely moved as scarlet stained his chain mail. He said between gasps, "Your neck, your leg, their damn arrows can pierce armor. No, no, don't speak. We're almost there." Gilles stumbled but kept upright, and Jehanne hardened her grip on something, a flutter of white. A standard, she had her white-knuckled grip on a tapering flag, the pole dragging the ground, scoring the dirt. She wouldn't let it go, no matter how far Gilles carried her, and he didn't say another word to her. Wind hit her scalp, and she realized her leather cap had fallen somewhere. She imagined it as a hurt kitten on scuffed earth.

Gilles faded, and her vision melted till she was crouching by a fire. The air smelled of woodsmoke that night at camp. She sat alone with Gilles. They were wearing simple jerkins and pants. Gilles was a handsome man, to be sure, and not much older than Jehanne, though she hadn't taken in either of those observations fully while they'd been comrades. His hair was almost silver in the firelight.

When she caught his eye, he rubbed her cheek. She was too tired to flinch away. Besides, it felt good to be treated softly by one of her companions. At least there was this bit of goodness left in the world, this and her hope that God would deliver them all and let them win this war.

"The angels were gracious to us." Gilles' blue eyes flickered black and gold. "I thought you'd die, and I would've never forgiven myself."

Jehanne traced an arrow wound on her leg, then shifted to the bandage on her neck. "I thought I only owed my life to God, but I owe it to you too."

He laughed. "You gave Le Basque a scare when you stormed back into the battle after you were wrapped up."

She pouted. "He had my standard."

"You were supposed to rest."

Jehanne lifted her chin and scowled. "It's my standard. And the English commander called me Satan's whore. Was I supposed to take an arrow and that insult in silence?"

"If you curse any more men, the English may think you're a witch."

Jehanne snorted and rubbed her fingers against her hose. "Let them think that. God knows my heart, in the end."

"How did a girl of your raising learn to be so bold?"

Jehanne leaned back, brow furrowing, her mind elsewhere. Let the rich man think as he wished. "I don't know. Is it boldness? How is it that the swords and arrows can make me so terrified, yet full of life and meaning all at once?"

In the middle of battle, as she rode with her armor, standard, and little else, Jehanne couldn't think much past the angel Michael's words to her. His wings were like the fire pouring from Heaven's spigot, and his song congealed in her blood. His face was a star-pocked amalgamation of a jackal, a frog, and an owl; it made her cry in wonder to look upon it. The saints Catherine and Margaret were her water, her hands tight against the standard. The river of their songs flooded her like she was a penitent, wrapped in savage grace.

"I want you to follow me wherever I go. You're my guardian now. My flesh-and-blood one, anyhow." Jehanne had had a dream that the sky darkened to a violent, thrumming amber and a man with a lion's head, a ruby-studded mane, and a melting crown threw her into a seething abyss. But so long as Gilles was by her side, Jehanne was unafraid. Between God and him, her life stretched harrowing but long ahead of her. She'd show Maman and Papa how cruel, how dismissive they were in their errant attempts to protect her. She couldn't wait for their humbly accepted apologies.

"Is that meant to be a reward?"

Jehanne half-smiled. "You could consider it an honor. You saved my life. I need you with me as my protector. Will you promise God and Mary that you'll be at my side when the worst's to come?"

"I promise you I'll follow you to my death and after, if need be." He changed the subject abruptly, his voice an urgent whisper, "What are angel voices like?"

Jehanne grunted. "Why would you want to know?" His eyes were an uncomfortable blue, their color heightened by the campfire. Without stars in the sky, he was the brightest thing there.

"Who *wouldn't* want to know if they had the chance?"

She stared at the languid flames. "Like this."

"Fire?" Fire, the fire in her blood, the fire that wedded her to God.

"Yes, the flames of Heaven. You'll hear them one day. It's not the same when I describe them."

"You're an odd one."

"Is that an insult? Do you doubt me?" She had faith better than anyone; she knew God better than anyone. That may've been prideful, but after the court indignities she suffered, she deserved to boast what she could.

"No. I wouldn't have asked if I was—God forbid and save my soul—atheistic in any way."

"Then why do I hear judgment?" She kicked a pebble by her foot and fidgeted. She needed her needle and thread; they always calmed her.

Gilles lifted one side of his mouth. "Like I said, you're odd. You weep for the English devils. You have a soft heart."

Jehanne frowned. "It's terrible to die before you can have a final confession."

"They don't deserve your pity because they wouldn't return it. Do you know what they'd do to you if given the chance? If you were in one of their prisons, do you know what the guards would do to a girl?"

Indeed, it'd be better to have a way to defend herself. She had had a sword she never used in battle, but she had broken it when she smacked the flat of it on a camp follower's backside in a fit of rage. Whether the blade was weak or the woman's hind too firm, Jehanne didn't know. Her men were meant to pray and fight for France, not lech about; nevertheless, her anger cost her the only means of self-defense.

Jehanne grunted and removed her cap. "I do know. I suppose it's just the same as what we would do to our enemies." She scratched the base of her shorn hair.

If I should die, best to die serving God. My men won't forsake me, God won't forsake me, ever.

The world was streaked gold, a vibrating globe of lightning, and she stood in a crowd with all eyes on her.

A crowd, a crowd, yes, yes, she understood now. After the throne room spectacle, after the Siege of Orléans. She was God's warrior meant to save her people till her death. The summer day, so perfect, smelled of sweat, wood, and anticipation. A good day for a kindling. For a second, she was standing next to a man in chain mail making a wooden cross, then a man in white robes wordlessly offered the cross to her. The priest's skin was wrinkled, and his eyes were sad.

A man with a black hood over his head walked to her and said in English, "Forgive me."

"I forgive you," Jehanne offered in the best English she could manage, touching his chest with her palm, and he shuddered.

In a stuttering flash like God's run, she was bound to a wooden pillar and dressed in white as she pleaded with the people near the wood to back away, so they wouldn't be burned. She couldn't hear her own cries. Her throat ached. She wanted to talk to the sullen priest, though she didn't know what to say. He looked like Papa; he looked like he would listen. She considered talking about the relief she'd feel once she died, and she could be with Catherine again, sitting in the old lavender field and tickling stray cats' chins till they purred.

In the smoke and blood and tears, Jehanne knew who she was. She stopped gasping. The heft of her body didn't falter because she could see the Son, could feel the Virgin's warm hold shielding her from pain, an embrace so like Maman's before Catherine died. The smoke billowed black. Tear-obscured faces of dead soldiers in the sky. King Charles. Visions, fleeting as raindrops hitting hot soil. She said one word over and over until she could speak no more.

"Jesus. Jesus. Jesusjesus*jesusjesus*."

Christ hung before her, his expression twisted, but his eyes kind. The worst of everything was over now. Her meager flesh fell away, as simple and yielding as linen, exposing her bones. She was no longer Jehanne, but united with God, God staring at Creation with all his hydra flowers, and she saw the pyre dampened briefly so the executioner could tear her clothes off as a final humiliation, as proof that a witch couldn't escape judgment. The cap she was forced to wear, a meager thing with her crimes sewn into the felt, dropped away when her head dropped to the side.

Jehanne's soul returned to her body, that husk of original sin. She was still coughing and crying from the smoke. She choked on it again and again. Far from shaven away, her hair sheeted across her vision like rain on glass. Her nose bled, and when she wiped it, she streaked Clair's blood on her skin. The manor reeked of death and sulfur, and Jehanne opened her eyes to witness the dead, the bodies littering the main hall. Only two beings moved: Fa—Gilles and Moreau. Gilles stood like a sentinel, a cemetery statue, frozen, observing.

Moreau was like a loup-garou. Though his appearance hadn't changed, no long fangs or wide nose, he was a pretty, golden-haired beast of teeth and nails with inhuman quickness. He lapped up a near-black puddle with his tongue and all fingers, sucking on them like sticky candy coated them. God, he was riddled with bullets, and so was Gilles, but they gave no indication of pain.

Moreau crawled, latched on to a headless officer's shoulder, ripped the thick fabric off as if it were parchment, and sank his teeth into the man's throat, slurping and crunching his way through.

Did he and Fa—Gilles really kill them all? Kill everyone but me? Devils, the both of them.

Gilles ascended the stairs before her, one hand sliding along the banister, sword wielded in the other, till he came to where Jehanne held Clair—and Clair, she worked to breathe as her eyes dimmed; she still lived as Jehanne mourned and cradled her close like a sick infant.

An unwelcome voice broke through the grief: "He likes the taste, it seems." To her former war companion's credit, he had aged well after five centuries, and his terrifying beauty disgusted her, that calm, unmoving paleness that, with the spilling of blood, became unlined and unstressed.

Jehanne asked, attention on Moreau below, "What is he?" She looked at Gilles. "What are you? What did you do to him?"

He dropped the sword, and if Jehanne wasn't clutching Clair, she had three-quarters a mind to skewer him, if that'd do anything.

"It's amazing what one does when faced with a forever-life, or dying in obscurity."

"And how much of that was his choice, Gilles?"

Eyes flashing with wolfish glee, Gilles fell to the floor beside her. "Do you remember?"

That didn't answer her question. "Remember what? You—I . . ." He set a hand on her cheek and she flinched away. "Get off, you beast!" He persisted and was unfazed when she punched his bloodied shirt, the skin and bone beneath hurting her knuckles, as if Gilles had an iron carapace. "Go—Gilles, stop!"

"Do you remember everything?" To himself, he muttered, "Will nothing I say make you forget this?"

"How could you? I was. . . ."

"Jehanne, and you still are." The hay, her tiny little home in Domrémy. Her sister. "The Maid of Orléans. You couldn't forget Orléans, could you?"

She wouldn't have, but if she'd been brought back unnaturally—had she ever been truly sick? Had the teas she'd been given only been there not to better her health and assist her sleep, but to make her permanently forgetful? Had her nosebleeds been her head fighting its locks?

He took my wings.

"No, it's not true. This can't be true. It can't be. *I* can't be." But these visions of her first life—the ringing, which she realized, in terror, were voices. Terrible, beautiful voices.

Kill the demons. All of them. Cast them in fire.

"And why not? Isn't this a miracle?" He reeked of blood and wine.

Kill them all.

"I was in Heaven. Why are we here? Why aren't we dead? And how could you, Gilles? How could you be like this? How am I here? How did you bring me back?"

"I was like this before we met, and I'll explain." He shook his head and chuckled, as if in jest, despite his ruined clothes and hair matted dry and black.

"What happened to my real maman and papa? My brothers?" The only person's fate she knew for certain was Catherine.

He sighed. So cavalier, and she loathed him for it more than she loathed anyone, even the English captains. "I don't know. Your mother helped overturn your conviction after your death."

"And my papa?"

"I don't know." Jehanne tasted blood, and Gilles' widened eyes made her realize it was her own.

"Oh, darling, your nose."

Yes, I noticed.

Cast him in fire.

A bone-splintering cold entered her body and sent spiderweb tremors down her arms. "I am not your darling, or your pup." Jehanne snarled. "How could you not know what happened to them if you've been alive so long, you useless beast?" She had run away to pursue her divine duty to France, and it had been the first and last time she disobeyed her parents. Their final wish, had she strayed, was her death. "I was—what happened to my ashes?"

"You were dumped into the Seine like trash!" His face contorted in agony. "And I left you, spied on you for the Crown, betrayed you, left you to die. We all abandoned you when you needed us the most."

"What have you done?" she asked once more, having no time for this tripe. Her burning had happened in the 1400s; she was past it by now. "What could you've possibly done to bring me back to this Hell?" She couldn't imagine. Even as a disobedient child, Jehanne had tried to be good, to not suffer like this. As the angel and the saints had instructed, Jehanne had donned a cap, surcoat, and hose. If Papa had seen her, he would've cuffed her ear till she was half-deaf. She sewed Mary and Jesus' names into her standard and kissed them before her prayers. She had been good, and she had died.

"You murderer, you devil," Jehanne gasped, fixated on Clair's shining eyes.

Kill every devil. Kill them all.

"Wasn't I a murderer then, in our time together? Didn't I kill more men for our cause?"

Supporting Clair's head with a palm, Jehanne wiped away the woman's tears with her other hand, though she only smeared more blood as she tried. "Not like this."

"How was the war more just than this? I've been in Hell without you. My masters gave me life again, so I could give you a second chance."

"And how long has that been, your time without me?"

"Centuries."

"I never . . . you want me as your, your . . ."

266

Gilles scoffed, as if out of all his sins, her insinuation offended him the most. "It's more than *that.*"

A statement he'd made caught up with her. "Your 'masters'? Gilles, no, don't tell me you . . ."

His pupils darkened as he withdrew, voice rough and deeper inside his throat. "At first, it was only silver I wanted for my soul, because of the mad spending I did while I was alive, but then it was never enough, and so I— that was so long ago."

"What?" Jehanne shot him a glare. "What did you do to bring me back?" She yanked on his ruined tunic, hoping the half-undone collar hurt as it tugged against his bruised neck.

He closed his eyes. "I can't."

She cast an arm to the ruin around her. "You've done this, yet you can't say—God, what did you do? You told me of your wife, and what could be worse than that and this?" Horror sank in. "Where is Marcy? The wine cellar? Under it with the demons?"

Casually, Gilles remarked with a blank stare, "You need to bathe and rest before I tell you everything."

"D-did you kill her? Did you kill her like you've killed everyone here?" All Jehanne had wanted was an end to her loneliness, a companion not obligated to serve her, and now she could've very well killed Marcy by inviting her friend here because she hadn't taken "Father" seriously, had tried to reason away all the strange happenings to something wrong with her head.

"No, she's alive."

"Are you lying just to make me calm?" She could still hear the crunch of Moreau eating bones. "Because, given the circumstances, you'll have a poor time of it. Take me to her. The wine cellar, that's where, isn't it?"

Gilles' breaths were rapid. "I can't. You can't see what's beneath the manor."

"What, the demons? Is that it? Are they your friends?"

"I wish."

"Is that how we're alive? You serve demons under the floor and sacrifice innocents to them?" She needed to find Marcy, needed to go to the wine cellar. No time. The manor only had so many halls.

"Close. Not quite." He was infuriatingly coy, but no matter, she'd make him confess after she saved her friend.

Both Jehanne and Gilles swerved their heads when, in the near-silence, Clair's gasps became starker.

Jehanne ground her teeth together. "I need to pray for her."

Gilles reached for her shoulder, but she jerked away. "There's no use in it." Because of him, and he didn't sound remorseful. Not for his wife Catherine, not for those who died, and not for Clair. "She's hopeless."

The monster. Yet, for all his murders, he still looked like Gilles. She didn't know what she expected of Gilles, besides outward ugliness. Demons were meant to be hideous, but what did that say about her and her own knowledge of holiness, when many demons were once angels themselves? If God loved the imperfect, Jehanne thought as she looked upon Clair's open throat, she shouldn't have aligned deformity with damnation.

"All the more reason she needs it." No matter her part in this, Jehanne couldn't let Clair die alone.

Then, she had a plan. Of course she did, didn't she always, eventually? Pray and then run to Marcy. Go to the wine cellar, where Gilles kept his doves. If she could stand. Her legs were lead. She had to go, to stand, to run, but she could only remain with the dying woman.

Gilles persisted, "Jehanne, I'll wait for you in the study, where it's quiet." He casted a glance at Moreau. "Promise you won't disappear, and I'll explain what I've done all these centuries, what I am, how we're alive. Please, as long as you're here, I can live, and I'm certain you'll forgive me with that heart of yours."

"I promise," Jehanne lied. Well, half-lied. After she disappeared to find Marcy, she'd definitely meet Gilles again, but not for the reasons he hoped. Thankfully, he left them, Jehanne, Clair, and Moreau. She rested one hand on Clair's cheek, the other on the woman's neck. Her own neck throbbed, and she still heard Moreau feeding below. Though the smacking and splintering uneased her, his attention never diverted from the corpses.

When Clair's heartbeat left her throat and her soul left Jehanne's hold, Jehanne still prayed through obligation. She wanted to think Clair's death had meaning, peace and forgiveness, but it was cruel, meaningless.

Peace. Forgiveness. It reminded Jehanne of Gilles by her side moments ago, him and his desperate pleas for her to rest, for her to give him a second or third or fourth chance. Did he ask God for the same so long as he thought he could repent and absolve everything? Was that why he raised his head to God with demons under his boots?

It all needs to burn. The bastard, the bastard. He needs to burn.

Death was needless here, needless and empty, and even if Clair flew to Heaven, God had given her the potential for a full life for a reason. Her own motivations, and, yes, He had planned this too—no, she couldn't think of it, her head swelled like a rat was curled inside it. She wasn't meant to be alive. If God needed her to protect others, Jehanne had already failed.

You can save so many by turning this all to ash. No time to think anymore, no time to adjust to this new skin stretching across her bones.

With Clair still in her lap, Jehanne jolted when the front door creaked open below.

22

Marcy

"André?"

"Marcy?" He croaked. "Oh God, how the hell did you . . ." They stopped and took each other in. She had no words for how he looked. Whatever the original color of his shirt was, it was black now.

She asked, "What are you doing here?"

"Funny thing, that." He coughed, a rough and deep noise that made Marcy nervous. "I was in the woods, after visiting a friend and playing cards. I think I—it was night. I walked into the woods to take a smoke without the smell bothering anyone. Was drunk and cursing Tante like the fair-minded lad I am. Saw men accosting a-a little boy with this shining, this cross around his neck. Two—three men? Beating him over the head with a wooden club. Blood, the boy's mouth, everywhere. Tried to fight. Went to punch—him, the leader, and he laughed off a hit to the nose, and next thing I knew, it was dark and hurting. Can't feel my legs."

"Hurting?" Marcy's stomach roiled, and she meant to ask about the boy, but her gaze shot to André's bare feet, particularly the left one. "God, André, why is your foot swollen like a melon? And it's purple." Like a berry.

"Reassuring, thanks. Twisted it fighting. That luck of mine, you know."

"I think I can—it needs to be wrapped, right?"

"I'd say so," André said, dryly. "But not much'll be done with me like this." Half his face was bloated, and his breaths were strained. "Are you intact?"

Marcy tilted her head, dizziness making her see double. "As far as I know."

He wheezed, and it might've been a laugh. "That's as good as anything, I suppose."

Scrabbling (claws?) came from behind. Marcy seized, and yet the possibilities gripped her so tightly she couldn't bring herself to panic.

Maman, I think you're about to receive your wish. Marcy shook her head and banished the dark thought. No, bigger issues, priorities. War, darkness, screaming, her cousin chained up. Escape.

André's cheeks were wet, his eyes pink and wild in the lantern light. Blood had crusted under his nose, but it seemed whoever had damaged his nose had also reset it, as if they could handle the blood but not any crookedness.

"What happened to your nose?"

André's mirthless sneer was a startling black. "The monsieur was kind enough to reset it after he broke it. Didn't want me to be ugly."

Uncomfortable with forcing the issue, Marcy focused on his restraints. "God, how do I get you out of these?"

"We need to go before something gets us. There's something, the key, the doves, where he keeps his doves, it's, it's. . . ." André choked.

"Doves?" The footsteps were closer than ever. "Do you hear that? The demons, or whatever's down here . . ." Marcy turned.

Small figures emerged into the light, bodies covered in grime and scuttling oddly, like crabs. The lanterns cast grotesque, bruise-like shadows on them.

André coughed, drew a long, loud breath. He shook in his chains.

Children, three, no, four shaking children. Three boys, one girl, all in torn, disheveled clothes. One of the boys had busted lips and an eye swollen shut. The other two boys had dried blackness on their chins. Marcy couldn't register the truth, even when everything confirmed her suspicions about Rais. A fissure split in her head. The stories of the man who professed to be her only friend's father—

It couldn't be, but it was.

André said of the children, "We've kept each other company for—however long it's been."

Children, no chains, limping freely. A dark voice said to her, *Easy to catch and subdue. The monsieur can fend against children well.*

Christ. Remembering herself, Marcy said to the children, "What are your names?"

"Addie, Jacques, Jules, Isaac," the girl answered, pointing to herself and each boy.

"Well, I'm happy to meet you all." She took more note of their clothes then, and whatever color they once were, the garments were now indistinguishably gray and black. In places, gems glinted on the grimy fabric like flies.

"I saw where he put the key, the key to the circles," Addie said, and Marcy leaned forward.

"Where is it?"

"In the mouth."

Marcy's brow furrowed. "Where?"

"In the mouth, the one in the chair, through there. He stuck it in the mouth."

"What? Who put it there?"

Addie wept. "The blue man stuck a key in the mouth."

"Whose?" she asked, meaning whose mouth.

"The blue man. He—he doesn't—he likes to chase us before. The master and his servants."

Before what? Marcy would've asked, but thought better of it. She tried to embrace the upset girl, to comfort any of the children and listen, but they moved away from her touch.

"Marcy," André said, his voice ragged. "Don't leave me."

"The shackles, I can't get them off without the key."

274

"No, dear God, you might not—please stay where I can see you. Please. Please don't leave me." Begging, he was begging in a tone she'd never heard from him.

"I'm so sorry," she said, and to the children, she muttered, "I'll find our way out, but can you show me where the key is? Show me, please." She pivoted toward André again. "I'll come back, I promise."

"Please, please don't go." He released a sob. "Don't go, I'm begging you." She noticed a dark stain on the inside of his slacks.

With a pinprick chill creeping up her arms, Marcy swallowed. She didn't know what he'd gone through or how to comfort him, and she thought it rude to ask while he unraveled. She crossed the distance and rested a hand on his dirt-crusted cheek. "Oh, trust me, cousin. I'll be back. I promise to God."

André made a noise between a scoff and another sob. "Might want to ask someone who'll actually listen."

Marcy didn't have time to question his lack of faith. "I promise to Papa, then." With a watery smile, though it hurt, she left André there in the dark and followed the children to find the key, the way to André's freedom.

None of the children offered their hands to her, but they led her, five little Virgils with strange gaits. To speak to them, Marcy stopped and settled on her knees. Because she was becoming taller than Maman and almost Papa, she thought she must've dwarfed the children while standing, scared them if she got too close.

"It's okay. It'll be okay, sweet ones. If someone comes, I'll kick them for you. I've a heavy kick." Her words fell as flat as a book page.

"There, in there," one of the boys said, a boy with tawny hair and a swollen eye.

The children stopped as Marcy went forward. They refused to follow Marcy past a certain point. Inching forward, turning her head, Marcy realized she no longer saw the children. A sensation bothered her throat, the phantom tickling of when she saw a spider and then jolted at every sensation because she'd spared it, and her mind told her it lurked somewhere on her body.

Marcy followed the lantern trail, picking up one of the bulky things. Earthy mounds protruded like turgid worms, light passing over them like a watery reflection. As she traveled, shoes scuffing along, her headache worsened, and the smoother rocks rotated like the eyes of a flounder. A glow emanated down the tunnel, a kind, hopeful light brighter than any of the underground prison's other glimmers. Warmth, welcome, the end to the struggle. After Marcy found the key and saved André, they'd find a way to climb out. She could taste freedom, as green as an apple's skin, and it made the aches in her chest worth it.

She stood and sprinted as her lantern and the lights on the earth gave way to—

Marcy halted and lost her grip of the handle. The lantern didn't break, but the flickering light died.

Urine ran hot down her legs.

23

Rosalie

Waking up beside Roger that November morning was the worst thing she'd experienced, and Juliette and Maman's deaths crushed her further. But what Rosalie saw when she opened the leering manor's front door came a close fourth.

"Christ." She didn't think she'd ever see this many bodies at once. Was this like Anatole's experience in the morgue? Even then, those bodies were clean. This was utter madness, carnage she thought she'd been numbed to after reading enough in the paper about men's faces melting behind masks, and their feet rotting away like spoiled meat after weeks in a trench carved out by the Devil's pitchfork.

A man, a man who looked like a demon. Blood drenched him so much, Rosalie couldn't tell what his hair color was. He bolted his head up, his pupils so large his eyes were only gold with the light glaring on black.

He lurched upward by some power other than his feet and stepped forward with a half-ring of cartilage in his mouth. She pointed her pistol, yet before she could shoot, or before he could accost her, he looked to the stairs where a girl sat with a body in her arms. The girl glowered at him, and he trembled, meat and blood falling from his mouth as he wheezed.

When he looked back to Rosalie, they stared at one another for what seemed like a minute. She could die now, she realized, but Marcy was here and needed help. Her finger grew heavy on the trigger.

He looked again at the girl on the landing. Eventually, as if deciding Rosalie unworthy, he knelt and returned to the scraps of the—God, it was one of the officers Marcy had called. She could tell from the dim glow of the badge.

Marcy. She had to cross this sea of bodies.

No blood, no death, nobloodnodeath.

Blood—Roger. Juliette with blood on her pillow, and her squalling babe calling for her as the doctor covered her head with a white sheet.

Her walk was slow, a childhood song playing in her head to help her cross. When Rosalie ascended the steps, a hand covering her mouth and nose, the girl's sullen face changed little. It had the wan shroud of mourning.

"Are you Jehanne?"

The girl sniffed wetly. "Y-yes." She coughed once. "Yes."

"I'm Marcy's mother." Looking to the woman in Jehanne's arms, Rosalie asked, "What happened here?"

The girl straightened. "I don't know how to explain it, other than there was a fight."

Jesus, Mary, and Joseph, I'd say so!

Rosalie swallowed, doing her best not to smell or taste anything. "Where—where's my daughter?"

Jehanne's voice tremored, and yet her expression was eerily still. "She isn't here, but I—I think I know where to find her. The wine cellar, I think we can find it."

A cellar?

"So, you'll show me to it?"

"I'll try." After she stared warily at the pistol, Jehanne's eyes roved down to the woman in her arms. "She was my, my . . ."

Jehanne leaned down to kiss the woman's temple before setting the body down and working to stand. She then patted the woman's apron to find something, it appeared, a bump in a pocket; she fished out a napkin crumpled into a ball. She sobbed, looking at them.

Unsure how to offer proper condolences, Rosalie said, "I'm sorry. I—" The poor girl almost fell and, with the woman's body between them, Rosalie reached forward and worked to steady the blood-soaked, distant-eyed girl.

When she righted herself, Jehanne croaked, "Thank you, Madame Deibler."

"Please, call me Rosalie. We're well past formalities."
She looked down. "This woman . . ."

"Her name was Clair."

"I'm sorry you lost her. I wish I could be of better help."

Voice lifeless, Jehanne said, "It'll be okay. It'll all be over soon. The worst is over."

As they went down the stairs, Rosalie keeping a wary eye on the man-demon, they limped arm in arm together until panic lit a fire under Rosalie's pace.

She wouldn't bury Marcy.

"This way, I think," Jehanne said, and they took a left and kept silent for a good minute. When they'd made it halfway across the hall to the cellar, the girl said, "Gilles killed everyone, everyone except . . ."

Rosalie tensed, unsure who Gilles was. Or if he was still here. "What is that thing, that man?"

"I wish I knew. Or maybe I don't, not anymore." She heaved a raspy sigh. "And Gilles, I thought he was my father, but everyone I loved is dead. I have no one."

The poor girl. "Marcy cares about you."

"You think I'm mad, don't you?" It wasn't said in indignation. If anything, she sounded distant. After what Jehanne had witnessed, Rosalie couldn't blame her.

"No—"

"It doesn't matter. This will all be better when Gilles dies and never hurts anyone again."

Rosalie's brow furrowed, shoulders going upright. Though she didn't mind company, homicidal company was another matter. "Yes, well . . ." Marcy mattered most.

Although, really, she should be gentler with this girl after what she'd endured. "Marcy, we . . . unless you need to rest, and I can go alone?"

A light returned to the girl's eyes, a flicker like steel, which Rosalie took as a good omen.

As they checked hall doors, Jehanne grumbled, "Most of these doors are locked." She froze. "I need to go back and find the keys."

"Where would those be?"

"Gilles must—damn him."

Rosalie's throat burned, but she held the panic at bay. Instead of dissolving, she set her pistol on the table and undid part of her hair, taking the pins and bending so she was eye level with the keyhole.

"Pray this'll work," she told Jehanne, who made a noise that was half-grunt, half-question. With the pieces of metal pinched between her fingers, Rosalie worked the lock until it gave.

"How do you know that?"

"My maman had her tricks when my sister and I tried to lock her out of our rooms."

"But how did that teach you?"

"She taught us when we were older in case we needed it."

"By God, you'll need to teach me that." A lighter tone, hopeful.

When Rosalie unlocked the door, the wood gave way to a barren room with a crooked curtain festooning a window and resting defeated on the carpet. The only other object of interest was a piano with dust layering the keys.

Jehanne huffed. "This isn't it. This'll take forever, and when *he* comes back to look for me—" Before she had finished, Rosalie brushed past her with her pistol and pins. If it would take forever to find Marcy, they'd best be quick.

Eventually, after checking door after door, they reached the end of a dim hall with a single white door with two paper notes. Rosalie read the first:

Do not open to preserve quality of wine.

Convincing. The second note:

Tristan, if you drink yourself stupid and vomit on the study upholstery again, please clean it yourself. I have other important matters to attend to at the master's behest, and I do not wish to be distracted from fulfilling my important duties. —M.C.

"Here we are," Jehanne said, shoulders falling as she finished reading the second note.

Rosalie hoped Marcy would be on the other side of the door, running toward them with a relieved grin once the wood creaked open.

After Rosalie unlocked it, they climbed down the groaning, mildewed steps. When they reached the bottom, her first thought was that, despite being a wine cellar, there was no wine at all. Instead, a fetid stench permeated the air, and she swiftly found the source: a gray wheelbarrow stained with brown matter so clumped together it looked like black welts. Strands of hair stuck to the sides.

How could this filthy, bodiless wheelbarrow fit down the stairs? Why did it smell like that? What was here?

Blood, so much dried blood.

Who was here?

Rosalie clamped a hand over her mouth. "Can this be?" She gagged.

Jehanne trembled. "She—she—he said she was alive. She must be. God, he—I'm supposed to protect her." She began whispering, "I need to be strong. I need to be strong."

Rosalie was nothing. *Love is the mother of death.* All her life, the more she wanted to voice her grief or love, the less she could. *God, You can't let her die too.*

Babel, all her life was Babel. Fractured and crumbling, scattering into incomprehensible pieces, buried and forgotten in the sand like Ozymandias. Gone, unable to be rebuilt.

She had nothing. The dead have nothing and shake dust and spiders at Charon.

She couldn't bury Marcy—

She couldn't—

She couldn't—

All her thoughts were of the past because the present and future had ended, but the past always trickled, always rippled like the Lethe, and now she was drained. Rosalie murmured, "You—you said this was where she'd be, didn't you? This is blood, blood and other—other . . ." Bones poked out of the black mass.

"I don't know. I don't know. I don't know. I'm supposed to protect her," Jehanne said.

That was the end of it. Rosalie crumpled, body hitting the ground with such force it rattled her teeth. She wasn't blessed enough to faint, staring into the pit. The darkness.

The terrible stench became her world. Marcy was hers, hers to carry wherever God led and buried them. And so here she'd stay. The more Rosalie tried to calm her breathing, the worse it got.

She broke.

She died that day in spirit, that day when she wept in the washroom and she leaked milk, blood, tears. Death was a long, ragged scream still ringing in her ears, still Hell.

I had a dove and the sweet dove died. Jehanne needed her; she was just a girl, but Rosalie was dead. *O, what could it grieve for?* Marcy needed her, but she was dead. *Its feet were tied, with a silken thread of my own hand's weaving.*

Her daughter couldn't be dead when Rosalie was alive, or was Marcy alive while Rosalie was dead? Marcy, alive. Alive in the blue-silver vaulted ceiling when the entire world was dead in this morning star Hell. God, what would she tell Anatole and André?

Rosalie rusted over, and she barely registered the hand on her back or Jehanne's words. Though she tried to regain sense, make a plan, all she thought of was Roger, pale and still, a flood of old, burning images smashing through with relentless force. The severed tongue the officers mentioned. It could've been Marcy's, discarded like trash by her murderers after a failed escape attempt.

Did the timeline fit? (It couldn't.)

Did it matter anymore?

Marcy, year-old Marcy giggling when anyone tickled her belly. Marcy rattling the crib gate with her meaty fists, wailing and glowering, as if saying, "You tried to strangle me with your sadness, and I hate you for it."

Rosalie would spread her fingers in Marcy's thick, curly hair. "I'm sorry. I did the best I could." She would take a handkerchief and wipe the mucus and spittle from Marcy's face. The child reached out and babbled as Rosalie picked up the fallen pacifier and went to clean it.

Marcy liked the old American trick Rosalie's own mother had taught her, dipping clean linen in sugar and honey and twisting the cloth into a bulb for her daughter to suckle, which gave Marcy a taste for sweets Anatole happily obliged. But that would ruin her teeth, the sugared cloth, so Rosalie stopped allowing it for her fierce child, squirming, sanguine.

Mine.

"Mumuh," Marcy would whimper before she accepted the pacifier in Rosalie's grip. She liked hearing Marcy, hearing the life vibrating inside her. She didn't mind the sleepless nights and soiled clothes. There were worse pains than a noisy and messy child.

All Rosalie thought of was Marcy, her silly four-year-old girl who, as Rosalie read on the couch, had startled her when she curiously peeked under Rosalie's dress and tried to pluck the dark, coarse hairs off her maman's legs. Rosalie always recoiled, and Marcy would cry, as if struck, and they'd sit there, surrendering to that long space between them. It was the space that yawned and gnashed ever since Marcy had passed through that silver membrane between her maman and the world, left the peaceful, comforting dark to scream at the harsh, biting light snapping at the cord that bound them.

"Madame Dei—Rosalie?"

Jehanne is looking at me. She needs me. I'm supposed to protect her.

All Rosalie thought of was seven-year-old Marcy who, when she informed her daughter she had her winter boots on the wrong feet, simply twisted her legs to make an X.

All she thought of was twelve-year-old Marcy pouting and curling on top of the closed commode with a towel under her, complaining about how she'd never chosen to bleed, especially so early in life.

All she thought of was Marcy dying alone in the blackness, Marcy dying alone and thinking her mother believed her better dead.

Is death what's best? Is that what you want?

"No," Rosalie wept. "*No.*"

24

Marcy

"No . . ." **Urine soaked Marcy's socks.** She was both cold and hot, and she stank, the puddled light stank. Jerking forward, her foot knocked against a rock, only for her to look down and realize that rocks couldn't have hair. She clutched her throat, vision flashing a ghoulish yellow, and she returned to the morning she'd decided to watch a man die.

She'd been stealthy, too stealthy for her own good, and she hid in the back of the auto Papa drove to work. That frosty morning, André was ill and couldn't assist with bringing the guillotine parts to the front passenger's seat, so Papa did everything himself.

Her elbows shook when she opened the auto door. Papa said "yes" easier than Maman. He was kind; she'd never seen him angry, yet she still feared his reaction if he discovered her. But Marcy deserved to see Papa, see him truly, and see the world too. The world, in all its wonder and cruelty, couldn't hide from her forever.

Between the time Papa kissed Marcy goodbye and the time he lugged the guillotine parts to the auto, she was under the backseat. Her legs cramped, and her palms sweated, a chilly pins-and-needles itch prickling her feet and hands. As Papa drove, she bit her bottom lip and felt the road's blemishes and tumors. When the auto stopped and she waited, waited for the footsteps to cease, Marcy knocked her head on the seat as she lifted herself to her knees and stumbled out onto the crunching gravel.

She saw a cluster of people and, after a jolt of shock, approached them in a haze. It was still dark, close to dawn, so they were all blots of brown-blue and black-gray. The people swelled around Marcy. A woman stood closest to her with a jacket slung over both shoulders and the eyes of a spooked mouse. Spittle lingered like hazy pollen clouds. Marcy held in a sneeze, and her nose burned. Smoke, cologne, the scent of fresh loaves. Her mouth watered despite herself. A glimpse of what looked like school uniforms. A group of boys younger than her, all dressed in charcoal-gray. It was so early for schoolboys to be out. The stench of people, the collective of swarmed, perspiring bodies shouting her last name, though none of them saw her.

By Mary, Marcy hated mornings.

Papa, there was Papa by the undone guillotine with dozens of circling eyes seeding themselves in him. Her gaze caught the red carnation in his jacket pocket. It drooped like a question mark. His brows, eyes, mouth were unmoving as he and his assistants, four valets dressed in identical black frocks and hats, silently assembled the guillotine, the Maiden of Death, the Widow. There was a time, Papa told her without emotion once, when children played with tiny replicas of Her. It was normal, nothing to fret over, Marcy had been told. Death was as mundane as Papa.

Though it was hard to discern the assistants' features, Marcy recognized Henri, her father's one friend, the quiet man who joked even when the corners of his mouth sagged. Once the Widow was erect, Marcy's gaze rested on Papa's hand, which gripped the rope controlling the blade. Papa seemed to take note of the crowd without looking directly at them, no meeting their eyes, but Marcy's heart pounced to her throat when, instead of drifting past the spot above her head, his gaze settled on her.

He paused for a second, tilted his head down only a fraction before averting his eyes without so much as widening them. All along, Marcy had expected him to see her. Once she sneaked out, it was inevitable. Not only that, but Maman would also notice her absence.

Marcy had to see. She'd been kept in for so long, and she couldn't be a child forever. She deserved to see Papa as he was to the world.

And yet . . .

In that natal time of day, the scraggly, orange-haired man dragged to the Widow was Christ-like in his half-nakedness. Men in black flanked him like a murder of crows. Marcy wondered then why nobody in the crowd even suggested she, a young girl, should shield her view. The criminal was positioned on the bascule like wood for a fire, his limbs arranged just so. Under the buzzing streetlight, the condemned man's hair was the brightest thing there. That, and Papa's carnation, as stark as his rosebushes. The crowd jeered, oppressive and close to ravishing every side of the Widow. Marcy tensed to keep herself from falling forward.

Papa's hand tightened on the rope, Marcy saw it well. He might stop, might let the criminal live. Her fists clenched like his. The condemned man resting on the bascule had the tears of a widower shining on his cheeks. Spit dribbled down his purple lips. Papa cocked his head, eyes glossy and distant, a shadow, a different half of the man who picked wild strawberries with her, who played with Jolie, who danced with Marcy in the living r—

Rush of noise, silence, noise again. Laughter, like the kind after an uncomfortable joke. Talk of how the body would be moved before the pallor set in.

Marcy covered her mouth, might've yelped like a wounded pup. A wave crashed through her, thoughts and images she couldn't explain to herself, much less another person. The almost-dawn was mothy and tattered like an old blanket abandoned under a bed.

The head plopped into the basket, and the crowd broke into various reactions: slow applauding, grumbling, murmuring about the morning chill. No gasps, as if standing around a public guillotine would end in any other way. "Always too quick for the likes of these bastards," an aged man beside Marcy complained.

There had been no preamble, no pause for effect. Papa was not one for spectacle. Marcy gulped as he spoke to his assistants. Not all the blood fell into the basket. The shiny-eyed, spooked mouse-woman took a handkerchief, walked forward, and bent to dab some of the blood on the cloth. The flickering streetlamp shone on her, made her glow. One of her coat sleeves fell into the black-gold pool, and she brought the handkerchief to her nose.

Of course, Marcy knew what her father did; despite sheltering her, Maman and Papa tended not to brush off her questions, but this was different. Once she saw him by the guillotine, it became a facet of her life with nerves and legs.

The people surrounding her laughed and snorted and joked. Marcy was little, crushed beside them all. She noticed the ghosts in the air and grew dizzy. Both her grandfathers, whom she never knew, had a blood anxiety after performing executions for so long, or so Maman told her, and maybe Marcy had it too. A headsman's curse, always seeing blood on the ground and faces in the walls.

What had she expected?

Gulping down her sick, Marcy sprinted to the right before Papa could find her again, slipped her way between the bodies splintering the space, and fled to the back of the building where the parked auto lounged and smirked, knowing. Even away from the Widow's glare, Marcy saw the spilled curtain of that dead man's life when she lurched and crawled into the front passenger's seat, the Widow's seat, not caring that she bumped her elbow, and it throbbed. Papa came back to the auto with his hat and coat intact. Despite the strong scents of his cologne and the seat leather, the crowd's stench still lingered on Marcy.

When Papa came and got into the auto, he didn't falter, even when schoolboys raced past and threw rocks at his door. As he drove home without a word, Marcy stared at the windshield and squinted when day broke. He offered his hat to keep low over her eyes because she hadn't brought hers. She accepted. That was all he did.

It was maddening, that bladed silence. Marcy clutched her throat, massaged it, thought of the Widow behind her, and asked Papa to stop the vehicle. After he pulled the auto aside, she flung herself out, wilted on the grass, and vomited. When she thought she was done, she retched again. Papa knelt with her, rubbed circles into her back, and spoke, but she couldn't hear what he said, only how he said it. His words were warm honey, but also gravelly like a crumbling headstone.

No, she wanted to say, he'd get grass stains on his pants, but it was too late. They were both stained. She tucked her hair behind her ears and sniffed, which came out more like a boarish snort. A string of mucus dripped from her nose to the grass. So much for composure.

Papa cleaned her face with the handkerchief pinched in his hand, as he did when she was small and waddled about with a pool of green mucus settling above her lip. The bitterness of her breath lingered until it was all she knew for a silver-blue stretch of time. Marcy picked up her papa's fallen hat. Papa helped her stand, gripped both her arms, and a wave of embarrassment crashed through when she thought he would offer to carry her back to the auto. He would carry her when she was tinier and fit well in his hold. When the park's grassy orchestra lulled her to sleep. When dusk made the grass as red as scone jam. When Papa's heartbeat was against her cheek and fireflies fuzzed the air.

As she returned to her seat and they resumed the drive, she shook from exhaustion, but kept the tears at bay. With the Widow, they were a company of three, and there was this distinct sense of eavesdropping.

It looked like it hurt, how tightly Papa gripped the wheel.

The lanterns returned her to Hell. The cavern walls eyed her, and she knew she'd never see Maman or Papa again, never laugh and kick up dirt in the garden, never feel the tiny little curls on Jolie's body, the little mats before Maman or Papa combed out her undercoat. Blue lips and blue silk and the mouths, oh God, their mouths. Mouths on the walls, but no throats. No way to scream.

Shackles, jewels, and eyes gleamed in the light, smirked like Herod perusing the annals of the Chapel of Holy Innocents and finding himself aroused. Eyes, devil-eyes, but not. Too little, too human. As her vision blurred, the lanterns grew long, misty limbs along the cave walls.

Closest to her were lumpy, soiled blankets. The blanket, hands, curled hands poked out, and she imagined dozens of small bodies folded together. Squashed, bloated, grubby. Could be mangled. They, the children under there, could look preserved like little angel statues, but the rancid odor said different. Rancid was too tame a word.

Marcy was trenched in mocking light, which lingered like sun-yellow smog, trenched there with the blanketed bodies, the faces molding the black dirt. The piss, blood, and soil on her like brains on a stretcher-bearer's elbow. Feral, crazed thoughts insisted that she flee, flee as far as she could. *Need to take them, take André and the children out of here, take them.* If she could move, if she wasn't killed. If she wasn't already dead.

She couldn't bring herself to lift the blanket closest to her, that piece of fabric flung aside as if in momentary regret. The belt of time, a cancerous wick, hissed like a whip. Abyssal pockets of earth yawned before her, graves likely not so different from the ocean's bottom, where bulbed devilfish writhed. And Marcy, dizzy and ill, became aware of something, a kernel of the universe watching her, neither holy nor wicked, but cold as an iron tongue. It pulsed through the walls and poured down on her.

She tried to walk forward, but a heavy ache below her navel stopped her, reminded her of when she had her first menstruation. When she had angrily informed God He had chosen wrong because she'd never have a child, Maman offered a rare smile. A forlorn one, since Maman's happiness always carried a salty, bereaved air. Stewing like a bitter, steam-huffing toad, Marcy had fumed as she sat half-naked on the towel-draped commode, betting Maman was too mannered, too clean to suffer like this. As she drowned in humiliation, Papa had peeked in bashfully, only to ask if anything new had happened. Then and now, she wished the leaking bullet wound between her legs would kill her.

In the middle of the cavern, a blue boy hung his head in a chair, his mouth gaping wide. "You'll catch flies like that," Papa would say, and Marcy swallowed her sick.

In the mouth, Addie had said. *The boy in the chair, through there.* Marcy stepped forward, her legs wet, plodding planks. She was in front of the rotting boy. The key, she needed the key to free André, would need him to try to help the children climb out of this pit. She feared jostling this poor, poor boy would make him catapult awake.

The silence sliced through her like an electric bell. A crucifix, silver as Judas' palm, hung from the dead boy's neck, burrowing into his tented throat and stained collar. Marcy inched her hand into the boy's mouth, past his teeth. His body was as rigid as a dry board. No, more than that, as if Medusa had hardened his flesh. He couldn't have been older than ten. She expected worms, cockroaches, maggots, yet nothing startled her, let her know it was time to scream. Only the quiet guided her. Her fingers brushed something she mistook as wet, but he was so dry and the smell—

She thought she heard a sigh. She gripped metal, and pulled, pulled, and then the key shone in the light. Shone like the dreams where Marcy went down a candlelit corridor with no end. No monsters, no blood, just the finger-thin fires casting bony light on the melting walls.

Clasping the key, Marcy collapsed to the black ground and retched until she was hollow. She only dully noticed the shattered bones beneath her fingers. Even as she expelled all she had, all that belonged to her, she moved away from the blue-gold cave and back into the winding labyrinth where the living children waited. The key dug into her palm like some unholy trinket. Her hand, her body shook in a frantic pendulum, the rhythmic *twick-twack* of a woodpecker, forward-back, forward-back like a nun's habit in the autumn wind. Before she tumbled out of the dove room, the execution room, she went back to the boy and took the cross; she and André would need it.

As if it helped this poor little soul. She swore the cross burned her palm, Cain's mark, sensed her filth, but she only clenched her fist harder.

In Marcy's stories, men died all the time. In the Great War, men died all the time. That's what she read. Black on white, the crisp, bloodless newspaper accounts of the trenches, sulfur, and melted faces. Cold numbers like letters, letters like bodies blackened to ash. All the letters were just pieces of a dismembered word, right? Write, letter, letter, let her, let her. Let her, let her, let her. What did those words mean? She couldn't stop; she had to focus on them and nothing else. Her thoughts hindered her escape. They were like medicine, a cure and a poison.

What would Papa say when he saw the taint of this place on his daughter? Or Maman? Marcy was marked by a filth that she'd never wash away. When she found the children again, staying in a single spot like Jonah hovering before the whale's gullet, Marcy said, "Don't look, don't look back there, please. Tell me all of you didn't see what was in there."

"He already made us see," Addie replied.

"Who? Who made you see?"

The girl said, "The blue man and his friends." One of the boys pointed to his own torn tunic. Marcy's heart plummeted to her shoes. If the servants were all on his side, then Jehanne was alone with him.

Marcy thought of Papa and the Widow again, but no, she couldn't. She shouldn't. She shouldn't think of Papa here, of all places, when he could be the one thing of unabashed good in the world.

Rais and all the guilty servants will go to the courts, and Papa will have them. Even the women. I don't think Papa has ever killed a woman before. Rais, that evil man from *Là-Bas*, that devil, the knight who took children like

Bluebeard took wives. He spun sweet blankets of lies to net children away from desperate parents. *Each man kills the thing he loves. The coward does it with a kiss, The brave man with a sword.* If anyone deserved death, it was him, and that sent a shock down her spine.

The rest of that day, the day she had watched Papa kill a man, flooded her. Marcy didn't realize they were home until the vehicle sputtered and lurched to a stop. When she and Papa entered the house, they had barely crossed the threshold before Maman launched off the couch and straightened, prim and tight-lipped like a lady in a painting. Her dress was a faded burgundy. André coughed in his room, but it was only the three of them. Maman never slapped her, even for discipline, but Marcy hunched her shoulders anyhow.

"I . . ." Papa swallowed, removing his hat and squeezing the rim with both hands. "It was my mistake."

Marcy stepped forward. "No, it wasn't. I sneaked into the back of the auto and saw." Papa, the one who planted roses and sang, killed a man. Killed men. Marcy knew of his profession. Maman and Papa had told her, and she would sneak a look at the postcards with gray, illegal pictures from executions, but she didn't truly know until she saw. She saw that the blood Papa spilled had lived with her all along. Lived at her feet, lived in her head, lived in her sheets. Lived in her veins. She expected a small, formal crowd in front of the guillotine, a filmy image in her head, but instead everyone had packed around her like starving wolves.

Maman spoke to Papa, words leaking out at a furious pace like blood from a dead man's neck. "Did anybody take her picture? Did they see you with her?"

Papa said, a bit uncertainly, "I don't believe so. I wasn't aware of her for a long while."

Maman pursed her lips. "What did that man do?" What an odd shift. Papa leaned and whispered the answer to Maman, as if he hadn't already tainted Marcy with his knowledge, as if he could preserve her after that.

Maman pursed her lips again. "Good, then." She became somber again. "Did she see? Truly?"

Marcy stepped forward. "I did." The rope and the Widow and the mouse-woman, and the man, the man was dead.

Maman rubbed her temple, mouth quivering. What had once been solid as stone was fractured, and it startled Marcy. "Why did you sneak out? What did you hope would happen? What did you think you'd see? Why, Marcy, why?" God, would Maman cry? "We tell you about these things so you never have to see them. Of all things, why sneak out to see that? *That?*"

Marcy stepped back, she couldn't answer. From the exhaustion etched deep in Maman's face, Marcy saw she had aged her mother considerably on that sherbet-colored morning. For an instant, she wondered if Maman had ever seen death, but she knew she had. She had lost so much, in another time.

Gently, Maman said, "Marcy." Papa was there between them, hands reaching toward them both. His left hand toward Marcy, the rope hand.

"Sorry." Marcy repeated the same word. Maman bowed in the armchair with her head in her hands; that seared Marcy's memory. And she fled to her room; she was thankfully left alone until supper. Her family, all four of them, ate and never again acknowledged what happened, and so much as broaching the subject would've been like cursing in a church.

Part of her, especially after the shock she'd endured, couldn't accept that the courts controlled life and death, that Papa pulled the rope. As the executioner's daughter, it was infused in her blood, the blood of hundreds of alleged criminals. Horrific, monstrous men suffering horrific, monstrous justice.

Retribution, vengeance. That was the word, the last one. Vengeance wasn't neutral, even legislated vengeance, yet was death a penalty when it ended pain? That thought scared Marcy, the appeal of death. She wanted to die now.

Who was a judge, a mortal, to determine if one of God's children, one of His little words in His winding story, needed to be cut away?

Did Papa doubt himself? Was Papa afraid to go to Heaven because he might meet an innocent man he killed? But she couldn't go to Heaven if he wasn't there. She didn't care how perfect Paradise was if she didn't have him.

To calm herself as she and the children made their way back to André, Marcy tried to recall that old folk song Maman taught her, the one about the woman who loved another woman, but lost that affection because she didn't give her lover a rosebud.

Under the oak, I lay and died. Couldn't remember, the words like snow on her lips, already gone. The ground was too cold. *On the driest bough, a nightingale cried. Sing, nightingale, sing. Your heart's to laugh, mine to die. I lost my friend to a rosebud I kept from her.* That song, even with its comfort, hurt Marcy because of how it showed love for what it was: yet another chance for grief. That austere, lonely, thankless sort of love when Maman would chide Marcy for walking around with her gown undone because she could catch a cold, and Maman would kneel to tie the sash of Marcy's gown twice.

Maman would then fret over every sneeze with a furrowed brow and twitching fingers, and, huffing, Marcy said during one of her little colds, "You know, this'd go away quicker if you gave me the right dose of medicine." Despite all her past pain, Maman had risked loving again, and Marcy never understood despite knowing what Maman had gone through. She had understood the way one knows how something works without thinking of why. She'd seen the pain Maman went through like scraping a knee, not losing a limb, or losing yourself. She had thought Maman not talking much about those she lost meant she had moved on, or had forgotten, only to stumble again.

Marcy blinked back tears, and more followed. She was a foolish girl. Even in reaching for freedom, she was giving in. She would marry her cousin because only executioners and their relatives could legally intermix with first cousins. Nobody else would want them; nobody else would want her. In her attempts to be free, she'd be a bird in a cage again. Maman had known that.

She had to get home. After years of resenting the walls and clean floors, she needed to go home the most when she might never see the house or Maman or Papa or Jolie again. She was as doomed as a hungry Irish Catholic in an English factory. She'd die here, and maybe she wanted to if it meant her suffering would end, if it meant she wouldn't see little eyes in the corners of her room as she tried to sleep.

When the children led her back to André, she couldn't meet his eyes, and he looked as if he wanted to speak, but his eyes were hollow in the lanterns' glow. With sweat-slick hands, Marcy freed him. He grunted painfully and slid to the black ground. She joined him, so that only the children stood and stared with the lanterns.

Marcy ripped off a piece of her dress skirt and held out the makeshift bandage. She teased, more than a little forced, "Help me do this, big army man." He did, impressively quiet as they wrapped his foot.

André's face crumpled. "I don't think I can go on."

"What do you mean? As in 'walk'?"

He rubbed his hands over his temples, wrists marked where the shackles had bitten into flesh. "Live. Not after what happened."

Marcy didn't want to press André about what Rais had done to him or made him do while he was in this pit, especially if it would hurt him.

"If you need to speak about it, me and Maman and Papa'll listen. Or give you sweets, whatever works best."

Abruptly, André said, "I have a daughter."

Marcy didn't know how that was pertinent, but she didn't want to stymie André. "Yeah." That was the most she could offer as she swallowed the taste of residual vomit.

His attention snapped to her, and it burned her. Too many eyes here, too many in the light. "You knew?"

Oh right, she wasn't supposed to have heard about that. Marcy stared at her knees. "I eavesdropped when you spoke to Maman."

André kneaded his forehead. "Oh, God. And you heard—"

"She said she'd rather have me dead than married to you."

He paused, and she hated the pity in his eyes, that pity like he knew what she'd seen, knew her sin of witness like Eve shamefully removing the palm leaf below her navel. "God, you didn't deserve that."

"Yes, well, after all of this, I think that's a little low on the list of things I'm fretting about, maybe number nine or ten."

"You really aren't bothered that I had a child with a woman I met in Strasbourg? Didn't you want to marry me?"

She had, not that long ago. But now, he was convenient, yes, convenient was the word, as terrible as it sounded. Before Jehanne, André had been the only person she knew well who wasn't Maman, Papa, or Papa's friend, Henri. Her cousin had a rugged handsomeness to him, and he was, when that seed of infatuation sprung its spindly legs, Marcy's only chance to create a bond and start her own life.

Before she met Jehanne. Marcy finally answered, "I thought I did, yeah." God, what would Jehanne do if everyone survived this and her father (father? was that even possible?) went to prison? She wouldn't have anywhere to go. Marcy wouldn't stand for that, not for a second.

"It was a mistake, one I can't take back, a debt I can't repay. Tante and Oncle would be better off without me, better with me dead, especially like this. A useless burden, the family putain d'idiot."

That sent a chill down Marcy's back. "You aren't useless. They'll be so happy when you're back and all right, trust me. It'd end them if you died."

"I doubt that, given my enviable position as the disappointing replacement."

"Did either Maman or Papa say you're only a replacement for little Roger?"

"They don't need to. God, I'm sorry. Look at me, sitting here and doing nothing. We all need to leave."

"It's all right. Take your time getting up; going too fast might hurt you more. We'll figure everything out when this is all over."

André grunted, rubbing at the mucus bubbling out his left nostril. "Suppose I should attempt to stand." He slid up a little and grimaced. "Christ."

"Here." Marcy offered both hands.

"No, no, I've got this."

Marcy urged, "Taking my hands won't burden me. Please, if it'll help."

His voice was quieter than a whisper. "Maybe I deserve to die here alone."

"Don't be so dour. If you die, it won't be alone," Marcy joked, her laugh nervous and faint.

Dryly, André said, "Thanks, cousin."

"And I'm not leaving here without you, so get that out of your head." He took Marcy's hand and leaned against her.

The children surrounded them, and they, Marcy, and André supported one another like the mossy, crumbling pillars of a Roman temple. They looked and smelled awful. Marcy again tried to think of herself as one of the poised heroines in the movies she read about, but she assumed her hair and clothes were decidedly less dashing.

André said, "What's that in your hand?" When Marcy lifted the cross with her free hand, his expression broke, but he extended a hand. She dropped the cross on his palm. "I didn't save him."

"Oh, but you did the best you could. You could wear it to honor him."

Her cousin put the cross in his shirt pocket. "This belongs to his parents." They resumed their leaning into one another. Best to focus on the itinerary: escape.

Marcy asked, working to fill the silence, "Do you think we can find our way back to the surface?"

"Yes, or die on the way, I suppose. Or starve."

His encouragement worked as well as hers. "Great."

"Never fear. If anything, thirst would get us first."

Marcy snorted. "I'm glad we have that comfort, at least."

"I suppose I do have my uses, after all."

The children were quiet and walked funny. Every one of them, Marcy and André included, limped past the glowering lanterns. Her poor cousin shook with each step, so she was strong for the two of them.

Eventually, they found the opening from above.

"Need to be with her. Need to, need to . . ." Maman.

Jehanne's voice came next. "I'll need to find a ladder. There may be one in the shed outside."

Jehanne. The blue in Marcy's heart brightened to yellow-white, yet she was unsure the voices were real until André tensed beside her.

He shouted, his tone urgently hopeful, "Tante, that's Tante!"

Maman said, not noticing them, "I have to go down and find her."

"How can we get back up?"

"Can you find that ladder? Will someone try to hurt you?"

"Only Gilles is here, and he—I—oh God."

Marcy shouted, "Maman! Jehanne! Hey! Can you see us?"

Faces appeared. And she supposed they did see them, with the deer-stares she and André received. Maman's hair was undone, which made her look strange, and it fell over the edge of the pit. Marcy mused that Maman was like Rapunzel, except her hair was too short, and what a terrible thing anyway, to burden someone's scalp with your weight. Maman looked like someone had doused her in cold water. She blinked, then blinked again.

Jehanne asked, "How many of you are down there?"

Maman reached down to them and said to Jehanne, "Hold on to me." With Jehanne's help, she was closer, her elbows scraping the shining blackness.

One by one, Marcy and André helped the children up as Maman strained to pull them all up without worry or complaint. When it was done, André looked to Marcy. "Get on my shoulders."

She huffed. "No, you get on mine."

"No."

"Don't argue with me. You're injured. I won't put weight on your shoulders."

"I—"

Marcy stuck her bottom lip out so that she imitated an offended frog. "André!"

He sighed and acquiesced. And while Marcy regretted her decision immediately, he didn't stand on her for too long, and she survived. It seemed impossible for anyone to reach her. None of the hands seemed close enough, and the pit was steep.

She dug her sole into the black and when she peered up, she feared Maman would fall into the pit with her. As she climbed as much as she could without sliding down, which was a pitiful distance, Marcy's fingers brushed Maman's palms. She gave all her energy to a single lunge. Maman caught her wrist, and Marcy's body yelped like a frightened dog, telling her to *stopstopstop*.

A final twinge in her elbows and legs, and then warmth covered her, arms holding her close. When she craned her neck, the children were gone. Maman murmured in her hair, "Oh, my girl." And Marcy was okay for a second. Suffocating, but okay. She couldn't remember the last time Maman had held her like this. When Marcy leaned back, it took her a minute to take in everyone. André panting and on his hands and knees; Maman with her blotched face and tousled hair. Jehanne covered in blood and looking a decade older in the curve of her cheeks.

Marcy asked, "Where did the children go?" André said nothing.

"They ran off. I don't understand. Why were there children down there?" Maman shifted her focus to André.

"My God, are you okay? Don't take this poorly, but what are you doing here?"

Too many questions. Marcy wanted her bed now, too tired.

André coughed, which rattled the air. "I lost my cigar, so I was digging around in the pit when Marcy found me."

"I'm glad your tongue is in good order." Maman's voice was rough, but not with ire. It was affection.

The four of them stood together, lifting like a quilt in the wind, rippling up as dovetailed threads.

Marcy warily looked at the floor. "Maman?"

"Hmm?"

"You might want to pick up your gun."

"Yes, right." Maman did.

Something was different about her friend; Jehanne's eyes were fogged like a window on which a seething ghost had breathed. Jehanne was haunted, but Marcy supposed they all were. Nevertheless, Marcy lunged into Jehanne's stiff arms. No time could've been long enough, and though they both reeked of blood, Jehanne reciprocated the tightening embrace and released a quiet sigh into Marcy's shoulder.

"Where's Mlle Clair?" Marcy whispered, and when Jehanne's silence answered her, she adjusted so both her arms were around her friend's shoulders, and she pressed her cheek to Jehanne's. It was so warm, the two of them as one.

The four of them went up the stairs, and her relief remained as tenuous as a plank bridge. It snapped more as, when they hadn't progressed even halfway down the leering hall, André fell in a sudden procession, from arms to knees to feet. Marcy, Maman, and Jehanne hovered, a wary swarm, a web of hands wanting to help, but afraid to unravel fragile silk.

He wept in long drawls, and only a few words were clear. "Tante, I'm sorry, m'sorry."

"Oh, André," Marcy said softly.

Maman knelt close, still not touching him. "Why are you the one who's sorry?"

"I'm sorry I'm not good. I tried. I tried to fight."

"I'm the one who called you . . ." Maman trailed off, unable to repeat it.

André gasped, "I can't go on anymore. I can't." He buried his head in Maman's lap, fists making crushed orchids of her dress.

Basking in her friend's steady hotness, Marcy clutched herself to Jehanne, this Jehanne more silent than Marcy had ever known her to be.

Marcy said, "Sing that song about the nightingale."

Maman's forehead scrunched. "I don't quite remember the words."

"That doesn't matter," Marcy said.

Maman gave the air a string of words and hums, smoothing her hand down André's hair and neck.

Jehanne whispered, and even that thundered in Marcy's ear, "What did you see down there?" In that instant, Marcy and Jehanne were the only people in the world.

"There were dead children, a whole cave of them. Maybe more—but I only saw that one place."

Maman entered Marcy's little globe again, but only as a voice. "*Sacré Dieu.*"

Marcy looked to her friend for reassurance, but none was found. Jehanne was a sickly white, but more than that, she fidgeted as if she wanted to be somewhere else. That was okay, because so did Marcy.

How good home would be; how good her bed would be.

Marcy asked Maman, "What about the police I called?"

Maman's hazel eyes were the bluest they'd ever been. "Oh, poupée, I'm so sorry. They were all killed."

Tears pricked her eyes. "But—but—I did what I was supposed to do."

Maman said earnestly, "You did. It's not your fault. It's no one's fault."

Jehanne tensed.

Marcy sniffed. "Jehanne?"

"You're wrong. Someone is at fault, and this place needs to burn. It all has to burn. I need to go."

"I'll go with you."

Maman gently tugged on Marcy's sleeve. "Splitting up isn't wise."

As if frustrated, Jehanne heaved a long sigh. "You all need to leave this place. This is my duty. This is why I was brought here."

"I don't—it doesn't make any sense. I read your father's diary. He's Gilles de Rais." Jehanne gave a somber nod. Marcy stared. "How long've you known?"

"Only today."

Maman frowned. "That's impossible. That . . . man died centuries ago." To Marcy, she asked, "Did you really read that dreadful book?"

"I was bored." Marcy asked her friend, "Is he really your papa?"

Blue ringed Jehanne's owlish, never-blinking eyes. "No, as I just learned."

"Did he kidnap you?" Marcy persisted.

"In a sense."

"Please explain. What about your real parents?"

"There's no time. God put me here for a reason." Jehanne's voice shook with weight to it. "And as much as I don't want to put another foot forward, I have to stop Gilles."

"No, we can all just leave and get help."

"Help, and then what? Have the officers who haven't died sacrifice themselves? I have to go. I was born for this."

"Jehanne, please, don't be a martyr, not now. You can come with us."

Her eyes gaining that usual spark, Jehanne pulled Marcy into a crushing embrace, but the smell of blood and mildew blotted all that happened next.

Marcy whispered when Jehanne's breathing hit her strangely, "Who are you, really?"

With the same quietness, Jehanne said, her hand on Marcy's neck, "Do you know who Gilles served?"

Baffled, Marcy answered, "Yes, Jehanne d'Arc, but . . ." She froze, stunned. "I don't . . ."

When Marcy blinked again, which may've been a minute later, Jehanne was gone. She took in everything. Her head hurt.

Urgently, Maman said, "Poupée, let's go."

Even at their fastest, fatigue and injury burdened their advance.

The only words were from André when they came close to the entrance and a stench, different but like that of the pit, settled on Marcy's tongue and made her gag.

He asked, "Where's Oncle?"

Maman rubbed her temple. "That's another matter. Best to focus on leaving here." Marcy couldn't argue against that.

In the main hall, it was quiet madness, and Marcy's belly roiled at the carnage. She couldn't understand this. Moreau scavenged a body with his teeth like a vulture did with its scythe-like beak, and when she saw who was smoking a cigar on the stairs like a gentleman at the park, her heart plummeted to her toes.

25

Jehanne

She sprinted to the shed behind the manor. To her knowledge, there was still an auto out front, and despite not knowing much about modern things, Clair had told her oil brought it to life, and oil could catch fire, so best not to touch it. When she had asked Clair what an auto ate to stay alive and the woman spoke about an oil canister, she said it was a metal bird with a long nose. The mental picture had reminded Jehanne of a hummingbird. It was a guess, a madly rushed one, that the container would be in the decrepit wooden building.

Her heart sank when she thought of Clair, but she couldn't focus on Clair or Marcy or Marcy's poor family— or the children Gilles had hurt, she realized with an encroaching migraine, to bring her back to life. Jehanne hadn't the slightest why an honorable man would become so vile when he had his moments of affection. She couldn't explain everything, like why Gilles would hurt children, even conceive of it, and if his reason was to bring Jehanne back, why didn't he stop hurting children after her rebirth?

When Jehanne found what she believed to be the oil canister, it was bigger than she thought, as big as her chest. She undid the top and sniffed. The liquid inside wrinkled her nose. Good, she had all she needed to cleanse this earth.

Doubt crept in like a fox slinking through the dark brush at the bottom of her skull. No matter her bravado, that doubt always crept about. All she wanted were the hours when she and Marcy had rested in bed together. Clair rubbing her back and half-embracing her. Papa with dirt under his nails in the garden where Michael, Catherine, and Margaret had told her to save France. Catherine, her ever-beaming sister, cross-legged by her on the family bed as Maman made them memorize hymns they knew from sermons instead of books.

Jehanne could just run off. Forget Gilles, not worry about his whereabouts or if he'd follow her to her second death. She could live with Marcy and her family. Yes, she'd have a family, a normal family, besides certain quirks, of course. She knew better than anyone that fire was a terrible thing, and she didn't have to listen to the voices telling her to light the pyre.

As well as that, she didn't even have matches, which impaired her plan, to say the least.

But if she left, Gilles would hurt more people for his own means, for his own pleasure. He'd follow her wherever she went.

In this war, the cause had splintered, but even though Jehanne couldn't protect those who'd died, she would champion their souls and all those endangered by Gilles. He was, after all, her companion, her knight, and only she could relieve him of his duty. Hunched, Jehanne lugged the canister as fast as she could, and only as she carried it did she realize her fatigue, but faith stoked her resolve. She tried not to slosh the oil on the grass. For an odd moment, she wondered if, in Heaven, she had met her parents and siblings, and if they had said their apologies and lived happily until God had allowed Gilles to steal her.

As Jehanne sprinted as fast as she could down a tapering hall, she lingered on what Maman must've thought when she received news of her last daughter's execution and the casting of her ashes into the Seine.

It'll be over soon, Maman, Papa, Catherine, Pierre, Jacquemin, Jean. I'll see you all again today.

As she entered the main hall, her vision tunneled, and she ignored everyone and went to work pouring the oil. If anyone had tried to gain her attention, their voices failed to reach her. Her pants were soaked where the oil splashed. She only paused when Gilles crossed the frozen space to stand above Moreau, who slurped at marrow and bone without regard for anyone around him.

With two sure stomps, a crunch, and a smacking pop, Gilles leaned over and caved in Moreau's skull, as if he'd lined his boots with steel. Rosalie jerked a hand over Marcy's eyes.

"It needs to burn," Jehanne said to herself until it became a litany. "It needs to burn."

"Jehanne," Gilles called. He came close.

"Get away from me!"

He looked at what she held. His eyes grew somber. "Is this what you want?"

"I—"

Before she answered, André came alive, or, more aptly, he went mad. Rosalie almost slipped on the oil and the fabric of her dress in trying to reach him as he half-lunged, half-hobbled. And when he flew at the devil, Gilles went down, eerily nonplussed as André relentlessly hit him in the face, throat, and chest. As Gilles stood again, he reached for Jehanne, but before he could step close, André landed a punch to his jaw. It only made Gilles stumble a little, but it was a valiant effort.

Marcy was there, too close to the monster and tugging on André's sleeve. "André, he's not fighting back! Let's go!" In a hectic procession, Rosalie came from behind and tried to steer both Marcy and André away.

Jehanne tried to gaze into every glazed eye. The dead were most of those Jehanne saw every day, even when she was too stuck in her own bonnet to learn their names as she ate well and rested on clean sheets. She swallowed and closed her eyes, even when she had nothing left to spill. She was as empty and drained as the canister she dropped at her feet.

Gilles called to her, "Jehanne, darling, if this is what you want, I'm more than happy to oblige, if you follow me." He glided up the second floor and around, the balcony with its half-open curtains. André followed, eyes silver and face scarlet. Rosalie tripped on a hand and the long skirt of her dress, falling to her knees before Gilles, which frenzied André's ministrations.

"Dear boy, are there parts of you I haven't broken yet?" Gilles ground his foot on André's bandaged one, and André howled. "You should find a cane. It'll do you good." With a flippant grin, Gilles swerved another blow. "I really wish you had been this animated down in the dove room. It's really not pleasurable to insert yourself into a limp toy. If I'd wanted that, I would've used one of the corpses. Mary knows I have enough." Again, Gilles ducked a hit with obscene grace. "It's a shame my old castle is in ruins and everything confiscated, or else I could've used my instruments to make you more excitable."

Jehanne tensed when Gilles, seemingly bored, gripped André's throat and lifted him up as if he were paper. A single squeeze could end him. Rosalie, still on the ground, lifted her pistol, and with a jolt, she shot it once. The bullet entered Gilles' wrist, rippled through his arm and blew out at the shoulder. His entire arm splintered open, the once-blue sleeve pouring red. André fell and scrambled away, gripping his throat and coughing. Gilles flinched, but smiled at the wound as if a child had pinched his arm. Rosalie shuffled backwards, regaining her footing and throwing an arm over Marcy's shoulders.

"Well done, madame," was all Gilles said.

Jehanne wondered why he wasn't fighting as he had with the officers, why he embraced her spilling of the oil.

You're not a pile of ashes anymore. Go!

Jehanne kicked the empty canister aside. Damn her inaction. Going toward the steps, she tripped over an arm, or maybe it was a leg, but she quickly recovered out of the sloshing mire and climbed the first steps. *God is a consuming fire.* She tried to move to the landing, but halted.

Moreau stood between her and the rest of the ascent. He had been patting Clair's temple when he caught sight of Jehanne and bolted up. (When had he gotten up?) Snarling, he lurched once and stumbled. Her knuckles tightened, and when she gazed down, a faint gleam by her left foot caught her eye.

The braquemard crusted black, Gilles' sword, her sword now. It must've been knocked down the steps in the current struggle. The sword he'd sliced through an Englishman's neck, a soldier who had towered over her as she bled from the neck; in that moment, Gilles had looked every bit like a softer, terrified Michael, his eyes blue and bloodshot for her.

She hurriedly grappled the sword and pointed it at Moreau, but it was then he made a sound that was neither a growl nor a curse. As he sobbed, she realized his mouth was contorted not in a snarl, but a grimace. The sight of him, a bloody, lost wretch, didn't terrify Jehanne; it was sad, the way his crushed head looked where his ruined skull, brain, and eyes protruded forth, half his scalp sloughing over an ear.

"Make it stop," Moreau begged. "Please."

Without closing her eyes to prepare for the blow, she lifted the sword, said a prayer, and swung at his neck, and so Moreau fell to the floor twice, mercifully released at last. The faint descent of him rolling down the stairs afforded little of her attention as she climbed. By the time she reached the stalled conflict, Gilles leaned with his elbows on the banister across from the balcony, the curtains lashing out with the wind. Jehanne stepped between Gilles and the family, lifting the sword to be the steel distance between them.

It has to be me. It was always supposed to be me. God wanted me; God let me leave for a short time to help those who needed my love. And I tried, did the best I could.

Marcy whispered, "The trellis, let's go."

To Gilles, Jehanne said, "Why do you hurt others if it makes you drink and cry? Why would you hurt so many? Why would you when you had me again?" The taste on her tongue soured.

"Habit, I suppose. What else could I do? What else was this life of mine worth? So long as I repent, fleshly acts

321

can be forgiven, even when they're done for the Devil. And I'll stop, I swear, now that you're here. I'll stop if it means never seeing the faces in the walls again."

"A habit is biting your nails or sucking your thumb. How could you? How could you?"

Gilles clenched both hands and raised them, and Jehanne couldn't help but flinch. "How could the king leave you to die? How could God and His angels sentence you to burn when you were a flicker of light in a dark age? How could God and the Devil keep you from me for centuries? I spent money on cathedrals, sacrificed many to gain silver and accrue a blood favor, and it still took me ages. Does 'why' matter at this point? Is this what you want, truly, for us to die? I could be your father, if that's what you want. A home, a family. I can love you and tell you everything now." Jehanne stiffened. "No more secrets. You could even find your own way, have a husband and children."

She erupted not in a shout, but a whisper. "Is that what you think I want? And you'd let me stray from your side? What makes you think I don't understand you'd keep me caged so you could gawk at me?" Rage consumed everything. *I'll chase you into the fires of Hell myself if it means I can ensure you won't hurt anyone again.* Fire cleansed. Jehanne knew better than anyone, didn't she? All she needed was a match because she hadn't thought that far. Fire, the ecstasy of release in the throes of agony when she, a small tear, traveled upward upon the path of

Creation and melted back into God's eye. And then, after everything was ash, she'd . . .

She'd what? What could a martyr do after she'd already suffered and died? What could a runaway do when everyone who had loved her died centuries ago?

Jehanne glowered. "When did you start hurting children? When did you first start killing?"

Gilles' jaw set, but his shoulders eased. "I suppose I've nothing to lose. All will be forgiven by the Lord. After I lost the last of my silver on a theater piece, ah, his name was Jeudon. The last name, can't remember the first, not that it matters, anyhow. He was a poor furrier's son, and I offered him a job as a young page after I saw a wolf pelt on his charming little shoulders; I said he could be trained to read and write, and his parents were ecstatic. I still remember that frightened peace on his face when he bled nude on the hook. He had stopped struggling and accepted his flight to God."

"How old was he?"

"I don't know. Twelve, ten, I suppose." He shrugged. "Forgive me. They all blend together, after a point." His eyes glistened, but not from tears. He looked behind Jehanne, as if thrilled by Marcy trembling against Jehanne's back. "I loved that expression, the one when he realized his predicament, that shock, the sorrowful gleam in his eyes. If I could freeze that moment forever, I would. Forgive me, darling. I know how it sounds, but I couldn't help myself after your death. The blood, like when we were at war, their fear was—" His expression grew solemn, voice quieter. "No, I suppose it was only my second greatest joy, second to you."

"Children, Gilles. You've hurt *children*! And you hurt the people who swore themselves to you, too. People who once trusted you."

"I know, but the woman and Moreau were complacent and willing."

"Her name is Clair, and when would you ever realize when someone isn't, as you say, willing?"

He leaned forward like a child with a well-loved secret. "You should've seen what I made Moreau do in the depths, how I made him coax the children so he and the others could beat them unconscious with whatever tools at hand. Then you wouldn't pity him. And the woman, well, she could've tried to stop me, or she could've denied the money I gave her and left, but no, she stayed and kept quiet."

"What did you threaten them with if they didn't comply? Do I even need to ask, when you've already carried it out?"

"Does it matter? If someone gave you the choice to torment a child or die, wouldn't you choose the latter?"

Heat rose in her throat like a song. "I'd say so, it matters. And for your last question, I want to say 'no,' but I don't know what you put your servants through before you made them hurt others. I can't blame them. Now that their souls are gone, they've faced their judgment, for better or worse—"

"Jehanne, you truly are too pure for the world if you think that."

"—but you haven't faced yours."

"I understand your anger."

"You do, do you? How noble." Suddenly, the hotness in her throat died. Was this anger, or acceptance? She would've preferred anger to this.

What am I accepting?

"You were always a righteous one, but you were also close to God, and He loves even men like me. Can't you find it in yourself, that grace? That saintly forgiveness for a poor, repentant wretch?"

Jehanne snarled. She hadn't asked to be a saint, and she wasn't about to pray for his sake. "Go to Hell."

Gilles bowed his head. "I was always an obedient soldier, wasn't I?" When he looked at her, she didn't see regret or a plea, but this closed scrutiny. "Is this what you really want, for us to fly to Heaven together? All my powers—they were meant to amount to this, you know. To us being together for eternity, and to think, in the times ahead, though you're furious now, I can prove how gentle I will be to you." He grinned, arms outstretched like the Madonna.

You sale con, so that's where you think you'll go.

"Yes," Jehanne said, voice low. "That's what I want. We can be together in Heaven without this pain. And then I can try to understand."

He leaned as if he meant to fall over the banister, which would've—she wasn't sure if it'd harm him.

Marcy shouted, "Let's leave!" But, after the jolt of remembering other people existed in the world besides Gilles, Jehanne ignored her, hoping a day would come in some other life when all would be right between Marcy and her again.

Marcy pressed, "Jehanne."

She said to Marcy, allowing Gilles to gutter from her mind like a candle. "I need to do this. Go down the trellis."

"Do what? You can't stay here. He's not your responsibility."

Jehanne twisted around and kissed Marcy's forehead, clumsily holding her sword hand away. Her dearest friend, with what strength she could give, reciprocated with a gentle christening on the mouth. When Jehanne pulled away, she said, "I was born to do this." She rested a hand on the back of her friend's head.

Blinking, gaze swampy, Marcy whispered, "Please."

Jehanne's soul split. As she turned away and stepped closer to the banister, Gilles granted her a longing look. His eyes, flickering and as blue as the Devil's, were tear-filled. He shrugged, fumbling in his breast pocket with his uninjured hand and producing a cigar pack and match. It was a mundane feat, his ability to hold them both without dropping them. He stuck the cigar in his mouth with some effort, took his near-ruined arm—now looking better than it had seconds ago—and worked to light the match on the banister. If Jehanne hadn't endured the past few hours, his efforts may've been comical.

Marcy tugged on Jehanne's elbow, another hard grip on her opposite shoulder. "We need to leave. Now. Please."

Gilles took a step closer to the banister.

Jehanne said, "I'll watch over him. Like I said, climb down the trellis."

"No, no splitting up again," Marcy replied, "no leaving without each other. Come with us."

"This is my duty."

"You don't need to help him."

"I'm not. The police will come to check on their missing men and find this. I won't let him disappear."

"Please stop being so stubborn," Marcy pleaded, voice breaking. "We all love you. I love you. We want you to come with us and be safe."

Oh, Marcy, but I will be safe.

Before anyone could stop him, Gilles dropped his lit cigar over the banister. The oil ignited. The space under Jehanne's ribs churned as the scent of burning wood and meat overwhelmed her world. Marcy, Rosalie, André, Gilles, their mingled words were soup. Jehanne was Venus in the sea, ready to be born from the roaring foam, the slick and seedy mass threatening to drown her; she was Saint Margaret in the great dragon's belly.

But now Jehanne's story, like the tales of Venus and Margaret, was over.

Jehanne raised the braquemard, and though Gilles tensed, he didn't do anything to thwart her, as if preparing to be run through. The calm settling in her was both bliss and agony. As the stench of sulfur grew, her bones settled and reformed anew, and she swore they poked out of her back to grant her flight.

She dropped the sword. Marcy and her family would be okay, and that lifted Jehanne up. They would escape, and reinforcements would come soon after an extended absence of the dead officers, all of whom would be avenged. Gilles twisted around, body like a serpent's, and Jehanne steeled herself. For the sake of who he'd been by the campfire, she didn't meet his smoldering eyes. This was for his wife Catherine and Clair and Moreau and all the children she couldn't protect in her old life and now.

With a burst of force, she left Marcy despite a desperate protest, crossing the distance between her and Gilles. Before Gilles could sting her with any blackberried promises, Jehanne clutched his shirt and shoved him with all her strength and, feet ungrounded, they both tumbled over the banister, plummeting headfirst into seething light. She knew pain, purpose.

As she fell, she flew.

26

Marcy

Marcy wailed.

Before she could stop herself, she stared over the banister, but she didn't find Jehanne.

Hands reaching in the flames—God, there were hands and nails and eyes and teeth in the fire.

Hands reaching, reaching for Marcy in the scorching, reeking pit that swallowed Jehanne like an angry, swollen bat devoured a wasp. The lights below, pointing at her like an imperious king in yellow with a molten crown dripping down his hair, made her vision blue, and she could fall so easily and forget, fall back into the dirt she'd scrambled through with blood and filth and urine coating her like it did now.

She could be clean, clean in Jehanne's light like she hadn't been when the lanterns sneered at her. The manor's filth had burrowed its way inside her, staining her in such a way that she could never be clean. She could scrub her flesh, but not her soul. But with fire, she could cleanse herself and make everyone hear and see her love, the love Jehanne hadn't comprehended before she chose to die instead of staying with her.

All Marcy had to do was fall into the bed of fingers like it was Papa's rosebushes. The thorny sting would last far shorter than her memories. Too many lights, like what Papa would say about Versailles. Her foot rose to meet the banister, but hands stopped her. She wanted it to be Jehanne, hoped her eyes had been wrong.

"Marcy!" Maman shouted, and Marcy understood what it meant to be petrified as Maman looked to her with pure terror; Maman lay open before Marcy like a wound exposed to cruel wind.

"Marcy, love, please. Come with me."

Though Marcy realized she wasn't the only person who'd ever lost someone, or the only one who could lose life if she stayed, she insisted, "You go. I need Jehanne."

Maman's visage crumpled. "Jehanne wanted you to go down the trellis with us. Please."

Trembling, André teetered over the stone railing outside, and Maman gently guided her to the balcony.

Maman squeezed her shoulder. Marcy drew a breath deep into her lungs.

"Go on, André," Maman said.

"I can't do it," he replied, voice high. "I'll break my neck."

Maman said evenly, "I know it'll be hard." She looked back at Marcy as she spoke, as if Marcy would fade into smoke if she turned away. "I'll go first and catch you both if you fall, all right?"

It took a long while before Marcy felt the hand leave her shoulder. Maman tentatively made her way to the trellis, which shook but proved sturdy. Before Maman descended, however, she looked to the both of them and said, "I promise to catch you."

Neither Marcy nor Andre replied with anything beyond nods; with the fire growing, it would have to do.

Once Maman had reached the ground, André said to Marcy, "You go first."

"I don't. I can't . . ."

Hurriedly, he clasped her hand in his, which made Marcy feel nothing as sweat poured down her temple and arms. "You can. I couldn't have done this without you. Believe me."

Marcy said, her voice somewhere high above her body, "Please go first. It'll put me at ease to have you both safe. Do it now!" The last statement came out harsher than she'd intended, but it was all she could do not to cry.

Despite his concerned look, he obeyed her wishes, and as he descended, Marcy froze, stuck between the scowling, pinkening world and the fire's gnashing grin.

Please don't die, André. Please don't, not like—like, don't die, please.

André couldn't die, not after all that had happened. In her head, the trellis cracked and he fell, his head splitting on the dirt and feeding the worms. He couldn't die; she'd already lost so much, and perhaps the only person who would understand was Maman. Not even Papa could because though he saw death in his job, he hadn't seen Marcy like *this*.

When there was no war, Marcy had smacked her heels against the couch and said, "I wish I had a brother."

Maman had looked up from her bloodless newspaper. "You have André."

"He doesn't count. He's . . ." He was outgrowing her. The more he trained with Papa, the greater the chasm between them. If only she knew a way to keep him, to keep the boy who'd played with her by the sea, those days when she tasted sweat and salt on her lips as she ran.

Maman stared into the distance for what seemed like thirty minutes. "You had a brother. His name was Roger." Her face moved oddly, and she choked on the last word like she'd bitten her tongue or swallowed something sour.

"What happened to him?" Marcy asked, perking up.

As usual, Maman avoided looking at her. "He went away."

Marcy pouted. Roger was lucky to leave and have his own adventures. "Can't he come back?"

Maman pressed her lips into a thin line, and she averted her eyes. "He died."

Marcy wanted to ask how, but she thought it'd be too much, so she said, "What did he look like?"

She should've asked how Roger died because it would've had the same result.

Maman's face shattered. So many lines she hadn't thought her mother was capable of with her smooth stoicism. "Please." With that, they never spoke of Roger again (she almost forgot his name), and Marcy had returned to the comfort of Papa with his scratchy beard and poppy ankles.

She didn't understand Maman's distance and secrecy. Honestly, it was infuriating that she wouldn't trust her own daughter with anything. Then again, Papa hadn't spoken much about her big brother either, so it was unfair to blame Maman for everything.

She felt something leaking down her neck, shoulders, and back. The manor was falling like a stubborn, ancient forest beast finally submitting to age.

Water. Even in fire, she was drowning.

Marcy blinked. It was her turn to escape, but she couldn't climb down. The smoke billowed, black and omnipresent.

Instead, another memory assaulted her, and a crack in glass formed until she realized it wasn't glass, but a gray April day when she'd tried to climb a pitiful birch in the corner of Papa's garden. The bark gave way under her nails, and she fell with a loud grunt without reaching a branch; her frustration had overwhelmed the *oofgh* of the fall.

"Marcelle!"

Marcy froze as Maman was upon her. Maman was wearing a white dress, which was crinkly and ugly, but that wasn't the point. The point was that the dress made her ghostly, like the limbs below her neck were fog tapering down to the dewy grass.

Maman shook her shoulders once, and it jolted Marcy's heart like she was a rabbit watching a wolf emerge from the dark brush. "My God, what were you thinking? You could've broken your neck! Is that what you want? How could you be so unbelievably stupid?" Marcy's eyes hurt with tears, and Maman deflated. "Oh, poupée. I didn't mean—"

Marcy ran off, and in the evening during supper, neither of them acknowledged Maman's outburst. Maman's folded her fingers together in her lap and focused dully on her nearly full plate ten minutes into the meal.

"Marcy!"

"Stop, Marcy, *Marcelle*!"

Maman—André?

Marcy snapped her head up, but Maman was gone, leaving only smoke and gray light in her wake. She lurched, and something cold and hard grazed her hands and pressed against her stomach, and she had the sense of falling until she frantically shuffled back.

As she returned to herself, the calls bordered on screams and the air grew acrider.

Eyes stinging, Marcy could barely see Maman when she looked down, could only see her palms extended like a porcelain Virgin statue, but when the world focused, Maman's hair was a mess and her face shone where blood hadn't marked her.

Despite what she and André had witnessed, they'd climbed out of the underground tunnels. She could do this. Marcy's eyes watered, and she gagged as smoke billowed out into the open air. The manor groaned when she made her way down the trellis. The uneven edges of the wood bit into her skin. She ignored the splinters, not through will, but because of her fading awareness of her own body. She could only hope someone would catch her if she fell, if the wood cracked, if she tangled her feet in the vines.

She climbed and climbed. The smoke wouldn't leave her nose and mouth. Before she registered the ground at her feet, she stumbled, blood thudding in her ears at the pace of a horse's run. Even then, an eerie calmness invaded her, and hands steadied her.

Lurching, Marcy could not free herself of the stench of smoke, of cooking meat, or the sight of Jehanne falling. She curled deeper into Maman as the world was smoke. The sky, threatening rain with its intense violet, shunned them, and she rocked against her family.

When the rain hit, it clup-clopped at their knees. Marcy was only aware of one sensation: the lead weight of a full burlap sack spilling needles down her thighs and her belly swelling like a rot-sweet apple. No matter what she had just endured, her body thought it was a good time to keep bleeding like the world hadn't fallen apart.

Maman motioned toward the auto (had she really driven here?), but Marcy didn't have the strength to climb into it. Maman carried and settled her into the backseat with André.

"I didn't know you could drive," Marcy mumbled.

Maman set a hand on her temple and brushed the sticky hair back. "I'm adjusting, poupée."

As her vision blissfully faded, a heavy slosh pooled in her until the fiery chill gave way to wheels unsteadily beating down the road and the mourning banshee wail of sirens.

27

Rosalie

Holding a newspaper, Rosalie sat on the front porch and collected her thoughts. The front image: an ash-gray photo of children huddling together by an officer's car. In the dying dawn, crow caws and birdsong mingled. The leaves skirting the trees and scattering across the chattering lawn were as scarlet and gold as the tips of waxwings' tails, yet the wind had the taste of winter to it.

A week, it'd been a week since she, Marcy, and André were scrubbed clean at the hospital and interrogated one by one about their experiences. André snarled and broke when anybody, from the gentle nurses to the soft-spoken doctor, touched him. He didn't allow anyone near, except for Rosalie and Marcy. Even Anatole, released within a day of the manor's collapse, couldn't go near him.

"What happened, my heart?" Anatole had asked Rosalie when they found themselves alone in bed, which felt both more welcoming and more alien than it had in decades, this little cradle for all her sadness. They each kept taking turns watching over their silent daughter and nephew, and sleep seemed a long-deprived dream, the water after a forty-day desert journey.

"Can I tell you? It's all too much and too little. God, it'd be better if you never heard everything we saw, all of us. I can't . . ." Rosalie didn't know exactly what was under the manor beyond André's fractured account and eventual refusal to speak, Marcy's few words giving way to stunned silence, and newspaper reports of the national police investigation.

"Anatole," she whispered, "in the wine cellar, I saw blood and rot. I thought Marcy had died, and I couldn't move."

He rested his hand on hers.

"You saved them. Marcy and André would've died without you. And the children too."

"Oh, I'm your hero now, am I?" she teased, though her fatigue sapped away the lightheartedness.

"You never stopped being my hero."

"Flatterer." Rosalie huffed and spent a second too long straightening a loose curl. "I'm sorry. I'm sorry for being such a, as my sister would say, femme chiante."

He rubbed his thumb between her knuckles. "You never were."

"Then I'm sorry for my hurtful words."

"You were grieving."

"So were you, in your own way." She swallowed. "If you ever think you can't cry or act strange with me, please know you can because—because you've always let me break. You've always let me be strange."

"I should've told you the truth about André's daughter," Anatole conceded, and they clung to one another; he smelled of his cologne and faint petrichor, and they fell asleep like that. Before the dreamless rest, she thought sourly of Jehanne and the man who alleged to be her father, their black, crumbling limbs webbed in the cold grave of the fire.

In the morning, Anatole left her side for a job, and she supposed then he had gone to the Rennes square alone, given André's trouble walking. When she looked in André's room, before she picked up the neglected newspaper, its date going three days back, her nephew's dozing form confirmed her suspicion. It was just as well because the cold only agitated André's recent injury, and the last thing he needed was the onset of illness.

She needed to face the chronic dread in the house. How strange for her haven from the world to seed fear, but she supposed the shadows had been alive all along.

Most importantly, more important than her fear, Rosalie didn't like how close Marcy, her body like stone, had come to the fire.

Had come toward the balcony's edge.

I had only held her moments before, when she smelled of death and urine, when I thought she'd died and was

unsure she wasn't but a fading vision—I haven't held her
that close since her birth. And I almost lost her again.

Even then, they had established a trust, no matter how meager; she had trusted Marcy and André to find their ways out, and she had promised to catch and guide them.

When they returned home after their stay in the hospital, Jolie capered about and celebrated, and neither Marcy nor André afforded her a glance as her tail went back and forth like a frenzied clock pendulum. Despite the distant reception, Jolie hardly left either of them, but rather alternated between the beds and only reluctantly padded away to mess outside or eat.

And it was often in Marcy's room where Rosalie found her daughter and the dog resting together, refusing to part.

Rosalie went inside, the front door shutting softly as she glowered at the newspaper crumpled in one clenched hand.

On the paper she held, the words and blurry faces had their own little black heartbeats that sped together. The dead children, some in odd clothing unfit for the times, others nude, most had their tongues and hands removed, some had their heads separated from their bodies.

Rosalie tossed the folded newspaper into the fireplace.

When she would go to André and ask how he was, he spoke of anything but his time below the wine cellar. He had a fading red mark on his wrist where Rais had clutched him, another on his shoulder, which she'd seen when his clothes were torn at the manor.

340

Rosalie didn't know how many burns he had, and she feared asking would provoke a sobbing fit or uncontrolled violence against himself or the furniture.

And it was while thinking on this Rosalie stood outside André's door. His room was simple and clean.

Resting on his side, eyes bloated strangely like a tired frog's, he waved carelessly. "Salut."

She went to sit by him, making sure not to knock against the chair André balanced his horned cane against. As she settled beside him, he moved awkwardly to join her. André's breath reeked of wine.

"Do you want a piece of candy? There are a few in the oven."

Looking lost, André asked, "Is that all you came for?"

"I didn't make them."

"That's not what I asked."

"I wanted to see how you were. I suppose it's stupid to ask."

"Did I tell you about my journey to the appliance factory? I think I may be hired there."

Rosalie patted his arm and smiled, though she was unsure how to feel, having never been familiar with factory work. "I'm glad for you, if that's what you want."

"I think it'll go better than past endeavors." André rubbed his hands together.

Rosalie shook her head. "Don't worry over that today. Just rest."

His gaze flickered around the room, as if scouting for hidden threats.

To comfort him, she said, "If you want, I'll bring you milk." It sounded foolish once she heard herself.

André released a small laugh. "I'm not a boy any longer." He was once a soldier, and now he was a father, and he might've believed she saw him far removed from the little boy who'd follow her around the house once he'd learned to hobble.

It was a mistake on his part.

André may never, as long as he lived, reveal that he needed someone to care for him while he recuperated, somebody to give him what he couldn't ask for. In time, André may decide to reveal every aspect of his trauma, but she couldn't force his willingness. He could snipe and deflect, but she wouldn't be so easily deterred in helping where she could.

He offered a faint smile that reflected the remnants of her sister's cheerful son, the child always so eager to please, whose energy turned to anger and a need to surpass, to wipe out his insecurities and the fear that he was potentially not enough.

She briefly touched his cheek with the back of her hand.

André clasped it. "I'm not ill."

"Your temperature says otherwise."

"Tante?"

"Hmm?"

He squeezed her hands. "Thank you. I'll do the best I can to repay you and Oncle. I know I'm a pain, but I'll make a worthy nephew out of myself."

"There's no need for repayment. We took to the duty of raising you, not requesting a loan for your life." She exhaled through her nose. "I'm sorry."

His wandering eyes settled on hers. "For?"

"For telling you your choices were stupid." She, out of anyone, should've known what it meant to shrink in a mother figure's shadow, to think nobody thought her worthy.

André laughed, and it was hard and empty. "You weren't wrong. After what I did, I ended up in a nightmare."

"I was cruel. You didn't deserve that, nor did you deserve for me to call you a whore."

André corrected, "Less than a whore." With biting joviality, he spoke in what may've been an attempt at lightheartedness. "Look at me now. I probably couldn't find someone to pay for me."

"You don't think you deserved what happened in the manor, do you, whatever it was? Because you didn't. Nobody deserves what that monster did."

"Forget what I said."

He was withdrawing. In time, maybe, he would trust her. She would wait. After all, it had taken her two decades to find what words she could.

"I've never despised you, neither you as my sister's son nor you on your own."

His smile was watery. "That's good to hear."

"Do you mind if I ask why you were there, what happened?" Because of the stains and the comment Rais

343

had made, she could assume what had happened to him, as much as she wished her thoughts were hyperbolic. She didn't want to dredge this up, but she thought if she didn't, such trauma would be neglected.

"I was dragged there after I tried to stop a child from being kidnapped." André dragged his palms down his face. "I—he . . . I can't, I'm sorry."

"You don't have to speak about anything that hurts you. It's all right. I'm sorry to have brought it up."

"Part of me wishes I had died there so I wouldn't have to relive it. If it weren't for Marcy or Oncle or you, I might've just let myself die."

Stunned, Rosalie stared at the floor and let a burgeoning silence pass. "It would've ruined us if you died."

André's voice was coarse, the dark hair on his face deepening the shadows of his scowl. "I'm ruined. I was less than nothing to him."

Rosalie insisted, "*He's* nothing, not you."

"He—he took me, and nothing I knew could stop him, none of that hay I sliced, all those times I saw Oncle pull the rope. Nothing prepared me."

Rosalie's eyes burned, but she didn't interrupt him.

He continued, "And that bastard took all his victims with him. Except for those few children." He swallowed. "Except for me." He clung to her.

"Listen to me, whatever happened, you are blameless."

Roughly, André asked, "Am I?"

"Yes."

Rosalie let André cry against her, harsh drawls making him tremble, and she touched his head like she had done when he fit into her arms after she fed him. She'd rub his scalp, his little neck, and his eyes would roll back in contentment. She settled her hands on his head and back and stayed that way.

Sitting with her nephew, she wanted to take his pain and discard it where he'd never find it. She imagined if she had been shackled and endured what he did, she'd be in the very same state. For the first time in years, she sang her nephew to sleep, even when he requested no such treatment. Besides the children, only he and Marcy could say what they witnessed beneath the wine cellar, and rage spilled through her thinking of it.

Deeper into the excavation of the manor's ruins, the police had discovered two of many bodies, described to be holding each other in a shadowed, webbed embrace, a ghastly, splintered mirror before they settled into one another as ash to blacken headlines. Lurid visual evidence to pore over. Rais and Jehanne.

How many years of little cadavers were in that horrid place? No, Rosalie couldn't believe that man's story about being alive for hundreds of years. A madman, that was all he was, all he could be, a man who thought himself old, the original Bluebeard. An elaborate refraction, and he had manipulated his daughter, caused her to doubt her identity. Jehanne had martyred herself rather than leaving her mad father and living a fulfilled life.

Her heart cramped as she read the newspaper reports of the bodies found both above and below the ashes. The men who sacrificed their lives to save her daughter, the children, the sheer, callous waste of it all.

Leaving André, Rosalie went to the kitchen and retrieved candies from the oven. They dimpled and caved on the cloth napkin. Pain came to her then, and she leaned against the stove.

Again, Marcy—red, blue, and purple against a moony frown of white, the black smoke veining behind and around her, and the scarlet of her almost-fall, the dim, accepting gray of her brow.

Even from that height, she had noticed Marcy's eyes were entranced with a force that curled her bones. That moment had taken at least a decade off Rosalie's life, thinking her daughter as bewitched as she had been during her early sleepwalking episodes.

Worse, as a week passed, Marcy refused to look at her papa. With a shaking voice, Anatole recounted how she would always feign sleep when he tended to her bedside, and not even a good-hearted joke stirred her to relent. Rosalie didn't understand it; Anatole had nothing to do with the atrocities a supposedly undead man created.

When Rosalie knocked on Marcy's open door with a free hand, her daughter twisted her head, eyes swollen and half-lidded from lack of sleep, tears, or both. A precarious tower of books obscured the lamplight, making her eyes dim. Her hair was an overturned basket of unraveled yarn. Jolie raised her head and, as if intuiting Rosalie's purpose, padded off the bed and past her, likely moving to join her other patient.

Rosalie paused, unsure, and then entered, sitting by her daughter on the bed.

"I brought you candy." Marcy took the napkin and stared at the debased chocolates. "They were more intact when I fetched them from the oven."

"Thank you." Purple circles shadowed Marcy's eyes as she rubbed a finger along one glossy, round shell and set the gift on her nightstand. Rosalie brushed her thumb against her daughter's knuckles.

"I'm sorry about Jehanne." Bad idea, too direct. She should've let Marcy mention Jehanne first. Swiftly, she added, "I'm so glad we didn't lose you or André." The room had a thickness to it, a rank heaviness like their last seaside visit; the weedy air had been heavy with salt, and she imagined the shells in the water, tangled with siren hair and fishing wires, love knots.

"I'm glad we didn't die too." Marcy seemed to force herself to laugh; it came out as a hoarse croak. Her smile didn't match her eyes, and it cut Rosalie. An ache claimed her, a piddly desire to return to the oceanside, the half-formed shore that haunted her dreams, a dreamy solstice veil with strings of seaweed and crab eyes and mermaid hair.

Then, Marcy darkened in a way that could only be felt. She said, "I just hate that he won, that demon. All he wanted was to die with Jehanne."

"How do you know?"

"Because of his eyes during the fire. He didn't want to die alone."

"He didn't win. Listen to me, darling, you can keep Jehanne's memory alive, and she'll matter and go on, even if she's not by your side."

"Maman," Marcy croaked.

"Hmm, poupée?" Rosalie worried her words had hurt more than she intended.

Marcy's eyes flitted between Rosalie and the floor. "I don't want to be broken for love. I don't want it to be like in the stories. I don't want to end my life or marry some man and forget." Breaking because of love, that agony that smelled of a hot summer when the lilies were in full bloom and the air tasted of pollen and smoke. Rosalie remembered a faint, misty little scene of Juliette snoring, her hair sprawled on a book of Baudelaire poetry.

Marcy asked, "Do you ever think what things would be like if we didn't lose anyone?"

"I do." Rosalie thought for a long time. "I do often wonder, if things had been different, how everyone would've gotten along." But the remorse hurt too much, the phantom never-images of Maman and Juliette holding a newborn Marcy and patting her hair.

Marcy exhaled, which made a short whistle through her nose. "I think they loved you. Your maman, Juliette, Roger. I think they'd be proud. Or they are, wherever they may be."

"Thank you. I suppose they could be, God willing." Rosalie rubbed her thumb into the wool of Marcy's gown, her daughter's fingers twisting the dark fabric of her skirt. When it looked as if Marcy's eyes would spill over, Rosalie gave her the crumpled handkerchief, for what it was, resting in her pocket.

"What was your sister like?"

How odd. Nobody had asked that after Juliette died. There was too much to tell. "She'd chew on her hair and stick out her bottom lip whenever she wanted me to do something. I called her Fat Lip."

"You made jokes like that?"

Wryly, Rosalie said, "Yes, back when I knew what jokes were." Pity stirred to the forefront, pity that Marcy never grew up with her only sibling. "Before Roger." Because silence would sting, Rosalie let words flood the air without direction. "I—my child, I want to say you'll heal from Jehanne's death, but—well, you may not, and that's just as right as if you do recover. Your papa and I will help in what ways we can." What those ways were, they'd have to discover.

"It isn't fair she thought she had to die for everyone else. She should be here and safe. I should've let her know I loved her too much for that."

The space behind Rosalie's eyes tightened. "But love, you did. You said as much. I don't see how she could've not known."

Marcy put her head in her hands. "I just wish I had something like a picture to remember her by."

"I know, poupée. I know."

"Do you have a photo of Roger?"

Rosalie hesitated. "Why?"

"Because, well, I always wondered what he looked like, but I was afraid to ask because it'd hurt you and Papa. But I thought it'd make him real, which doesn't make any sense, I suppose, but, uh, forget I—"

"I do."

"Can I see him?" When she received no answer, Marcy added, "Is that . . ."

Too quickly, Rosalie replied, "Yes, you can. I'll retrieve them." She left Marcy and ventured to the master bedroom. She felt under the mattress, and she unearthed the key. With the care of a pallbearer, she stepped to the desk and knelt in front of the locked drawer. When she unlocked it and freed it of two small, gray photos, she squinted to blur her vision.

When she returned to Marcy's room, she found the handkerchief had fallen to the floor.

Rosalie started, "In this one . . ." She swallowed. "I—I know to you it's likely a bit morbid." Roger was not alive in this particular photo, and she couldn't imagine how such a thing must seem to her daughter. A grotesque parody.

Marcy took the photos, staring at the first.

"He looks nice."

"Yes," Rosalie replied with a roughness in her voice, "he was handsome." Even though she had never let Roger go, she had forgotten how beautiful he was, beautiful in his simple, sleepy contentment.

"His hair is really dark," Marcy observed, as if her brother were warm and pink in her arms now.

Rosalie looked at herself, younger and infinitely sad, wanting to die and sure she wouldn't survive to the next year. A premature weariness had lined her eyes and mouth.

Now, she was grateful for the years she'd been given, even the ones she worried she'd wasted.

The second picture was Roger alive and reaching out. She swore he was smiling, no matter what the doctor said, that newborns couldn't smile.

Rosalie in the photo had upturned lips. Happy, for lack of a better word, since elation didn't quite describe it, yet still saddened. Even with Roger alive, her post-birth lull nourished a seed of melancholy, yet it was happiness all the same, feelings uninformed by the dismal future.

Marcy gulped and wiped her nose with her knuckles. "Thanks for showing me. I know it isn't easy."

Rosalie remembered to breathe.

Marcy bristled, so Rosalie asked, "What is it?"

"These—I still—Jehanne didn't deserve to die, and— but she gave up her life, and for what?"

"For us." A black, scorching hatred numbed Rosalie's more positive emotions. "I would've killed that monster for you." If she could've, but it was clearly futile when she had tried with the gun.

Marcy rubbed her cheek with the back of her knuckles. "Don't talk like that, please, not you too."

"Too?"

"I need at least one of you not to kill someone."

Rosalie wrapped her arm around her daughter's shoulders. Marcy leaned into her mother's touch as a child should. After a minute, she breathed so slow and soft that Rosalie thought she was asleep, until she spoke—

"Maman, I loved Jehanne like she was my wife."

Rosalie didn't know what to say. "You'll find others to love" would be dismissive, like telling a mother who lost her child that at least she could have another.

She hesitated before saying, "When I said what I did about death and you marrying . . ."

"Better off dead than marrying André." Indeed. Good thing her daughter and nephew had such pristine memories.

"I—I meant I wanted you to live and be free instead of being trapped and miserable."

"Are you miserable?"

"No, I'm not, at least not because of you, André, or your papa, but I knew you'd be, and I wanted you to have more opportunities."

"I guess you'd know more about marrying someone who will . . ."

Rosalie wasn't sure she wanted to follow that thread of thought. "I love your papa, and I'm—I'm so sorry I hurt you. I only wanted you to keep away from public attention enough that you'd be able to walk around without judgment one day." She added, though her skin prickled

352

as she spoke, "I never wanted you to be like me. It would be humiliating."

"Why? I thought you weren't miserable? I may not know many people—you know, outside of our family and Jehanne. But I look up to you more than any other person. You're a hero." Doubt tugged. Surely not.

"The police are heroes. You and André are heroes. I only came after . . ." The worst, she wanted to say the worst, but all of it had been beyond reckoning.

"You helped me after Jehanne fell. If you weren't there, I don't think I could've made it down."

Her girl's eyes were glassy like the film over Adam and Eve's after they'd betrayed God. Rosalie's heart quickened because she didn't know what it'd take to uncloud Marcy's eyes.

"Maman, I'm sorry about your valise."

Rosalie blinked, pausing longer than she thought she should. "Pardon?"

"The case I put my clothes in. It burned in the fire. Sorry, I just thought of it."

"It's nothing to fret about. I'll survive without it."

Marcy closed her eyes slowly before opening them and staring at the floor. Rosalie remembered one of the few times she'd left the house with her family. She waded through the sea as Marcy and André had laughed and chased each other on the shore. With the salty crust of the ocean's dried tears between her toes, Rosalie felt the water's force, its austere darkness and the sun's frosty glare. She saw that in Marcy now, that weight and searching as the tides pulled and threatened to steal her unsteady footing.

That day many years ago, Rosalie had been lost, and it'd been the children's laughter that guided her back. Ever-persistent, Marcy wrapped her arms around her neck, and their cheeks met before Rosalie shrugged Marcy away for fear of making her daughter ill from the wet cold.

Rosalie struggled to compose herself. "You've carried the hurt my words inflicted for too long, and I'm sorry. I'll do whatever you need."

Quiet swelled between them. *I am more like Maman than I realized, but no more.* Guilt followed her mother's memory. *Oh, Marcy, if only you'd met Juliette and her.* But Marcy could, in a way, if Rosalie continued to carry them with her in stories and gestures. In grief, she had absorbed every last song and prodding joke.

"André'll probably marry somebody else, in the end. But I don't think, I don't think I ever really actually liked him in the way I thought. Not like I liked Jehanne."

Rosalie didn't know what to make of that; Marcy and Jehanne hadn't known each other long, but she could only imagine if the subject of her childhood infatuations— who, well enough, became her husband—had died while she still pined after an ideal. Could it be that Marcy had loved another woman as Rosalie's own mother had secretly loved and grieved Anatole's mother? Maman had lived in shame and silence for most of her life, and Rosalie would be damned if Marcy would suffer the same fate.

Despite that, she didn't know how to broach the subject now.

"I'm sorry," was all she could say.

"Did you ever love someone besides Papa? Love as in, you know?"

"No. Our families and what we're involved with, it makes it hard to form bonds. I did—I did have men who fancied me, but I hardly reciprocated."

A buzzing filled her ears, then passed as quiet as fireflies.

"Did you want me?" Marcy blurted.

"Pardon?"

"When—after Roger passed, did you really want me?" From the start, Marcy was more difficult. She needed to be to survive in this world. A new exhaustion flooded Rosalie.

She let out a heavy exhale through her nose, and then cupped Marcy's flushed cheeks. Marcy closed her eyes and leaned into one of her palms.

"I was scared, but do you know how happy your papa and I were to have you? We were grateful."

Marcy's eyes were still shut. "Have I ever made you happy besides that? Proud?"

Had she made her child so starved for validation? Rosalie wanted to say, "You are so precious to me," but it swelled in her throat. She was terrible at sentimentality. If she said Marcy meant everything to her, "everything" would be too little a scope. Rosalie toyed with her own hair while she tried to come up with a more concrete sentiment, one based on experience. Instead, she only made a pitiful, strangled noise, but Marcy smiled a little, so the meaning must've stuck somehow.

"There's never a moment you haven't. Made me proud, that is. You've worried me, but I was never disappointed." Rosalie stopped fooling with her hair. "I thought I'd never carry another child, never see them survive."

"I expect you'll never let me leave the house again, after all this." Marcy wiped the tears from her cheeks.

"We can go outside and—enjoy activities."

"Like what?"

"We could go cycling. We, or I, would need to purchase one." Flustered, Rosalie corrected herself, "Or two, rather. It's been so long, and I'm not certain I like the riding as much as I once did." Marcy's expression fell further, if it were possible. Right, she didn't know how to ride a cycle. "But when your papa returns, we can go somewhere today. We could walk, whatever you prefer. Or we could—"

Marcy righted herself. "Where?"

"Wherever you like, though I suppose my purse will give us a limit."

Marcy grinned and lifted herself off the bed, eyes bright and clear, and it was the first time any of them had smiled since the horror they witnessed. Shared images that skulked like wraiths in the nightscape, strung together with painful, biting gold like Ariadne's yarn.

Rosalie's knees ached, as did her wrists, those senseless ghost aches that dampened and weighed down her body.

The day was, as many autumn days were, stubbornly bright despite the chill, though rain had come. It would come again, but they could face it.

"You'll really let me go outside after all that's happened?"

"I just—I didn't want to expose you to the looks people would give you if they discovered who you are, if they pay attention. In my experience, they do."

"Help me prepare for it. I don't care about people judging us, especially ones I've never met. I saw how they are, and I don't care."

Thinking about Anatole's work, Rosalie replied, "Best to wait until the day brightens more before we arrive at the square because of, well . . ."

"The stones need to be cleaned first," Marcy said, her smile carrying an aged bitterness that hurt Rosalie's heart.

Later, the walk to the Rennes square took approximately thirty minutes. Marcy's head lolled to the side as she stepped on acorns and kicked pebbles into the road cracks.

They passed people with clothespins in their mouths and damp bedsheets in their hands, but Rosalie, also in black to respect the dead, guided her daughter so she paid them no heed. As they approached Saint-Germain square, a wooden, rain-pocked sign postured the town motto:

Live in harmony.

Rosalie's belly coiled in tension as they approached the square. The wind smelled of fresh bread. They passed the fountain, and there sat a man with trembling hands and bandages around the top of his head. He would be one of many when the war ended, if the war ended. The wind, as cold as it was, didn't chill Rosalie, and Marcy didn't tremble, though she wrapped her arms around herself until she needed her hands to keep her hat on her head.

The more they walked, the more Marcy sauntered about, her eyes alight briefly as she inspected the shop windows, each beaming sweet tart and darkly grinning flower. A drowsy contentment washed over Rosalie.

"Maman?"

"Yes, poupée?"

Marcy's eyes were half-lidded again, and she crossed her arms over her chest. "When will I stop hurting?"

The calm faded. Rosalie paused, not wanting to make Marcy more morose, as if she could blame her, for what little her daughter recounted would drive most adults to madness.

Rosalie offered a hand, still sore and cut from when her pistol recoiled, and Marcy unfolded one arm to close that distance. "I'm not certain the hurt ever stops." She almost said it never stops, that all scars twinge a little, but she wasn't her daughter. Maybe it would be different somehow, yet Marcy cared so deeply.

"That's what I thought. Thank you for being honest." Marcy looked peckish, with little color in her cheeks, and

Rosalie didn't want her to fall ill on their expedition. When the girl stepped, she lurched forward.

"We'll find little blessings, I think." She hoped.

Marcy shrugged, not meeting Rosalie's eyes. "If such things exist."

"Are you hungry? Would you like to go inside someplace? Do you need to sit down?"

"I'd just like to look around some more." Marcy eyed a parked auto, and though it didn't connect to the previous thread of conversation, she said, "I'd love to learn how to drive."

Rosalie held her words too long for comfort; she was reluctant to have Marcy inside one of those loud monstrosities. She feared for Anatole, even, and hadn't enjoyed her own one-time driving experience, but she forced her body to lose tension, which was unsuccessful.

"I'm sure your papa wouldn't mind teaching you." Rosalie focused on the stones beneath them, the reliable tread of footsteps rooting their thoughts to the earth.

Marcy stopped and stared at the ground too.

Rosalie squeezed her cold hand. "What is it?"

Her daughter muttered, head bobbing back and forth, "Seven-five-one, seven-five-one, but there's more, aren't there? And I need to remember them all, seven-five-one."

"What do you mean?"

Marcy pointed at the cobblestones. "Papa killed a man here," Marcy said, her voice void of weight.

"Ah, yes, well, let's go look at one of the shops."

Marcy crushed Rosalie's fingers. "It's a good thing they built drains here, isn't it?"

Rosalie fidgeted, and Marcy came back enough to loosen her grip. "Is there anywhere else you'd like to go?"

"It looks so different now with the sun. I wonder how they clean the stains, everything that doesn't go below." Marcy's voice rose a pitch, and she pulled away. "Where does all that blood go, what doesn't drain away? Does any of it go under the stones?" She grew quiet and soft. "Do you think the stones are hungry? Do you think there are ghosts under there, ghosts who can't eat because they don't have heads? It drips, their blood, and rises under our feet like hungry water; it rises to eat us."

Ignoring her spasming legs, Rosalie knelt in front of Marcy. The manor tragedy had made all her limbs weaker, and she hoped she'd be able to stand again at the soonest convenience. At first, she gripped both of Marcy's hands and traced the open, clean palms with her thumbs. Then, with a palm on Marcy's shoulder and the other on her cheek, Rosalie said in earnest, "Please, poupée, stay with me. Would you like sherbet? Flowers? Books? I know how you are with stories."

Marcy's eyes cleared a little, pupils shrinking. "Can we sit down somewhere?"

Rosalie moved to stand, but her ankles protested. Testing the strength of her feet, especially after a walk, was a hardship. When she grimaced, Marcy came to her aid, extending both hands and letting her maman lean against her. Marcy supported her as best she could, and

Rosalie said, "Thank you." Pride swelled in her, stinging like thorns barbing her lungs, but the pain made her warm. What a pair they were as they limped to the closest bench and sat as one, a slanted tower.

The strolling people hardly afforded Rosalie and Marcy a second glance, consumed in the rigmarole of their own lives, and though the two of them would never be whole or normal (indeed, what a word), the day had its comforts: the incessant birdsong, the scent of fresh bread, the gentle, rosy touch of cologne in the air, and the heat of Marcy dozing against Rosalie's shoulder.

If only for an hour, they could forget what it was to be empty.

ACKNOWLEDGMENTS

Thank you to Mom, Noah, my loved ones, and to those who encouraged me throughout this journey. This book would not have been possible without my critique partners and first readers: Kelsey, Marí, Conner, Katie, and Professor Tony Grooms. Thanks to August for her support, and I am immensely grateful for the astonishing work of my cover artist, Victoria Davies, and for the hard work of my editor, Kristen Tardio. The support of those no longer here also immensely assisted me, so thank you Grand, Grandpa, Angie, Cathy, and Grandma. Leonard Wolf's *Bluebeard: The Life and Crimes of Gilles de Rais* inspired portions of this novel.

ABOUT THE AUTHOR

After years of crafting stories at home and in her grandparents' blue home in woods of Ellijay, Georgia, Emily Deibler gravitates toward macabre narratives. In her professional life, she studies social media and marketing, having earned a BA in English and currently pursuing an MA in Professional Writing, both at Kennesaw State University. Her short story "Papa's Work" won first place in the Kennesaw State University English Department's Undergraduate Creative Writing Awards, and her poem, "Turkey Hunting," appeared in Z Publishing House's *Georgia's Best Emerging Poets*. She lives in Kennesaw, Georgia.

Unlike her deceased relatives, she executes only her characters.

Made in the USA
Lexington, KY
03 October 2018